Honours of War

by the same author
WINTER OF THE EAGLE

Honours of War

by

K. M. Campbell

London
GEORGE ALLEN & UNWIN
Boston Sydney

First published 1981

GEORGE ALLEN & UNWIN LTD
40 Museum Street, London WC1A 1LU

British Library Cataloguing in Publication Data

Campbell, K M
Honours of war.
I. Title
823'.9'1F PR6053.A48/

ISBN 0-04-823176-2

Typeset in 11 on 12 point Baskerville by Red Lion Setters, London
and printed in Great Britain
by Billing & Sons Ltd, Guildford, London & Worcester

To My Father
Captain John Campbell

Honours of War

1

The adjutant of the 71st Highland Light Infantry sighed wearily and tried once more to balance the dancing figures on his weekly equipment return. His quill scratched over the paper and the nib separated, casting blots over the long columns. In despair he threw the offending instrument down on the dusty table.

It was hot, breathlessly hot, and the adjutant pulled at his stock to ease the sweat gathering round his neck. He leaned back in his chair and raised his tired eyes to the window. In the baked village outside, movement and sound were fading, driven into shade by the harsh Spanish sun. It was the time of siesta and only the cicadas were active, their interminable chirruping reaching its peak in these, the hottest hours. Only they seemed busy and – he, George Ingram, lieutenant and adjutant.

Ingram looked at his morning statement of the battalion's strength, and the neat strokes in the columns marked 'Alterations Since Yesterday'. There had been no change for days; he had last filled out a casualty return in May, after the action at Almaraz.

He turned his attention once again to those uncooperative figures, checking the company returns against the previous week's, but it was too hot to concentrate and he produced a third set of conflicting totals. The moisture ran and prickled under his shirt and he swore for the hundredth time at the distracting cacophony of the cicadas. The old figures would have to do; the form was waiting to be completed and sent off to the Assistant Quartermaster General. The faulty nib betrayed him again and splashed ink over the almost completed return. Now he had ink on his fingers.

'Corporal MacLeod!'

The chair in the orderly room scraped slowly over the stone floor. MacLeod had probably been dozing, and resented being disturbed. The door opened, smartly enough.

'Sir?'

MacLeod did indeed look as if he had been asleep, his eyes puffed, the sweat beginning to run at the sudden movement. He had discarded his scarlet tunic and was wearing his shirt unbuttoned to the waist. It was strange to see him so dishevelled as he stood at attention, chin out, arms tucked in, and the sweat pouring on his naked, hairy chest. Ingram realised that he was staring at the corporal's untidy dress and that the man was expecting rebuke. He raised the damaged quill.

'Can you cut me a fresh point on this, Corporal? And bring me a fresh form number seven.'

The corporal backed out, leaving Ingram to contemplate his ink-stained fingers. His eyes drifted back to the morning state of the battalion's strength. So many officers, so many sergeants, and rank and file; so many anonymous numbers – all of them now lying somewhere in the shade, perhaps in the squalid houses, or under a blanket screened against the sun. Companions of a thousand marches, now tossing restless in the heat. Only a handful of sentries and himself were at work. He could hear the corporal of the quarter guard trudging across the open square with the relief for the sentry at the well. The snick-snick of the shouldered muskets and the old sentry trailing back behind the corporal to the relative cool of the guardroom, leaving his comrade alone in the square to spend his hour's duty seeking what scant shelter the protecting screen afforded.

Here was MacLeod back, his tunic and stock neatly in place as was fit and proper. He laid the form on the table and placed a fresh-cut goose quill on top. His face was red and swollen and he gasped in the suffocating air.

'For God's sake, leave off your tunic, man. Remove your stock if you must – but, please, do not open your shirt.'

The corporal's eyes met him with grateful humour.

'Aye, sir, thank you. It's the ugly sight a sweating chest.'

'No sign of the post-horse yet?'

'No, sir. He's late back from Brigade today.'

'Probably won't be here till the evening now. Trust a Spaniard not to miss his siesta.'

It was an impressive indication of the efficiency with which the allied army organised its movements that there was a postal system at all. Yet every day the Spanish messenger came down to the regiment to deliver routine orders and dispatches and collect the returns and reports. Back up the long dry roads the reams of paper flowed, to Badajoz and Lisbon or north or east to follow Wellington as he moved. From all over Portugal and western Spain information came to him, telling him how many men were where, and how well fed and how equipped. And in the hundred offices of the staff pens darted orders, requisitions. But the post messengers were Spaniards, and on a day like this a reasonable Spaniard would seek shade for himself and his mount. If the post was delayed by siesta there would be time for Ingram to complete his next requisition. He addressed MacLeod, still waiting at attention.

'See if you can find the orderly officer. He'll be in some cool chamber, I'll warrant. My compliments to him and would he be kind enough to spare me a moment.'

'Yes sir.' MacLeod turned smartly and left him alone in the room with his empty forms.

Ingram picked up his new quill and, dipping it gently into his silver ink-well, he drew the form towards him and started to fill it in from the lists scattered around him. One camp kettle to every mess, heavy iron brutes that defied warmth. Billhooks, regulated at one for every ten men; seven received since last week's return, two unserviceable and one missing, to be deducted from Private O'Hara's pay, for simply losing it while cutting maize.

Column by column he worked, noting haversacks and blankets, shovels and spades, leaving a blank at pack-saddles, which were causing his arithmetical problems, and on to baggage straps and thirteen serviceable public mules. He sanded the sheet and stood up. Perhaps the orderly officer would have discovered something about the pack-saddles.

He walked over to the window and gazed across the village to the dim, brown folds of the Sierra Morena where Drouet's division still sat, guarding the passes. They had lain there for weeks, since the news of Wellington's victory at Salamanca had set Hill's Anglo-Portuguese army on the very marches of Andalusia, awaiting Soult's evacuation to the north. For Salamanca had opened the roads to Madrid and driven a wedge between the Bonapartist forces, threatening isolation to the Army of the South. Yet still Soult lingered in his southern province, dallying with sieges at Gibraltar and Cadiz, hunting Ballesteros's guerrillas from Granada to Ronda, defying King Joseph's orders to bring his 45,000 veterans safely to the succour of the north. Thus, as the fate of Spain hung in the balance before Madrid, the two armies in the south settled down to watch each other in the indecisive fashion of that long summer of 1812, which had seen them marching and counter-marching over all southern Estramadura and never coming into battle. And, while the blood flowed wide in Andalusia and Wellington lay outside Madrid, Bonaparte marched deeper into Russia. Ingram wondered what was happening there, on the broad steppe. There was no news of serious Russian resistance. He scowled at the distant hills and the tyranny they guarded.

Someone entered the room behind him and he looked round. It was his friend Fox, the orderly officer. His eyes had a certain defiance, guessing the reason for the summons.

'The pack-saddles? I've found one. A villager had it on his land. José Rodriguez. Remember? We've taken wine with him.'

'What was he doing with it?'

'Says he bought it from one of our lads. Myself, I'd wager it was one of the dago drivers . . . '

'Anyway you've got it back now.'

'Yes. Do you want a report?'

'God no.' Ingram's mind rejected the investigation which a report would occasion. 'What about the other one?'

'Aye.' Fox had just a glimmer of anxiety in his expression. 'Er . . . that's not so good, George.'

'What is it?'

'It's probably on the mule that's away.'

'Mule? What mule? I haven't authorised use of a mule.'

'Maybe it forgot to ask you,' Fox grinned. 'I beg to report Fourth Company's mule missing.'

'Missing?' He heard the anxiety, sharp in his voice.

'Aye. Missing. It's gone all right.'

'Christ! You know what a mule is worth on this front. How the devil are we going to replace it? There's not a mule to be had in fifty miles.'

'You're the adjutant; you'll think of something. Anyway, all thirteen mules were watered this morning.'

As orderly officer, Fox was treating the matter far too lightly. Ingram was furious.

'Good God, Humphrey, have you never read General Orders on the use of public mules. If some peasant is using it in his fields I'll have the people involved crucified. I'm holding you responsible. You get out there and find it. Now!'

Fox had listened with growing indignation and now he spoke

with venom. 'Don't you start giving me orders, Mr bloody adjutant. I'll take authorised directions from you, communications, postings and all the rest. But not bloody orders. Not from you.'

'For God's sake, man . . .'

'I'm three months your senior in this regiment and don't you forget it. Every time I'm orderly officer . . .'

'Some damned irregularity happens and I've got to cover for you. But not this – not a mule. Wellington'd break the man who lost a mule like this.'

'Christ, you're an upright bastard; the Colonel's perfect adjutant.'

'Man, it was stolen from under your damned nose!'

'Don't you . . .' Fox began, but Ingram turned from him in disgust and tried to control his anger. That mule carried the baggage of the entire Fourth Company and its permanent loss would impair battalion transport. There would be considerable inconvenience, not least in explaining the matter. The Commander-in-Chief had been emphatically specific about the uses to which battalion mules should be put. Irregularity led to endless reports and inquiries and possibly court-martial. Ingram glowered out the window and cursed the clerkish abilities which made him so efficient an adjutant. Otherwise he would be a company officer, dozing in the cool of some dark room.

Fox began, 'Look George, I . . .', and then stopped and the oppressive silence of the afternoon descended again. Ingram placed his hand on the jamb of the window and gazed into the biscuit-baked square. Nothing was moving; even the sentry at the well seemed asleep in his little patch of grey shade.

A horse clattered somewhere unexpectedly, coming in from the north and harshly cutting the sleepy afternoon. The sentry stiffened and turned quizzically to observe the rider approach along the narrow street. As Ingram watched, the horseman came into view, a sergeant of light dragoons. The horse was almost spent, its head bowed in exhaustion, and the dragoon was flushed, worn out by the heat. He nudged forward towards the curious sentry.

'Where's your adjutant?'

'I'm over here, Sergeant,' Ingram called, and the man turned his horse's head and clip-clopped over the square. At the window he saluted and reached for his sabretache.

'Orders, sir. From General Howard.' He rummaged for a moment in the pouch before withdrawing the sealed packet and proffering it to Ingram. 'They say the frogs has gone, sir.'

'Gone?'

'So they say, sir. Seems that raid the other day was just a parting shot, sir, and old Drooey's run off in the night, sir.'

'So there are no French in front of us now?'

'That's what they say, sir. I had it from a sergeant in the hussars who came in with the news. Says they was all gone this morning, sir.'

'Thank you, Sergeant. You'd better get your horse watered and into the shade. The well's over there. I'll send an orderly to show you a billet – if you're not moving on.'

'Thank you, sir; couldn't move no further if I had to, sir. This old nag's fair done in the heat, begging your pardon, sir.'

He saluted again, before dismounting and leading his horse over to the well. Ingram turned back into the room, examining the packet of orders in his hand. He saw that they were addressed to the Colonel, and looked up to find Fox staring expectantly.

'Marching orders?'

'Like enough,' Ingram acknowledged. 'I'll have to take them to the Colonel. Perhaps you'd find someone to look after the sergeant.'

'I'll do that, George.'

Amiably Fox made to leave the room with him but at the door Ingram paused and tapped the packet.

'You realise that this means you'd better find that mule.'

Fox bristled again. 'I'll find your damned mule. Don't you worry,' he snapped irritably and stamped back into the room.

Ingram passed through into the orderly room. Corporal MacLeod was sitting at his desk and shot to attention, eyes rolling with curiosity, as the adjutant entered, but Ingram ignored him and stepped through the open door into the square. The sunlight fell on his body as a physical blow; it was like stepping into the blast of an oven. He gasped at the heat and screwed his eyes against the glare. Over at the well the dragoon sergeant was sharing the little pool of shade with the sentry while he watched his horse drinking. God knew how he had endured the heat. Ingram continued straight across the square and entered the little house where the Colonel had established his billet.

The Spanish matron looked up from her pot with her toothless grin.

'It is too hot to ride in the sun like the fine sergeant there,' she said.

Ingram smiled: 'It is too hot to work in the fields, señora.'

Her husband and children were bringing in the harvest; there could be no siesta for them in their poverty. The woman bobbed her head ruefully.

'Sí, señor, it is too hot.'

She spread her arms and smiled again. They liked him, these people, for he respected them and could speak their language.

Ingram left the kitchen and climbed the stone stairs to the upper floor. It was stifling there, with the sun beating down on the roof. He paused at the door of the Colonel's room, before knocking and going in.

Colonel Cadogan was sprawled on his bed, naked to the waist, wearing only his white breeches. He had been asleep, but rose at Ingram's entry and reached for his shirt. Ingram tendered the packet.

'Orders, sir, just come in from Brigade.'

'Thank you, Mr Ingram.'

Ingram hesitated, wondering if he had been dismissed. He decided not, and amplified, 'The courier says that the French have withdrawn to the south, sir.'

'Does he, by God. Then Soult must be obeying Joseph Buonaparte's orders at last. Let's see what General Howard has to say about it.'

As the Colonel broke the seal and cast his eyes over the dispatches Ingram found time to wonder if Cadogan could pronounce 'King Joseph' with as much contempt as he managed to express in that word 'Buonaparte'. But then the Colonel had never brought himself to utter the words 'King Joseph'. Ingram found that he was grinning at the thought. Cadogan looked up and caught the expression but fortunately misinterpreted it.

'Yes, Mr Ingram, we're moving at last. We march in the morning. It appears that we are racing Soult to Madrid with orders to prevent his arriving.'

Cadogan pulled on his coat and stretched for his stockings and shoes.

'I'll come across to your office. The whole order of march is here and I want a look at your maps. We'll be busy enough in our arrangements.'

Ingram followed him as he hurried down the stairs and through the kitchen and strode across the square.

'By God, it's hot,' the Colonel growled.

Ingram nodded in agreement. He noted that the dragoon and his horse had moved away. Presumably they were in the cool shadows somewhere, reaping the reward for their journey. Until he had arrived there had seemed no hope of relief from the southern heat, and the bickering exchanges with Soult. Now they were going to rejoin Wellington. The British Army would be united again in its full strength. The 71st would be present at future victories.

In the office Ingram selected the map Cadogan required and, unrolling it, he spread it over the litter of forms on his table. The Colonel was just in time to move the ink-well before it was upset and with a wry smile at Ingram he placed it under the table.

'Let's see now; we'll be going to Trujillo first of all, then Talavera and up the Tagus to Toledo. We'd better have Major Cother in on this; perhaps you'd be kind enough to ask him to come here if he can spare the time. Then you will have to arrange matters for our early departure. I'll see the company commanders at six o'clock.'

In the orderly room Ingram found Corporal MacLeod haranguing one of his clerks for some minor offence. He stopped at the adjutant's entry and looked his long, curious look. Ingram relented.

'We're on a morning move, Corporal; you'd better start getting things together. We won't be coming back.'

'The morn's morn, sir. Yes sir.' He knew he could not be told where they were going.

Ingram remembered something he wanted to know.

'Is Mr Fox looking for that mule?'

'Aye, sir, he is.' A twinkle came into the corporal's eye. 'It's gey serious, sir, about the mule.'

'Very serious, Corporal,' Ingram snapped. 'Don't you forget it.'

'Oh, aye, sir,' MacLeod replied unrepentantly; 'I ken it is no wee thing.'

Ingram left him and once more crossed the square, in search of Major Cother. He found the major in the posada that served as the officers mess, where he was drinking wine with several of the captains.

'The Colonel would like to see you, Major, if you can spare the time.' He leaned forward and added quietly, 'We're ordered to march.'

Cother nodded in acknowledgement, drained his glass and rose.

'Weel, gentlemen, you'll have work enough now, gin I'm no mistaken.'

Ingram grimaced in agreement. There were so many matters requiring his attention: the company commanders to be advised; the heads of the various departments to see; the sergeant major; the quartermaster; the surgeon, to arrange transport for the handful of unfit men. He left the paymaster till last.

Hugh MacKenzie had been with the regiment for almost forty years and, having sold out his captaincy after the disastrous campaign in Buenos Ayres, remained with the first battalion as its paymaster. Now his face wrinkled in friendly greeting as he spoke in the Scots which all his service had not anglicised.

'I hae gotten aye damned dago in the toun coming in here after a warrant. Ye'd think we'd billeted troops in every hoose, aye and no left the puir bodies wi' a morsel tae themselves. Ye ken, I maun hae his Lordship Wellington's hale army kist tae pey ilka claim I hae had this hour past. Man, but they werena laggart tae conclude we'd no be back. Aye, and the sodgers will be wanting their siller gin they wad buy a junket or twa for the march.'

'I'll send MacLeod and the clerks over when I can spare them.'

'I'd be your obligant. MacLeod's a grand chiel at the sums.'

'I've got a problem, Hugh. I've lost a public mule.'

MacKenzie pulled a long face and tugged at his thick side boxes.

'Ye mean it's been purloined. Yin o' the dagos'll hae it hid awa for the harvest, my pledge on't. I'll speir at them whan they come in for settlement. They're honest bodies, ye ken, but close, aye and sleekit forbye. But man, ye'll ken I canna grant a warrant tae replace it. Ye'll maybe can borrow yin frae the ither officers but I'd hae my doubts on yon. They're no ower easy tae be had. Man, I can understand the folk for being awa wi't for there's scarce a mule in the village bar oor ain.'

Ingram nodded. 'There's a pack-saddle with it. José Rodriguez had another. Fox found it this morning. He claimed he'd bought it from a soldier.'

'Aye, maybe. There's gaol-men enough in the battalion, though there's a driver or three I'd credit first. Still if the beastie's no here the morrow's morn we'll can have it drap deid on the march and no questions asked, though ye maun gang wi'oot it for your transport. I daur say we'll manage; maybe ye can share the entrenching tools amang the company mules. Leastways I'll no be at ye for an explanation, but ye'll maybe let me ken gin ye find it?'

'I was thinking you could maybe adjust the peasants' claims but withhold actual payment until the mule turned up.'

'Man, but ye're the crafty yin. It's mair work, ye ken, and I'll need MacLeod, but I'll dae it. Damnation if I'll no. Ye'll hae yon mayor chapping at your door this hauf-hour.'

'I'll do better than that. I'll see him now.' He thanked the paymaster and pushed his way from the office through the crowd of villagers clamouring outside for payment.

The mayor received him with dignified courtesy as though honoured by his visit; the news of the battalion's departure was a matter for polite discussion.

'Perhaps there is some matter in which I may assist,' he suggested shrewdly.

'There is one matter, señor, which I am obliged to draw to your attention. I fear that one of our mules was stolen this morning.'

'Stolen?' The mayor was shocked. 'But there are no gipsies in ten leagues. Perhaps it has strayed.'

'Perhaps, señor, and no doubt some peasant will say masses to San Isidore for delivering a fine mule to his land.'

'No doubt that is the explanation,' the mayor sighed. 'Many of these people are very simple. It will doubtless be found when the harvest is in.'

'Quite. However, as the battalion marches in the morning that will be of little assistance.'

'It is unfortunate that I am unable to assist.'

'Yes. I have to advise you that the paymaster is withholding settlement of billeting warrants until the mule is returned.'

The mayor's eyes sparked with anger but his voice was calm. 'Surely that is needlessly severe. These people are poor and you would punish them for the negligence of a sentry.'

'I need that mule.'

'I see.' The mayor traced his thumb along a join in the wooden table-top and then drummed his fingers in decision. 'It shall be found. Pay the people, Lieutenant; the mule will be returned.'

'Your word of honour?'

The Spaniard's eyes met him proudly.

'My word of honour.'

Ingram smiled in acknowledgement. He could devote his attention now to more important matters.

It was later, in the evening, when the bulk of his work was done, that Ingram found time to visit the mess. The posada was overcrowded on this final night but he took the wine which a mess waiter offered and pushed his way through to join Fox.

'Well, Humphrey, have you found that mule yet?'

Fox shot him a warning look but he had been overheard. Walker, the captain of the Fourth Company peered at him.

'Do I take it, Mr Ingram, that my company mule is still missing?'

'I am confident it will be found, sir.'

'You've informed the Colonel, of course?'

'I saw no reason to trouble him, sir. The Spaniards will return it.'

'Pshaw! It's gone for ever, Ingram. Damned dagos.' Walker turned scornfully. 'What say you, Captain Hall?'

Ingram found his dark-jowled friend at his shoulder. Hall's Highland voice was deceptively gentle. 'I would say that George knows the dagos better than ourselves. If he is sure it will be returned, then no doubt it will be so.'

Walker snorted again. 'If it isn't I shall have to refer the entire circumstances to the Colonel.'

'Aye. That would be appropriate,' Hall agreed pacifically. 'You'll excuse us, Captain. Mrs Hall is waiting.'

For the first time Ingram noticed that the ladies were present and he followed as Hall led them over to where Catherine Hall sat amidst her customary court of junior subalterns. She smiled brightly at his approach.

'I wonder, Mr Ingram, will you be sorry to leave Don Benito?'

'Indeed not, ma'am, I . . .'

'He will, ma'am,' one of the courtiers teased. 'He and Fox have lost Walker's mule.'

'How d'you lose a mule, Ingram?' another called, provoking guffaws.

Ingram whirled the wine in his glass and watched it settle before he spoke.

'If you gentlemen have any constructive comment I shall be pleased to hear it. For my part I have arranged for the animal's return. I trust that you have attended to your duties with similar effect.'

Someone sniggered but Ingram's scowl stopped that. Slowly they melted away as he glowered round.

'There, Mr Ingram, you see,' Catherine teased, 'your gruffness has chased all my admirers away.'

'Not all of them, ma'am, I protest.'

'No indeed,' echoed Fox.

'Your gallantry is very fine,' Hall observed, 'for a pair responsible for a missing mule.'

'God, if anyone else mentions that damned mule . . .' Fox grumbled.

'There is no need to worry,' Ingram affirmed; 'it will turn up. I have arranged it so. It will turn up tonight.'

'Aye?' said Hall doubtfully, and then grinned. 'This damned town. Thank God we're marching at last.'

But the mule had not appeared by the time Ingram had seen the advance party off on the road, to ride ahead through the night and arrange quarters for the end of the first day's march. Irritably he cast it from his mind as he at last retired to bed. There were many more pressing matters to disturb his sleep. Reveille at four found him awake and when Ramon came in with the lamp he was almost dressed. There was a cup of hot water to wash in and shave. He took a last look round his room; there was no regret at leaving.

'Bring all my kit downstairs and have it packed on the donkey.'

Ramon nodded in acquiescence.

He found MacLeod waiting for him in the orderly room.

'A cup of coffee, sir?'

'Thank you, Corporal. You're up early – make sure you get some breakfast.'

'Aye, sir, I'll do that.'

Outside they could hear the stentorian tones of the sergeant-major and the clatter of hurrying feet. Somewhere a pipe drone squealed briefly and from the murmur of voices one sentence carried in through the open window in the rich accents of the Clyde.

'Whaur's ma bluidy buits?'

The Colonel looked in, his cap tucked under his arm.

'Ah, there you are, Mr Ingram. I see the men are at breakfast. Is the transport ready to move yet?'

Ingram did not know and had to admit so. He felt sure that the Colonel had been up no longer than he had, but that was no excuse. There was a nagging anxiety that the mayor had let him down. The Colonel nodded, satisfied that Ingram had everything in hand.

'I think I'll get something to eat. When is inspection? Quarter to five. I'll see you then.'

Ingram turned to MacLeod. 'Have you everything cleared up in here?'

'Och aye, sir. The paymaster's mule will be along in a while and we'll be loading up.'

Ingram stepped out into the gloom of the square and walked through the narrow streets to the yard where the baggage animals would be assembling. There was a gleeful bustle as the soldiers prepared to forsake the village that had been their home. Here and there a weeping girl had to be restrained as her lover took his thoughtless leave. Remarkably, Ingram remembered, one of them was coming with them, defying her parents and Holy Church to follow her man to the wars. Ingram wondered if they had contracted some form of marriage; presumably so.

The orderly officer was waiting for him, together with Gavin, the quartermaster, fussing over his supplies.

'Good morning, Mr Duff – did Mr Fox tell you about the missing mule?'

'When he handed over his duty, sir, but there's still no sign of it. Shall I divide the entrenching tools among the company animals?'

'Not yet,' said Ingram. He was certain the mayor would not have broken his word. But there was a growing doubt. The whole army distrusted Spanish promises.

'But sir . . .' The ensign was anxious to make his arrangements.

Ingram waved him to silence and turned to the quartermaster.

'Perhaps you'll oblige me with your light, Mr Gavin.'

He held up the lantern and peeered over to the Spanish drivers at the well, dimly seen, watering their beasts. Despite his confidence it was a nervous moment before he could count that there were all thirteen present.

'It must have just turned up, sir,' said Duff lamely.

'Damned dagos,' Gavin muttered. 'Never know what they'll do next.'

Ingram grunted philosophically. There would be only private satisfaction: no one would compliment him for his handling of the mayor.

'There is no purpose in gazing at it, Mr Duff,' he growled at the ensign. 'Have the animals taken round to the companies. We march in an hour.'

They left Don Benito before sunrise to catch the cool of the morning, and the pipers played them from the town. A thousand strong their column was and a trained eye would have known them by the incongruity of their dress. They marched to the pipes yet wore trousers and neither colours or drums were in their van, but bugles, and every cap bore the green plume of the light infantry. Yet the pipers had the kilt and feather bonnet and the men wore the red and white check on their caps declaring their Highland identity. Company by company they marched in quick time, falling into the steady rhythm that had carried them round half of Spain and now was taking them north again.

2

The troubles of war rumbled away from the south as Hill hurried his brigades north in the race against Soult. Through Mérida and Trujillo they came and by Talavera and along the valley of the Tagus. They marched by night to evade the blast of the sun, but nothing could evade the dust which rose from the van of every column and drifted back to suffocate the soldiers in the ranks, the trailing baggage and the servants, the women and children, and each little rearguard shepherding its stragglers along. Eyes became red orbs of pain and throats clogged with grit to crave every precious bead of moisture. Day brought rest but no relief, for then there were the flies and little shelter from the sun, and worst were the hours of siesta when the sun at its zenith drove thirst to the foremost of men's minds.

It was no better for the enemy as, to the east, Soult struggled to bring his army across the wasted meseta of La Mancha. As ever the French were encumbered by their baggage train, excessive and inefficient, cluttered with the booty of a plundered Andalusia. Worse were the hordes of Spanish followers, the *afrancesados*, jostling in terror of their countrymen. Military sense would have left them behind but common humanity prevented their abandonment to the pitiless guerrillas. And the guerrillas were flocking in myriads round the labouring army, a pestilence contagious with success. Soult's march was slow and painful, but still he came on.

By October, as Wellington invested Burgos and King Joseph fled his precarious capital, Madrid, Hill had reached the great fortress city of Toledo. Ballesteros had been ordered to reinforce him with his Andalusian army. Together they would be just strong enough to hold Soult on the Tagus and so allow Wellington to wrest Spain from the French. In readiness for Soult's arrival Hill deployed his troops along the northern bank of the river.

The pipes had been silent for some time and only the steady tramp of the marching men served to welcome the rising sun. The of their coats was faded to a light brown by the drifting dust and their faces were streaked with sweat. Weary eyes turned greedily to the river below, where it glistened in the early light.

Some way ahead of the column Colonel Cadogan sat mounted with Ingram at his side. They were on the crest of a rise and the Colonel was gazing across the wooded parkland where, some two miles ahead, the smoke of cooking fires drifted from the town and the roofs of the royal palace were dark above the trees.

'Aranjuez,' the Colonel stated; 'the end of our road.'

'Yes sir,' said Ingram, but forbore further comment. The bridge here was one of the few places where the French could force across.

'Well, we'll know soon enough.' Cadogan looked at Ingram wistfully.

Ingram smiled. The whole army was in mood for battle. He turned in his saddle to watch the battalion approach. Only the first two companies were visible, the other eight hidden in the dust. A horseman detached himself and rode towards them.

'Major Cother coming up, sir.'

The Colonel nodded and leaned forward over the bow of his saddle, watching the waking town. As Cother drew near, the pipers at the head of the column, sensing the reason for this activity, took up a favourite march and the music told the ranks that their destination was near. Weary men stepped out the prouder, squared aching shoulders.

'Weel, Colonel, are we here, at last?' asked Cother. 'It's no ower early.'

Cadogan smiled and pointed to the smoke ahead.

'Aranjuez,' he repeated. 'Let us three ride on and find what awaits us. It will depend on the height of the river.'

The River Tagus was running slow with its shallow waters picking their sluggish way through the weeds and mud-banks. Even now in this late season there had been little rain in New Castile and the river seemed to lie lower every day. At the weir in the palace gardens the merest trickle was falling over the top where in normal times the river would be roaring and gurgling on its way to Toledo. But now there was so little water that an errant boy could pick his way across without difficulty as he hunted the toads hiding in the mud. The two officers standing on the bank watched him thoughtfully. Here, just thirty miles from Madrid, the Tagus was the only barrier protecting the capital from Soult's advance.

'I'll wager it was higher this morning,' said Fox.

Ingram nodded; he knew what his friend meant.

'We'll never be able to hold them here,' Fox went on, 'the frogs can cross where they choose.'

'Perhaps the rains will come soon.'

'Well, they'll have to be damned heavy to have any effect, and anyway they'd slow Ballesteros up.'

'We still don't know if he's moved yet.'

Ballesteros was a question mark in everyone's mind. It was fully a month since he had been ordered from Andalusia to take his place in the line against Soult, and still there was no news of him. Even allowing for Spanish inefficiency, defiance on a grand scale was indicated.

'If he hasn't moved yet,' said Fox, 'he'll be too late to be any use to us. Soult will be on us soon enough. We can't hold out here; we'll have to fall back.'

Ingram nodded and they continued their stroll around the town. 'You've heard the news from Burgos? The siege has failed; Wellington's had to fall back before Marmont.'

Fox grimaced. 'I can see us back in Portugal by the end of the year. If only the damned Spaniards'd stand and fight we'd be able to hold on to Madrid. We'll lose it now, mark my words, and then by next summer Boney'll have made peace in Russia and be able to move troops down here. It'll be like Corunna again.'

'Alexander's bound to make peace now Boney's in Moscow,' Ingram agreed. 'We won't get another chance like this year.'

'Boney'll come back himself, you'll see. That'll make the Peer run. We'll lose everything we've gained.'

'Still, Wellington's never lost a battle you know.'

'Neither did Moore, but he couldn't stop Boney bundling us out in '08. Wellington's never fought Boney.'

'You're in a happy mood.'

'It's well enough for you. You can ride,' Fox grumbled, 'I'll have to walk back to Portugal.'

In time they reached the southern gate and stopped to look at the road south where it ran through the plane trees towards Soult's advancing army. The cavalry vedettes were out there, waiting, watching. On the road itself a sentinel of the 50th Foot paced up and down at his post while another at the gate slapped his musket in salute to them.

A hussar was approaching, well mounted on a fine grey, and

they stopped, curious, for his uniform was French in style. He paused at the sentry's challenge and spoke a few words before being allowed to pass. Slowly he entered the town with the weariness of many miles and as he acknowledged the salute of the second sentry they saw that he was Spanish with the epaulettes of a major. He nudged his beautiful horse forward to approach them.

His uniform had been gorgeous once, the trousers and dolman sky-blue, contrasting with the scarlet of his silver-laced jacket. At his collar the baton and palm of the light cavalry glittered despite the dust. His long-plumed shako was bedecked in cap cords and set at a jaunty angle. Now all was faded and worn by the road. His face had the same travel-weariness, but even the dust on his drooping moustache could not conceal his grim self-assurance. Yet his smile was warm and engaging.

'Good morning gentlemans,' he said incongruously in the late afternoon. 'General Heel, yes, is here, no?'

Ingram took mercy on the Spaniard's broken English and replied in the man's own language.

'Good evening, señor, are you in search of General Hill's headquarters?'

The hussar relaxed visibly and spread his arms.

'How excellently señor speaks Spanish. It is no easy thing to master another man's language. Have you been long in my country?'

'For two years – off and on, with the fortune of war.'

'Ah, then you will have had opportunity to converse with my countrymen. In the south, alas, there were no English with whom I could talk and . . . '

'You're from the south?' Ingram intervened, for the man had a Castilian accent. 'Have you word of Ballesteros?'

The Spaniard smiled politely at the foreigner's rude interruption.

'Generalissimo Ballesteros,' he amended gently. 'I have advices from him here.' He tapped his sabretache. 'Permit me to introduce myself; I am Major Marcelliano José-Luís Biarroco y de Orthez of the Hussars of Maria Luisa, on the personal staff of the Generalissimo.'

'Lieutenants George Ingram and Humphrey Fox of His Majesty's 71st Highland Light Infantry.'

They bowed, Biarroco achieving the feat in his saddle, but Ingram's mind was racing. Wellington had recently been appointed generalissimo by the Supreme Junta. Surely Ballesteros knew this and had marched north as ordered.

'What do you mean, "Generalissimo" Ballesteros? And where the devil is he?'

The Spaniard smiled airily. 'The Generalissimo assumed supreme command in Andalusia last week. He has remained in Granada to consolidate his position. I have here dispatches for Lord Wellington to that effect.'

'Good God!' Ingram was appalled at the audacity of the coup. That Ballesteros had not moved imperilled Hill's entire position.

'What the devil's he saying?' asked Fox petulantly, but Ingram ignored him.

'General Hill had better hear of this at once.'

'No doubt, Señor Ingram. It will be a great relief to him to learn that Andalusia is in safe hands.'

Ingram prevented himself from snorting in disgust and contrived to speak with polite formality.

'Then, if you will permit me, Major, I will conduct you to his headquarters. Perhaps you will accompany me to our mess while I have my horse saddled.'

The Spaniard inclined his head in assent.

Colonel Cadogan was in agreement with Ingram's suggestion.

'You'd better stay close to him, Mr Ingram. I don't know if General Hill's got anyone with him at the moment whose Spanish is as good as yours. But get back here as soon as possible; I've no doubt we'll have to retire now. Damned dagos – you never know where you are with them.' He glowered at Biarroco where he stood with Fox, taking wine and chattering gaily in a mixture of broken languages. 'God knows what Lord Wellington will do; I'll wager the Junta will have something to say. I fear you may witness General Hill in considerable displeasure.'

General Hill was indeed displeased. His normally placid face grew fiery red as he listened to Ingram's translation of Biarroco's light-hearted words and the flush rose even to his shiny bald head. At last, beside himself, he brought his fist smashing down on the desk so forcefully that the ink-pots rattled in their holders and his snuff-box leapt and fell to the floor. Biarroco wavered, his self-confidence pricked, but he rallied and tried to go on. Hill struck the table again to silence him.

'Granada! Does he say Granada, sir? This is treason, sir. Tell him so. No, wait! Have you seen his credentials? Then I'll have them – I'll have every damned paper he's carrying. Treason, sir, that's what it is – treason.'

Biarroco recognised the English word and drew himself up with lofty arrogance.

'I am . . .'

'My God, Mr Ingram, I'll not argue with him! Get his papers, sir, and tell him what I say.'

The Spaniard was outraged when Ingram translated and he argued noisily. It gave offence to be asked for his credentials and he presented them with bad grace. Ingram examined them briefly and tendered them to the general.

'These would appear to be in order, sir.'

'Yes, that's Ballesteros's signature all right – but his dispatches, Mr Ingram, I'll have his dispatches.'

Biarroco shook his head. 'My dispatches are for Lord Wellington.'

Again the fist crashed on the table and the voice was lethal.

'I am ordering him to release the dispatches to me.'

But Biarroco protested vigorously and Ingram found himself raising his voice to be heard. They stood there angrily shouting down each other's words. This time both fists came down on the desk and Hill rose, upsetting his chair.

'By God, I'll not have my headquarters reduced to a hen's rabble. Tell him that if he doesn't release his papers forthwith I'll have him arrested and searched.'

Sullenly Biarroco acceded, but as he handed over the thick bundles of documents he growled, 'The General betrays my position as a courier. It is his dishonour.'

Ingram's discretion forbore translation. He had never known the kindly old general to be so angry, had never heard of him swearing as he did now. He scowled his resentment at the man who had brought the general such hurt and who now sought to dishonour him.

'That is a remark, Major, which I will discuss with you at a more appropriate moment.'

The Spaniard inclined his head in assent, and Ingram found his mouth go dry in realisation of his accepted challenge. He wondered if Biarroco was an efficient swordsman.

'Perhaps, young man, you would let me see those contentious

dispatches.' The general's voice was almost gentle, as though he realised what Ingram had done. 'You might ask this – this gentleman to wait outside.'

While Hill broke the seals, Ingram stooped to pick up the snuff-box. He was only able to save a few grains of the scattered dust and as he replaced the snuff-box on the desk he found Hill smiling at him wistfully.

'The very last of my Black Rappee. You see what my wicked temper has achieved. I must apologise, Mr Ingram, for my outrageous conduct, but that scoundrel provoked me.'

Ingram could find no words to reply. Even captains were too lofty to apologise to humble lieutenants. But Hill had more urgent business. He handed the sheath of documents to Ingram.

'These are all in Spanish – can't make a thing of them and Harringham's gone till the morning. I've no one else whose Spanish is good enough for this sort of thing. Perhaps you'll see what you can do. Start at once. Ask Rooke to give you a desk. Oh, and keep that fellow Biarroco under your wing. He might be useful.'

It was late, very late, when Ingram finished his task and could lay down his quill. Biarroco poured coffee from the pot an orderly had brought an hour before and passed him the cup. It was cold and vile, but somehow refreshing.

'Finished, at last, señor, it has been a long night's work.'

They were alone in the office, with its litter of cluttered desks and maps and the oil lamp stinking in the tobacco smoke. Ingram's head spun with a weary jumble of high-flown and complex phrases. He had long since lost track of the significance of the words, concerned only to transcribe them into meaningful English. Biarroco's assistance had been invaluable and as they had worked together the constraint which their honour had imposed on the relationship had gradually relaxed. But now the job was done and memory of their dispute reasserted itself. Ingram found himself looking into the Spaniard's eyes and saw the pride reflected there. He had lost face and that demanded satisfaction. Ingram felt sympathy for the man and realised that he had grown to like him.

'Thank you for your assistance, Major, I doubt if I could have managed without you. I regret that military necessity rendered it essential to relieve you of the documents in your custody.'

'I understand, señor. I did not appreciate the importance which the General attached to the presence of Generalissimo Ballesteros.

On the other hand, General Hill threatened to arrest me; scarcely conduct towards a gentleman.'

It was touch and go, but Ingram knew that he did not wish to duel with this proud, amiable officer.

'You will concede that the General was provoked, but I can assure you that he has already expressed his regret at his fury.'

It was at least a half-truth and Biarroco looked at him evenly for a moment and then, leaning over the lamp to light another of his paper-bound cigars, he smiled.

'If the General has apologised, Señor Ingram, then he has behaved with consummate honour. I trust we may now forget the matter.'

Ingram felt his face break into a broad grin and he rose, gathering up all his sheets of paper.

'I must take these to the General, but then perhaps you would do me the honour of joining me for breakfast at my mess.'

'It will be my honour, señor, to break my fast with such distinguished soldiers.'

But they were not to have the opportunity for such a leisurely breakfast, for General Hill had further work for them. Ingram found him with Tilson-Chowne, the divisional commander, and the chief of staff. The General ran his eye over the translations and handed them to Tilson-Chowne with a grunt.

'We'd better get these into Madrid immediately and have them posted to the Commander-in-Chief. I'll send the Biarroco fellow with them. Give them to Harringham to copy.' He looked at Ingram. 'No rest for you, young man. You can take this Spanish fellow into Madrid and hand him over to an escort there. I want to be sure he reaches his Lordship in the north. I'll send word to Colonel Cadogan. You'd better get back as soon as you can. I expect he'll be needing you – Soult is in presence at last. We're falling back. I can't hold the frogs here now, with the river as it is. Get yourself something to eat – I'll have dispatches for you when you're ready.'

Biarroco was waiting for him in the office where Harringham now sat amidst sleepy clerks hurriedly copying the papers. The Spaniard shook his head vigorously when he heard the news.

'You have seen my horse. She cannot be ridden to Madrid now, she is quite spent.'

'Then you'd better take one of mine,' drawled Harringham, and turned to Ingram.

'There's a gelding downstairs. Tell the orderly. But mark'ee, Ingram, you bring him back to me – and I won't have spurs used on him.'

The orderly was sullen and reluctant.

'Well, he don't usually lend his horses, don't Captain Harringham, sir. T'aint like him, sir, if you know what I mean. Specially to a dago, sir.'

'Another word and I'll have you disciplined. This gentleman is a respected ally acting on the General's instructions. Get that horse out here.'

'Oh, if it's for the General, sir. Only doing me duty, sir, begging your pardon.'

Now Biarroco was arguing.

'But my mare – La Paloma – what about her? I can't abandon her like baggage in a campaign.'

'I'm sorry, Major, you will have to. You must realise by now the urgency of your news. Captain Harringham will look after her until I return, and then I assure you I will care for her until I can restore her to you.'

He was glad that Biarroco did not know of the impending withdrawal. It was so easy to lose contact in a retreat. Ingram wondered how bad things really were. It was rumoured that Wellington was having trouble falling back after the failure of the siege at Burgos.

'Your word of honour?'

Ingram paused and saw the concern in the Spaniard's eye. He remembered that this man was a cavalryman and would have a more than ordinary affection for the animal. He wondered how many desperate situations they had shared, man and beast, in the bloody attrition of Andalusia.

'My word of honour,' he pledged.

'My home is in Avila. I will be there.'

They had barely time to saddle up and snatch a quick breakfast before Harringham brought through the dispatches. Ingram was almost relieved, for he found tortilla revolting at that hour of day. He grabbed a handful of apricots and stuffed them in his pocket. Biarroco was thanking Harringham for the horse in flowing phrases but the reply he evoked was almost bored.

'Yes, very good Pepe, just remember – no spurs, h'm?'

Then they were down to the yard and mounted up and picking their way through the silent avenues where the population stirred nervously, awakening to fears of the approaching French. The birds were calling in autumnal chorus and as they turned out on the road to Madrid the two men heard the sounds of reveille beckon from a score of camps.

It was a sombre morning that broke over the plain of New Castile as the sun etched facings on the battalions of marching cloud. A wind stirred in the northern mountains and drove down the Jarama valley in forewarning of tempest. It would be raining in the north where Wellington was still ensnared in the aftermath of Burgos. Once, they thought they heard thunder and Ingram reined up and pointed south, across the Jarama.

'Now the rains will come,' he called.

But Biarroco smiled and shook his head.

'Guns.'

Ingram could hear them now, the subtleties of sound which Biarroco had so quickly identified. His respect for the Spaniard rose.

'Soult must be pressing the crossings,' he stated.

'Yes' – Biarroco's voice was calm – 'The river is too low; your army will not stop him.'

'We'd better get on. It's no good worrying,' urged Ingram, but his thoughts were back with Hill's little army trying to withdraw before an enemy three times its size.

Yet it was a pleasant enough change to ride through the meseta with its brown hills rolling into the distance and the grapes heavy in the vineyards. From time to time they would pass a ruined fortress where long-forgotten men had watched these selfsame marches. The hamlets that they passed were squalid biscuit-coloured dens, unchanged in centuries, where even the children did not stop to watch them go, so accustomed were they to the signs of war. But on occasion they came to blackened fields where the vines were burnt and the olive groves thrown down, or to villages where the buildings were broken and empty and charred to silence, and where there were no people to turn away as they rode by.

'All of Spain is like this,' Biarroco grieved.

It was so true that Ingram noted the destruction almost mechanically, without stopping to reflect on the death and suffering told by every such sight. But Ingram had seen the wasteland north of Torres Vedras, where Masséna had vented his frustration on the Portuguese people.

'Napoleon's soldiers care nothing for what they destroy.'

'They are the spawn of Satan. The things a man has seen. In

Andalusia. In Madrid. There is no end. In Avila, my home . . .' The Spaniard's voice broke with hatred. Ingram wondered what he had witnessed in his native city, but to prevent a recitation of the horrors of Spain he urged his horse forward again.

At Pinto they broke their journey and threw their reins to an ostler boy before entering the inn. Ingram found that he was stiff and Biarroco, seeing, teased him.

'My friend, you foot soldiers should learn to ride like true campaigners. Myself, save last night, I have been in the saddle for thirty hours. And riding for a week before that.'

'Perhaps today you are better mounted than you are accustomed.'

'Ah, the gelding is a fine beast, but my Paloma . . . she is a true horse.'

There was the usual fare on the table, a stew of chorizo, greasy potatoes in a mess of garlic, unleavened bread. But they ate with satisfaction. The wine was good. Biarroco picked up the porro and tilted back his head to let a stream of wine run from the narrow spout into his mouth. He stretched back and extended his arms until the distance was at its maximum and drank long and deep before stopping suddenly and thumping the beaker down on the table. The challenge was in his eyes as he reached for bread to wipe his lips and moustache. Ingram met his look, smiled in acceptance of the game and reached for the wine. He managed to start the flow easily and felt the cool liquid run down his throat. As he stretched his arms the pressure increased but still he managed to keep control. He was almost there, but as he tried to lean his head back he felt himself swallow and his concentration broke. Immediately his gullet was full of wine and as he broke off it spilled from his mouth and sprayed all over the front of his tunic. He spluttered over the table, laughing, and Biarroco roared merrily.

'What a man! A real Spaniard.'

He reached for the wine again but Ingram placed his hand on his arm.

'I've got to get you to Madrid, remember? And then you're going on north. Lord Wellington wants to see you.'

The Spaniard shrugged in resignation.

'No doubt he too will be angry. A soldier does his duty. I hear that he is a hard man to offend. But you will join me in Avila, and come to my home. We will drink many . . .'

In the street outside there were horsemen and their presence was disturbing the townsfolk. Someone screamed, a man cursed and there was a shot.

The ostler must almost have reached the door, for his hand was on the latch when he fell and his falling threw it open so that the two officers could witness the tragedy. The boy was dead, they could both identify that. There were horses milling around in the narrow street and a townsman was cowering in the shelter of a pillar. An unshaven man in ragged clothes was waving two pistols at people further up the street.

'The devil!' exclaimed Biarroco, drawing his sabre. 'Guerrilleros.'

'Bandits, more like.'

'The same. Undisciplined rabble.'

They were barely in time. There were men at their horses, one of them mounted on the gelding. Ingram found that he too had his sword in his hand, a useless gesture for there were thirty of them. It was appalling to see how cowed the people were. The riders had taken a girl, thrown her over a mule: presumably it was her lover who lay over there in his parents' arms, coughing the blood from his lungs. The man on the gelding kicked the horse forward.

'Stop!'

He had shouted in English, but they halted and looked at him.

'Leave those horses, they belong to me!'

'So! The Englishman speaks our language. My compliments.' The leader spat at Ingram's feet. 'Paco, bring the horses.'

Ingram felt his resolution waver, yet he began.

'If you . . .'

But Biarroco was speaking and his voice was sure and firm.

'Are you bandits or are you afrancesados? Do you act for yourself or France? You call yourselves guerrilleros, but you are scavengers like the Andalusian vulture. You cow the people with your threats and talk of Spain but you are carrion, and fit only to serve France.'

'I will kill you for that,' said the leader.

'Think well what you say, for I am on important duty for the Generalissimo.'

That impressed them, though they had no idea who was the Generalissimo, but the leader had committed himself and he slipped from his saddle, cutlass in hand.

'Have you no fear of the garotte?' Biarroco cried. 'I name you traitor.'

'Then, by Santa Teresa, name me well. I am El Abulense.'

El Abulense; the Avilan. Biarroco raised his sabre.

'I will kill you, townsman. I am Biarroco y de Orthez.'

The name was significant, Ingram observed, for El Abulense hesitated for a moment, but then with a snarl he closed for battle. Ingram would not interfere, but a man darted forward at Biarroco's undefended back and the Scot quickly checked him with a sword-point at his throat. The dagger dropped and the man stood pale in fright. Then Ingram saw the muskets and pistols trained on him, and knew that if Biarroco fell he would die also.

He could not turn his head to watch the duel for to do so would weaken him in their eyes, so he stood with his sword at the man's throat, listening to the clashing weapons, wondering what was happening. He tried to distract himself from the cries of the bandits, from the clash of cutlass and sabre and concentrate on the man at the point of his own sabre. The Spaniard's blood was pulsing by his ear. There was a mole just there with long black hairs. One of the hairs was white. If it comes to it, he thought, I'll have him just there, at the mole. He wondered if he could do it so coldly, if he would have time.

There it was again, the scraping of steel as the blades withdrew. One of them was hacking to the other's expert guard. He supposed the expert would be Biarroco; he hoped so. It took skill and strength to withstand such an attack. And I was going to duel with him this morning, he thought irrelevantly. The gang were shouting, urging their leader on again. An awesome ring of steel on steel. El Abulense must have swung with all his strength. The blades shrieked as they came apart. Then a thud and a hiss and the sound of spurting blood on the ground. The world relaxed; the deadly barrels lowered and he could turn and look.

Biarroco stood with his dripping blade over his victim, eyeing the horsemen in challenge. Sweat ran on his face and he panted in weariness. But there was no denying his challenge. The man at Ingram's sword-point eyed his surrender and backed away so that they stood there, alone together, facing all those ruthless men.

For a moment everything was tense, then one man snapped his fingers at the men holding their horses. Instantly the bandit leapt from the gelding and the little party scurried away, leaving the two animals free. The leader may have been killed, but now the gang had a man they obeyed instantly, without question. There was no doubt that they all feared him.

'Biarroco y de Orthez, I will not forget you. There are few who win the respect of José Perez. And you, Englishman, are a brave man.'

He nodded to his followers and they turned their horses. The girl screamed in despair.

'What of the woman?' Ingram protested.

José Perez stopped and turned on him and his eyes were like cold gun metal.

'Hombre, you are lucky to have your lives.'

Then they were gone, a mashing of flying hooves clattering in solid body into the distance.

Biarroco was wiping his sabre and he looked tense when he spoke. 'And now we ride on to Madrid.'

The capital was dismayed by the rumour of Hill's withdrawal and by the time an escort had been found for Biarroco the preparations for evacuation had already commenced. There were wagons being loaded in the courtyard and Biarroco watched the bustle for a moment before eyeing the Spanish dragoons waiting to take him north. He turned whimsically to Ingram.

'Madrid may fall, but these fellows will take care of me. They won't let me stray far, I imagine.'

It was embarrassing to meet his smile and know that he was virtually under arrest. The man was exhausted.

'You're very tired.'

Biarroco dropped his paper cigar to the cobbles and crushed it under his boot.

'A soldier does his duty. You're staying here tonight?'

Ingram nodded. 'I'll try to find my regiment in the morning.'

'Take the gelding back safely; he's a fine animal. Thank the captain for me.'

'Yes. And La Paloma – I'll get her back to you.'

'I know.' He smiled again. 'I dare say you'll be passing Avila shortly.'

'It looks that way.' The regiment had withdrawn through Avila before now.

'I'll see you there.' Biarroco swung himself up into the saddle. 'Goodbye, Ingram – and good luck.'

'Goodbye. We'll meet in Avila.'

3

The British army lay encamped on the slopes of the Sierra Guaderrama, miserable in the incessant rain, watching the French approach from Madrid. The vedettes were out, little groups of light cavalry with their capes drawn round them, the horsehair crests on their helmets sodden and heavy letting the water run down unprotected necks. The roads were rutted quagmires and the artillery would have a gruelling job crossing the mountains when Hill at last decided to resume the withdrawal. The hillsides ran with water and the fields where the camps lay were deep in mud, the grassy surface broken by the wear of the soldiers' feet. The men languished in their makeshift tents and made futile efforts to keep dry. Clothes, equipment, bedding – everything was wet and the mud clung everywhere, on their bodies, in their hair and even in their food, so that each mouthful was gritty and foul.

Above El Escorial Ingram stood in the battalion's tiny horse lines and looked around at the desolate scene. A cold mist lay over the mountains and the woodland enveloping the gorge was black in its nakedness. The last leaves hung dripping, limp, from the branches. Great boulders lay like sleeping tombs, grey and monolithic, stark among the rows of sagging tents. Most gloomy of all was the palace, sombre and ugly with its blank, unseeing windows, a symbol of misery.

Ingram shuddered and turned back to the horses. The wretched animals were patient in the rain under the scanty shelter of their blankets and he reached forward to stroke La Paloma's neck. She nuzzled forward affectionately, placing her splendid head against his shoulder. The animal was in beautiful condition, a fine beast with wiry strength, and Ingram blessed his good fortune in having Ramon to look after her. She would not be in his care for much longer for Hill must soon withdraw on Avila and unite with

Wellington in his retreat from Burgos. The main army would be suffering dreadfully in this weather; the roads were in appalling condition.

Ingram patted the horse's head and saw the sadness in the gentle eyes before turning away and trudging across the greasy field towards his tent. He saw a soldier scurrying out to the lower end of the camp and pitied the man. The latrines were stinking and overflowing, as he knew from recent unpleasantness. He would have to speak to the sergeant-major and organise another work party. Perhaps the commissary's people would be able to produce fresh quicklime in the afternoon.

He stooped to pull back the flap of the canvas hovel which he shared with Fox, and water cascaded upon him as he crawled inside.

'For God's sake watch what you're doing – and get that damned cape off.'

His disgruntled tent-mate was wrapped in his blanket, trying to pretend that he was dry despite the fine spray coming through the canvas. Ingram swore vilely as he struggled with the stiff buttons at his collar. He felt the mud soak its wetness through to his seat, and found himself hopelessly fankled. But at last he managed to undo the thing and opened it beneath him. He drew his blanket around him, swore again and wondered when he would ever be warm. Fox growled malevolently and tried to get back to sleep. But he was to be disturbed again.

'Mr Ingram, sir!'

The orderly's voice from without summoned him.

'Yes, Watson, I'm in here.'

'The Colonel's compliments, sir, and he'd like to see you.'

Ingram sighed and Fox swore.

The Colonel's tent was luxurious by comparison and he looked up from his camp table when Ingram entered.

'Ah, there you are, Mr Ingram. Sit you down.'

He seated himself on a chest and wondered what additional misery was to be heaped upon him. The Colonel handed him a sheet of paper.

'Our new route of march, Mr Ingram. Lord Wellington's had to run for it. The entire army is falling back on the Douro. You'll see from that we'll be hard pushed. Long marches, I fear. How soon can the battalion be under way?'

Ingram thought rapidly. It appeared that the French must be in overwhelming strength. The gains of the summer were being lost. He rehearsed the state of the battalion in his mind.

'Will there be time to cook, sir?'

'I think that is essential. I want the men to march on full bellies.'

So, while the dripping tents were struck the heavy cooking pots tried to get warm over sizzling fires. And, as the mud-coated veterans plodded around gathering their belongings, the women bustled about with food for their men. As usual they defied orders and moved off early with all their baggage, jostling ahead in a disruptive throng to be settled in, ready, at the next bivouac. The companies fell in, straggling over the uneven ground with the sergeants calling the roll. The sergeant-major stumped over to Ingram, halted with a muddy splosh, and saluted, arm aquiver, in the regulation time as though at a royal review.

'Three men missing, sir,' he barked, 'absent without leave.'

'Thank you, Sergeant-Major. We'll have to leave them behind; they're probably lying drunk in some bodega.'

'Very likely, sir.' Drunkenness was the pestilence of retreat.

Ingram climbed into his saddle and took a last look round the field. Everything was as it should be.

'Three men missing, sir. Otherwise present and correct.'

'Very good, Mr Ingram. Move to the right in column of route, if you please.'

File by file the battalion marched in companies from the trampled field and wheeled down to the road to take their position in the long trail of the retreating army. At their head the pipers charmed the stiffness from their chilled limbs and urged them on to the weary miles ahead. The other units of Howard's Brigade were also moving; their old companions through the years of war. The company of the 60th Rifles waited in their green jackets to form the rearguard, mostly exiled Germans hating the French. Ahead marched the 50th Foot with their squealing fifes and drums, and on their right as they passed, dearest of all, the 92nd Highlanders, the Gordons, stood ready in dripping bonnets to take their place in the column. By the roadside Howard was sitting with his staff, watching his men go by.

'Seventy-first, eyes left!'

The Colonel wheeled aside to address the General and Ingram followed suit.

'Morning, Cadogan. We're in for a march this time, I fancy. No more hanging about. I dare say we'll have the usual problems with discipline on retreat so be on your guard for stragglers.'

But the men looked steady enough as they tramped past. Despite the broken surface of the road, deep in treacherous mud, they contrived to look smart and their faces were those of men acquainted with war. Even the more unruly elements were behaving well, but Ingram knew that the worst characters could be relied upon to go astray, like the three men already missing, in the drunken disorder which afflicted every retreat.

Thus they left El Escorial with its sightless palace and made their way north, skirting the hills, to the great pass of the Guadarrama. For two days the column wound over the mountain road, which had almost defeated Napoleon, until at last the cavalry rearguard could break off its skirmishing and follow, vigilant for the hunting French. On they marched through the Sierras and the rain did not ease, but poured down upon their weariness, as boots let in the wet and worn clothes hung limp and chafing.

By night they erected their useless tents and scavenged for firewood to heat the heavy kettles, then lay exhausted in the chilling damp until, long before dawn, the sergeants called them from their half-sleep to begin another march. Day saw the weak fall from the ranks, and at every hamlet men slipped away to stupefy themselves with liquor and be left behind. Officers and sergeants did what they could to rouse the drunkards, persuade or discipline them into reason. And Ingram listed the men who had disappeared and knew that despite all efforts the morrow would bring more. There was consolation in reflecting that it was the more useless men who were being thus lost.

On one occasion he forsook his eternal forms to aid Hall in a search through the taverns of one of those squalid mountain towns. It was Hall's sergeant, Ross, who took the lead, guiding them along the narrow alleys.

'There is a terrible drinking place down here, sir. I have mind of it from when we were here with General Sir John Moore. There was the same devilment even then.'

'I remember it,' said Hall. 'A large place full of soldiers and a toothless old crone of a hostess. She sang beautifully.'

But the place was gone, sacked long since by the French. A man sat slumped in the broken doorway. They eyed him sadly as he lay in the rain.

'It was snowing when we were last at this place, sir,' Ross recalled.

Ingram scowled at the rain. 'Thank God it isn't snowing now.'

'It was the snow that stopped Boney catching us then,' Hall reflected. 'Back in '08 on the Guadarrama. I wonder how he's finding it now, in Russia.'

The man on the doorstep looked up and they saw that he was an officer in the hussars of the King's German Legion. His gutteral English was slurred.

'Not good in Russia. He retreats. All these damn years and the swine retreats at last.'

'Retreats!' Ingram exclaimed. 'From Moscow?'

'Yes. From Moscow. No good. There will be snow. Very cold. Many men will die. I know, once I have been there.'

'You're sure of this?' Hall demanded.

It was extraordinary news, tremendous in its import. Strange to learn it thus like ale-house gossip.

'I am sure. All change. In Hanover . . . ' He stopped and his eyes wavered. 'I am drunk, I am sorry. It is not good to be drunk, but sometimes . . . I fight all day. My vedettes are driven in. These damned lancers. Sometimes it is good to drink . . . These lancers . . . My sergeant is killed today. He has been a fine fellow. From my town. We are together always, since Bonaparte . . . sometimes a man must drink. I have here brandy. You will drink with me?'

'That's kind of you,' said Ingram, 'but we won't if you'll take no offence.'

'We're retreating too, don't you know,' Hall gently supplemented.

'Yes, yes. Very drunk, ashamed. God rot all Frenchmen.' He tried to stand up but was too unsteady.

'Come on, my dear fellow,' Ingram encouraged, 'let us help you.'

And they saved him, taking him back to his regiment. Somehow it made up for not finding their own men, a memory to encourage them through the following day's march.

It was during that day's weary blur that Ingram, bruised and saddle-sore, realised that the rain had rendered the road to Avila impenetrable to the army. They would pass ten miles to the north and he would be unable to do anything about his promise to Biarroco. The march forced on late into the night by broken roads that demanded the utmost of every man and woman. And still it rained and the mountains gave no rest. But the final gruelling day brought them to Villacastin and there, at last, they halted, for their junction with Wellington had been secured.

Yet they were not to stay long in Villacastin, for late on the following afternoon a message came down to Hill that sent the drums beating and summoned men cursing from their rest. Fox brought the reason to Ingram where he was superintending the collection of entrenching tools.

'Wellington's been driven from the Douro. We're falling back on Salamanca.'

'God, that's a hundred miles.'

'Eighty at least – and we'll be hurrying. The Colonel wants to see you.'

'Look after this for me. Corporal! If that tool's broken throw it away. Mr Fox is taking over now.'

Here was a sergeant to trouble him with some minor problem.

'McGuinness isnae weel, sir – Ah'll need anither man for the baggage detail.'

'That's up to you, Sergeant; you ought to be able to decide these things yourself. I'm sure Riley could be spared by Captain Hall.'

A few more paces before the next distraction, a medical orderly.

'Will it be the usual arrangements, sir? The surgeon's worried, sir; it's the dysentery, sir. There's two men awful sick, too sick to move, sir.'

So disease was back in the ranks again. He scowled for he could not help.

'Order of march as usual; he can follow his normal practice about the sick men. The field ambulance should be available.'

When Ingram joined him, the Colonel was in conference with the two majors, Cother and his junior, MacKenzie. Weariness had aged the latter, emphasising his family resemblance to the paymaster. They all looked worn and haggard, Ingram thought, as the Colonel leaned back from the map before him.

'I can see you've heard the news, Mr Ingram. The army's to stand united at Salamanca. I understand Lord Wellington's flank's been turned so he'd no option but withdraw. We are to be in Peñaranda in two days' time.'

'Good God, that's sixty miles, sir.'

'Yes, we'll be busy enough I dare say. But you're not coming with us, Mr Ingram.'

'Sir?'

'You're not going to like this, Mr Ingram. No more do I. But the orders have come from the Commander-in-Chief himself.'

'Sir?'

Cadogan lowered his eyes to the map, drummed his fingers and looked up again. 'You are being detached for a most unpleasant duty . . . ah . . . your friend Biarroco is in trouble. The Cortes ordered his arrest for his part in the Ballesteros affair. Did you know he was one of Ballesteros's most trusted advisers? His master's under lock and key now but Biarroco slipped his escort. It's desertion of course, so they'll hang him if he's caught. That's where you come in.'

Ingram listened in dismay, hoping that the exuberant hussar would retain his freedom, wondering where he was involved. Cadogan hesitated again.

'Ah . . . I regret, Mr Ingram, that you have orders to arrest him.'

It was appalling; Ingram shook his head in denial. Cadogan raised a hand to stop his protest and tried to explain.

'It appears that they want him very badly; he's got too much important intelligence to be allowed to run loose. Intelligence which must not get into the wrong hands. He's thought to be in Avila, which is where you're going. If he's not there come straight back to the battalion – we'll be somewhere along the road.'

'Sir, this is outrageous, Major Biarroco. . . .' But words failed Ingram.

'I know. I don't like my adjutant being used as a policeman, particularly since he's chosen for his friendship with the victim. General Hill has been acquainted with my views. I told him I could not do without you; he said I would have to.'

'That's the very devil, Colonel,' MacKenzie interjected. 'You cannot let the laddie go.'

'It'll no do, Henry, MacKenzie's right,' protested Cother. 'Damnation, it's unreasonable, man.'

'I'll thank you gentlemen to attend to our route of march. This matter does not concern you.'

The biting reply grieved them more by the clear distress of the speaker at addressing them thus than the cutting words themselves.

'Your pardon, Colonel, we forgot ourselves.'

'I'll do my duty, sir,' said Ingram sadly.

Cadogan nodded. 'They're giving you a half-troop of dragoons, though what use they'll be if you run into the French. . . . Try to come back in one piece.' The Colonel rose and led him to the door. 'This man's important, George, you've got to get him if you can.'

Perhaps it was Ingram's distaste for the whole operation that caused him to take an instant dislike to Fenborough, the cornet in command of the dragoons. He knew the breed; eighteen years old, with a confidence of twice his years and contempt for the improperly bred. The arrogance recalled to Ingram certain young members of Edinburgh society and their conduct when his father's estate was sequestrated. The bitterness was there yet. He was leading La Paloma and the youth eyed the mare enviously.

'I say, you Scotch fellows look after yourselves, haw. Where did you get a grey like that, Ingram?'

'You call me "sir",' said Ingram evenly and in the offended silence they rode from the town. It was an inauspicious start to their mission.

The journey over the mountains was terrible in the night, for the poor road was barely identifiable in the rain. In places it was merely a watercourse, running deep and so fast that the very stones were carried along in the torrent. Several times horses fell and one was so injured that they had to destroy the beast and leave its rider behind. They arrived at Avila before daybreak and found the gate closed against them, and Ingram had to rest patient while the wardens sought an officer of the town guard with sufficient authority to admit them.

'Apologies, señor, my men thought by your uniforms that you were French.' It was understandable enough by the continental style of the dragoons' blue coats.

'I must see the mayor at once.'

The man shrugged and Ingram knew that the mayor would not see him until the mayor felt ready to see him.

'Do you know a Major Biarroco y de Orthez?'

'Don Marcelliano? Naturally.'

'Is he here? I wish to see him urgently.'

The officer looked at him shrewdly. 'The hour is early, señor, and you have ridden hard. Perhaps you would care to accompany me to my office for refreshment.'

He led them up the street into a small square and entered the mansion on the corner. It had been some wealthy family's residence, Ingram guessed, before the decline of the city, but now it was decayed, in use as the headquarters of the little town guard. The Spaniard showed the two officers into an ante-room then slipped away.

'Damned dagos,' said the cornet, pacing up and down the room.

'You're deuced clever with their lingo, haw. Never could understand the devils myself, sir.'

'I suggest you make sure that your men are being looked after,' Ingram growled.

Later a servant brought them anis and coffee but otherwise they were undisturbed. Day was breaking and Ingram looked from the window over the decrepit buildings to the ramparts of the city wall. A lone sentry stood there gazing out at the plateau. He wondered how long they would have to wait.

'Old Francisco's taking the devil of a time,' Fenborough grumbled. 'Do you dice?'

Ingram glowered at the cubes rattling in the youth's hands.

'No, I do not.'

He wanted to think and wished his companion would stop fidgeting. He would have ordered him to sit still but that would have been quite offensive and he knew that he had already behaved in the most surly fashion. He tried to make amends. 'I have much to think of. Dealing with Spaniards always makes demands on a man's patience.'

'Laggardly fellows. Give me the frogs. At least they'll fight.'

The man was impossible, Ingram decided, and he sat down at the window to gaze moodily at the street outside. The whole unpleasant business required his thought, for clearly Biarroco was well regarded in his native city. It was infuriating to be unable to act immediately but long experience told him that a Spanish mayor could not be hurried in such a matter. To force an interview at this stage would be fruitless and likely to cause further delay. He wondered how seriously the city fathers would respect directions from the Cortes. It seemed likely that someone in authority knew of Biarroco's proscription and yet it appeared that he remained at liberty as a respected member of the community. If there was any resistance from the people of the town to the arrest it would be difficult to control the situation with only Fenborough and his handful of dragoons. He wondered how good a man the young cornet was in a tight situation; certainly his conduct thus far was unimpressive and he seemed to pay little enough attention to his men.

They had been waiting for just over two hours when a short man came into the room. He was a ragged fellow with bare feet and bowed perfunctorily at them. Ingram noticed the nasty-looking stiletto in the man's red cummerbund.

'You are seeking Don Marcelliano?'

'Yes.'

'Is it Señor Ingram? I see you have the horse.'

'I am Ingram.'

'Then you come with me.' It was a peremptory instruction, forceful from such a tiny man.

'Where?' Ingram demanded.

'To Santa Teresa,' he declared and, seeing Ingram remain still, he added, 'I follow Don Marcelliano. It is better you come.'

The man's tone was poisonous but there was no denying that it was important to accept the summons. There might be no other opportunity. As Ingram moved, Fenborough rose to join him and this caused the little man to scowl and hiss sharply through his teeth.

'Wait here, Mr Fenborough, and keep your men alert and ready for trouble. I believe the dons have suspected our mission. Don't unsaddle.'

He followed the man through the winding streets of the town, trying hard to calculate his direction and remember the route. They crossed a square and followed a meandering alley coming out at last into a broad avenue. The townspeople watched curiously, almost hostilely, as he passed, and Ingram was saddened to see the poverty in this once fine city. They halted at the door of a beautiful church and the little man knocked. It was a moment before the door was opened by a nun and Ingram knew that this was a convent.

'Santa Teresa,' explained the little man.

The nun beckoned Ingram within and he saw that his little guide had disappeared. He followed the nun in silence through the long cloisters until she led him into a little chapel. They stopped together at the door, waiting. Ingram looked around curiously. The interior was grotesquely ornate to Ingram's Presbyterian eyes and overladen with statues and reliquary. At the altar a priest was saying mass but only one communicant was present, a slim woman dressed in the inevitable black, but the style and quality of her clothes betrayed her wealth. The rites were coming to an end, Ingram's classical education enabled him to detect; he followed the formal Latin. The woman received her benediction, crossed herself and rose. When she turned he could see that she was young, in her twenties, but with tragedy written on her face, and the elegance of a true patrician. As she walked up the aisle towards him she looked directly at him and her dignified approach bade the nun move discreetly aside.

'Señor Ingram? I am Doña Margarita Ana-Teresa Menorez-Cabezon de Biarroco.'

He bowed, and tried to guess her relationship with Biarroco. The hussar had never spoken of his family.

'I am honoured to make your acquaintance, señorita.'

She half smiled, sadly. 'You flatter my youth, señor, I am a matron of five years.'

'Your pardon, señora, I . . . ' Ingram was flustered by his clumsy assumption of her spinsterhood. The name should have warned him. She would be Biarroco's wife.

'You have brought the horse. It is the act of an honourable man in these difficult times. Marcelliano will be happy. It was a gift from his brother. A fine animal.'

Ingram was discountenanced by this in view of his true purpose in Avila. He said nothing and the woman looked at him thoughtfully.

'You have not only brought La Paloma, but dragoons also. Are the French so near? Or is their presence perhaps connected with the disgraceful conduct of the Cortes? It would be strange if a man of honour came on so vulgar a duty.'

'A soldier cannot choose his duty, señora, though he may dislike what he does.'

'And you would satisfy your honour, first, before carrying Marcelliano to the gallows.'

'I would have it otherwise but he has deserted and committed treason. His secrets must not fall to the French.'

'So! They consider him treasonous.' Her voice was bitter, the tone low and angry. 'What do they know who have hidden in Portugal or Cadiz during the bitter years. They who fight among themselves for power, who raise an English lord to command the armies of Spain. These are the men for whom you act. Why do you not devote your duties to killing the French? Or would you rather hunt a loyal man?'

'Señora, I . . . '

'Let me tell you why Marcelliano would never betray his country or risk his secrets passing to the French. There was a man here in Avila whom the French would interrogate. They crucified him to the door of the Basilica de San Vicente with bayonets for nails and when he was silent they blinded him and then castrated him, and still he said nothing. They disembowelled him and yet his tongue was still, so they cut it out and left him there to die. And they would not let us who saw go forward to succour him.'

'That is a terrible thing to have witnessed, yet in Spain . . . '

'He was Marcelliano's brother! And my husband.'

It was horrible, too horrible to contemplate. He reeled with the shock of it, the image of the hussar's proud brother, the misery of this dignified woman. He could find no words.

'Do you think, Señor Ingram, that Marcelliano could betray Spain to the men who did that to Luciano? Would he die other than Luciano did with hatred and loyalty?'

'Señora . . . ' He had to overcome his horror, his sadness for her. 'I respect him, señora, but my orders are clear. His part in the Ballesteros conspiracy is deemed treasonous.'

'Indeed, señor? And what knowledge have you of the affairs of Spain?'

'Little, for unlike your good brother I do not consider a soldier has any part in politics.' He modified his tone. 'Like him I have my duty to perform. It gives me neither pleasure nor satisfaction.'

She looked at him coldly and he saw the bitterness in her eyes before they flashed with impatient resolution.

'Then you had better attend to your duty, señor, since you know no other guide to your conduct.'

She swept past him and left him standing there in the chapel, feeling clumsy and guilty, and very much alone. But the nun had remained and now she bade him follow her again. Ingram wondered what new secret was to be revealed to him in the rarefied confines of the convent, but then he saw that they were at the outside door and suddenly he was in the street. The door closed behind him with hollow finality.

There was no one in sight so he began to walk up the avenue and tried to remember each turning on his way. His instincts had served him well for in time he came to the square where the headquarters lay. Two of the dragoons had been posted as a picket at the front door. He was about to step from the street when his little guide appeared from a doorway and caught his arm.

'Don Marcelliano is well loved in Avila. We will never allow you to take him.' He spat in emphasis and the eyes that met Ingram were deadly with promise, then he was gone.

4

Ingram stood in the square. Around him was a bustle of movement yet no one could be seen save Fenborough's two sentries. It was obvious that trouble was looming and he decided to see the mayor at once. He would press the captain of the town guard to locate the civil leader without further delay. Having settled his mind, he walked smartly across the square and acknowledged the salutes of the sentries.

'Where's Mr Fenborough?'

'In that room there, sir, beside where you was before. The sergeant's with him. We been under arms since you left, sir.'

Fenborough looked up when he entered and Ingram could see the relief in his face.

'I thought we'd lost you. I've had a bit of trouble with the dagos; they didn't take kindly to being thrown out but they soon saw sense in a sword point. They've taken the grey though. Dunno how they did it, but she's gone from the courtyard.'

Ingram clicked his tongue in annoyance. Now the captain of the town guard would never co-operate. It had been very high-handed of Fenborough to evict the townsmen from their own headquarters, but in fairness, if there was trouble, it was a wise precaution to have the building cleared. He wondered how he would find the mayor and sighed in exasperation. Yet it was amusing to consider the missing horse. Some friend of Biarroco must have slipped La Paloma from under the sentry's very eyes. It reminded him of the missing mule in the sunny days down south.

'Well, have you found this dago fellow?' the cornet asked sharply.

Ingram restrained his reply in the presence of the sergeant. He was sure Biarroco was in the city and felt certain that the Spaniards were waiting for him to make the next move. But he did not know what he could do. A search for Biarroco would be useless and clearly the mayor's discretion was keeping him equally hidden. He cursed the cornet's lack of tact. Looking from the window into the square he noticed for the first time what an excellent viewpoint Fenborough had chosen for his headquarters; he had at least that degree of competence, though Ingram would have been happier if he could not have seen the half-hidden ring of armed townsmen surrounding the building. The situation was becoming serious and he applied his mind to seeking a solution.

In the end it came to him for the man he sought rode into the square on the familiar grey mare. Ingram gasped in surprise and hurried from the room to meet Biarroco at the door. He was just in time for one of the sentries had raised his musket.

'This bleeding sod's got your horse, sir.'

'That's all right – let him be.'

They met as friends in the square, Biarroco again performing his practised bow from the saddle before dismounting and clasping Ingram's hand. His face was wreathed in smiles, but there was irony in his eyes when he spoke.

'You have kept your pledge, my friend, and I am in your debt. But you have brought more horses than I might have wished. And I cannot keep my promise, for I promised you wine in my home and we have not the time to visit it. We must make haste.'

'Indeed?' Ingram was amused by the man's affability.

'We must make haste for the French hussars are but two miles from the gate.'

'Christ! How many?'

'Too many. Four squadrons at least. I saw them myself.'

Ingram was thinking rapidly. He wondered if he could trust Biarroco's assessment of the enemy strength; he had too much experience of exaggerated Spanish reports. As if he could see into Ingram's mind the Spaniard said, 'You doubt my judgement, Ingram? I think I'm competent enough to count only what my eyes see. Before the present war I was on Murat's staff so I learned my trade from the French. I was at Austerlitz and Jena. Not many of your army can say the same. There are four squadrons, my friend, perhaps more, and I hate every man of them.'

'Can we defend the city?'

'If we do they will slay every soul within the walls, as they will if certain people are found here. I and my companions must ride at once. Do we ride together?'

'Certainly. In theory I've to arrest you so I'd better tag along.'

He bellowed for Fenborough to have his men mount up and dashed back into the courtyard to find his own horse. The dragoons were tumbling out of the building and wasted little time in mounting, and Ingram told the corporal to lead them outside and form up. There were still a number of riderless horses but here was Fenborough at last with his sergeant.

'Three of my men are dead drunk,' he cried.

'God, man, cannot you control your own men? And you, Sergeant, I doubt if you'll be keeping your stripes. We'll have to leave them and shoot their horses.'

Fenborough began to speak rebelliously but Ingram cut him short.

'There are four hundred frog hussars at the gates of the town so get a move on. And use the drunkards' own carbines – you won't have time to reload, though I hope to God we don't have to fight our way out.'

The corporal had the remaining sixteen dragoons drawn up in two ranks in the square and on Ingram's order they turned and followed Biarroco through the city. Already the streets were empty and doors and windows barred as the townsfolk hid themselves from the first ravages of the conquering French. In a square they found a dozen riders, a motley crowd armed to the teeth, and Ingram saw among them the small man who had been his guide. They came forward and joined the little procession.

'Friends of yours?' he asked Biarroco.

'Yes, friends. I have many friends.'

The western gate was thronged with people fleeing into the countryside, but they pushed through on their horses and met outside another group of Biarroco's friends, half a dozen perhaps, and among them, in dark riding-habit, was the woman from the convent. She looked at him expressionlessly. Biarroco signalled to them to fall in behind and then turned to Ingram.

'You have met Margarita. A formidable lady, but bitter since my brother's death. And now, Ingram, my friend, we must ride.'

Their tiny column thundered across the wooden bridge, heedless of the river swirling below, and then swung right up the flank of the opposite hill. But the long slope was tiring for the British horses after their march through the night and the Spaniards soon passed them and disappeared over the crest. Yet Biarroco stayed and Doña Margarita and the little man, and when they reached the top they pulled aside with Ingram and let the weary dragoons pass by. It was a promontory that they were on and from it they gazed back at the town.

The rain had broken and the air was clear though the heavy clouds were foreboding, a grim setting for the ancient city. The great walls marched round the hill, a castellated grandeur emphatic of medieval origin. Moors had looked on this and Christian knights ridden forth in challenge. There were no heraldic banners nor pavilioned tents now, but an orderly mass of cavalry sweeping round the wall, riding full tilt for the bridge. They were moving with terrifying speed. They were a squadron strong.

'Some traitor has talked,' Biarroco exclaimed. 'They know whom they're after. Look, they've seen us now.'

'Can we hold them here?'

'No. The other squadrons would come out from the town. I know a better place, three miles from here, but we must ride like the devil.'

They were on the plateau now and could leave the road for the going was easier in the fields. But it was difficult terrain with great boulders to avoid and the tired British were left behind as the Spaniards streamed ahead. The woman left them, and the little man – only Biarroco stayed. Now the French were in sight again, hurtling down on them in frightening phalanx.

'On!' cried Biarroco. 'That scarp is the place.'

But the escarpment was still some distance away and their horses were flagging while the French were closing fast. The ground was broken here and the exhausted horses had to leap over hollows and swerve round boulders. One of them missed its footing and brought its rider crashing to the ground. His comrades would have stopped to aid him but Ingram yelled to them to ride on. There was no time to spare for unlucky stragglers. Now the Spaniards were streaming up the escarpment and Biarroco dashed ahead to organise their defence. And still the British soldiers urged their beasts forward in disciplined lines. They were in clear fields again and a peasant couple stood motionless by a hut near the road and watched the flying horsemen pass them by.

'On! On!' cried Ingram, but his horse was not of the mettle of the fine cavalry horses and in riding with them she was destroying herself. He knew that she was failing fast and suddenly, without warning, she foundered. He felt her stagger and she went down on her foreknees before rolling over so that he was able to leap free. He looked round in despair. The line of dragoons had surged ahead leaving him alone. The French were out of sight in a hollow, but he could hear the thunder of their hooves. He was in terror for there was nowhere to go.

'Hey, señor!'

It was the peasant who called to him, beckoning, his voice echoing over the tempestuous plateau. The man held the door of the hut open and called again. Ingram hesitated no longer but ran desperately towards them. His own sabre nearly tripped him, and his breath came in sobbing gasps and he seemed to be moving with painful slowness, but he reached the place.

'Thank you, oh thank you.'

He met the man's eyes and they were dark and proud, his swarthy young face framed in curly hair.

'Hurry, señor, hide.' It was the woman who spoke, a girl with all the weathered beauty of her peasant stock.

'Yes, yes, thank you,' and he was inside.

In the musty gloom he could see that these people had their farm implements stored inside and instinctively he lifted a heavy winnowing sledge and jammed it against the door. At once he realised that he was hopelessly trapped within the four stone walls. In his anxiety he noticed gaps in the unmortared wall and strained to peer through the holes to see what was happening without.

The hussars had arrived and the main body rode past without stopping, but a handful detached and wheeled into the field. It took the peasants a moment to realise what was happening, but then they broke and tried to escape their fate. Together they ran, the man and the woman, but it was useless in face of the lathered horses. Ingram did not see what happened, but he heard the screams. His stomach churned in fear yet he could feel anger rise within him and the heat of shame. He would not be slain in this place like a trapped rat. He moved to pull the winnower from the door but a new noise came upon him and he broke off to see what was happening.

Fenborough, his cavalry instincts free from the restraint of Ingram's command, had drawn his dragoons off to a flank and turned to face the French. Now his half-troop swept down taking the French in the flank. It was hopeless, of course, eighteen exhausted men against a hundred seasoned veterans. Fenborough was at their head, leading them like some avenging god in the madness of what they were doing. He was the first to fall, hacked down by half a dozen sabres. Then the handful of British dragoons disappeared among the milling hussars.

Ingram roared at his helplessness and wrenched the door clear. He drew his sword and rushed outside, but there was no one to fight. All the French were engaged in the massacre of the dragoons. Only the two trampled corpses of his protectors were near him. He was useless and he felt the fear beginning to flood back.

Then he saw that the fields were alive with armed men, stalking carefully towards the fray, and from the slope of the escarpment a band of riders came swarming down. Ingram recognised Biarroco's grey mare in the van. Cautiously the guerrilleros took up their positions while the French remained in unseeing combat with the stubborn dragoons.

The musketry was sudden and sharp, taking the hussars completely by surprise. A dozen men went down throwing the others into a confusion of rearing horses and shocked men. Before they could recover another volley smashed into them, and then a rippling fire as the Spaniards hurried to reload. An officer tried to rally his shaken men, and some followed him to scour the ground of these vicious Spaniards. But the officer fell, riddled, and his men wavered, and then Biarroco's men were among them bringing death and panic.

It was too much for the hussars, and they broke, flogging their horses to flee from the maniacal fury. The Spanish riders pursued them to make sure of their flight, but went no further than was prudent before returning. In the meantime their pedestrian compatriots were cutting the throats of the wounded left behind, and Ingram wondered what to do.

There was a sudden disturbance, raised voices, a clash of weapons. Ingram saw that the sergeant of dragoons had survived somehow, with five of his men. Now they were intervening in the Spanish bloodletting. He shouted in angry distress and ran over to the group.

'Put up your sword, Sergeant! And you, señores, stand back from my men.'

'They're killing the prisoners, sir. Wounded men.'

Ingram turned to the Spaniards. One of the men was fair with blue eyes, and features like an Englishman. Ingram met his eyes. 'Is this how the Spanish guerrillero wages war – on helpless men?'

The fair man held his eye steady and scowled and Ingram

wondered if the man was perhaps a British deserter, but there was nothing he could do about it.

Someone spat on the ground at his feet and a ring of blades appeared around them. Ingram read the anger and hatred in their eyes and remembered the young couple in the field.

'You see how it is, Sergeant. We cannot interfere.'

'Oh, I see how it is all right, sir. We wondered where you was, sir.' His eyes wandered over the bloody fields to the two lonely corpses by the hut. 'You'd be in the building, sir, wouldn't you? Mr Fenborough came back to look for you.'

'Then he was a bloody fool!' Anger flared in Ingram. 'Look what he's done to your troop.'

'Yes, sir. We only left men behind when you was in command, sir.'

'Attend to your wounded, Sergeant, and get ready to ride.'

'From the French, sir? Yes, sir.'

Ingram stormed away leaving the troopers muttering among themselves. He felt contempt for himself, for his terror and his inability to cope with the sergeant's patent insults. Yet he could have done nothing else. Nearby someone was screaming.

He found Biarroco by the hut. There were three prisoners and one of them was already crucified to the door, and to his horror he saw that one of the Spaniards, his little guide, was holding a saw.

'For God's sake, stop that!'

Biarroco looked round and his eyes were cold and blank. He pointed to the two pitiful, innocent corpses.

'You saw those people die. Think if Avila was your home.'

'They saved my life and I did nothing to help them.'

Biarroco looked at the Scot and understood, for fear was an old and constant friend. He laid his hand on the other's arm.

'You could never have saved them. You were in the hut; so would I have been. Unlike you I would have stayed there. You doubt yourself; I see it in your eyes. But you have no reason, Ingram. I saw you today and I saw you at Pinto. You know fear, so do all wise men. That officer of yours did not. He was a fool and but for him we would have exterminated them all.'

He turned back to the business in hand and the Frenchman screamed horribly.

'For God's sake, Biarroco. You are an officer. These men are prisoners.'

Biarroco actually grinned. 'I thought I was a deserter under arrest.'

'You have too many friends.'

'True. But for your sake, my friend, I will not torture this carrion. Fernando! Kill the swine!'

Ingram turned in horror and walked away but Biarroco caught up and put his arm around his shoulder.

'Oh, Ingram, how little you people know of war. The one we crucified, we knew. He cut down the woman.'

'But now we must talk of better things. You will rejoin the army with what that fool has left of your men. There are plenty fine French horses to choose. I will ride south with my men, where the Cortes and your Wellington will not find me, but where I can hunt the French.

'There is one thing I ask of you. Margarita cannot come with us. She is known to the French and so cannot stay in occupied territory. Take her with you to the army and find her a safe refuge. Her work in Spain is done.'

Thus it happened that Lieutenant George Ingram rode from Avila with a handful of disgruntled dragoons, three wounded men, and Doña Margarita Ana-Teresa Menorez-Cabezon de Biarroco. It was not a journey that augered well. The wounded were carried in litters and their slow progress was further impeded by the sullen conduct of their comrades. Ingram had chosen to ignore the sergeant's insolence but now he pulled the man to one side.

'You're still sulking over what happened this morning. I won't have it. It was a brave thing to do – no one'd deny that – but it was a mistake. Otherwise the French would've been wiped out. Now they can reorganise and come after us. As for the prisoners – that was a filthy business, but if it hadn't been for the dagos we'd all be lying back there with Mr Fenborough. As it is we've got to keep moving if we're not to be cut off. Do I make myself clear?'

'Yes, sir,' but the reply was resentful.

'Now, look'ee here, Sergeant, you get that tone out your voice. The men see it and behave like dago levies. Snap out of it and get your men in order. I won't speak to you again.'

He kicked his horse forward to join the aloof Doña Margarita where she rode side-saddle at their head. He sought for words to speak; it was gratifying to hear the snarl in the sergeant's voice as he dealt with the laggard soldiers.

'I dare say we'll make better progress now,' he confided. 'They were shaken by the loss of their comrades.'

'Indeed?' She spoke without interest. 'No doubt on the next occasion you hunt Marcelliano you will bring many more soldiers.'

'That is possible . . .' He stopped to control his impatience. 'Señora, no one is more glad than I that Major Biarroco is still free. I expect that the matter will be forgotten.'

'Then you do not know the people for whom you act. They will never forgive.'

'I shouldn't worry. I imagine he'll be hard to catch.'

'Particularly as he is no longer encumbered by the presence of a weak woman.' There was an edge of bitterness.

'His loss is my privilege, señora.' His shyness made the words cumbersome. Yet the woman almost smiled.

'There, Lieutenant, you flatter me for the second time.'

It would have brought a lighter mood to the journey had Ingram not been so inhibited in such matters. He felt tongue-tied and clumsy, conscious that the men were in earshot. It was almost a relief when the sergeant appeared at his side.

'It's young Alstead, sir. He's bleeding badly again.'

There was little they could do bar rearrange the youth's bandages.

'We'll try to find a doctor in the next town. We'll be stopping there for the night.'

But Alstead was dead by nightfall and the doctor could not save another of the wounded men. Wearily Ingram joined the woman where she sat over her frugal meal. Doña Margarita raised mournful eyes.

'Spain is drowned in the blood of your young men.'

He saw the sympathy which she bore and for the first time felt able to speak with her. Yet it was she who spoke, of her family and its suffering, of the two brothers, Luciano, the proud royalist, loathing Godoy, and Marcelliano, the dashing hussar, light-headed in his long service of the French, now embittered in his hatred of them. The tragedy reflected Ingram's own background, the gentle Lothian estate, Edinburgh nostalgic for the golden age of Hume, his classical education and sedate legal training, the bitter loss of it all with his father's ruin. Then the dreary days at Dumbarton Castle. Above all, the melancholy of war.

It was a bond between them when they rode out in the morning on a day that brought them to the allied lines before Salamanca. Catherine Hall was there, with the baggage column in the rear, and she took the woman into her care. It was a relief to be eased from the responsibility, to shed the strain of his mission and be able to return to the regiment. As Ingram forced his bruised body back into the saddle she came to him.

'I must thank you for all your attention, señor. My prayers will be with you in the dangers ahead.'

It was hard to leave her then, but he was anxious to be away in search for his battalion. He raised his old cap in salute to her and then, turning, he nudged his horse forward, down the road to the front.

5

The 71st were resting near a mill on the bank of the River Tormes when Ingram found them and reported to the Colonel.

'Well, Mr Ingram, you've rejoined the fold. Did you catch your fellow?'

'No, sir.' He outlined what had happened and the Colonel smiled wryly.

'You've let them have your report? Good. You seem to have had a more exciting time than your comrades. We've been on the march since you left – and on empty stomachs. The Quartermaster General's people have misdirected the commissary train so you'll imagine how things are.'

He turned from Ingram to watch the soldiers lounging by the riverside.

'We're on our way into Alba de Tormes where the brigade is to hold the bridge. Soult is very close now so I dare say you'll get your revenge for those dragoons.'

'Yes, sir,' said Ingram, uneasily remembering Biarroco's vengeance. He let his eyes wander and found distraction, for there was movement at the mill. Soldiers were scampering from the building. The Colonel followed his gaze.

'What the devil! The rascals are looting. By God I'll have them caught. Sergeant-Major!'

As they hurried over to the mill Ingram foresaw a long list of defaulters to be added to his backlog of routine work. There must have been at least fifty men in the building. They had spotted the Colonel descending in his wrath and were scrambling to escape. Ingram wondered how they were going to be caught for there were too many to stop, but Cadogan was quick to see his method.

'Sergeant-Major, and you, Watson. Bring that bag of flour to the door. We'll have those millers marked.'

As each soldier ran from the place they threw handfuls of flour over him, powdering him for later identification. Their more honest comrades laughed at their plight and cheered the Colonel as he walked away, dusting the flour from his coat as best he could.

'I trust it doesn't rain; a coat of dough would be most unseemly. Have the battalion fall in, Mr Ingram. We'll continue our march to Alba, but I'll have those millers' names before we go.'

The men were silent before Cadogan's anger as he rode down the line for they knew his dislike of looting and his rigorous attention to Lord Wellington's orders on the subject. There was no need for explanation, the soldiers understood well enough. The Colonel's eye sought out the powdered men from the ranks.

'Riley! Fall out and join the millers. And you, Crawford – I expected better of you.'

Someone began to laugh and another took it up, and in no time the ranks were filled with laughing and giggling men.

'Silence! Cackle like hens wad ye? I'll . . . ' the sergeant-major began, but his imprecations seemed to make things worse. Ingram saw Fox standing on the right of his company, grinning like an ass.

The Colonel was furious and turned in rage to Ingram and Ingram saw what was wrong. A chicken was peering indignantly from the folds of the Colonel's riding-cape. Ingram felt himself lose the struggle to keep his face straight and could not trust himself to reply. Cadogan was enraged but happily Cother intervened.

'Sir, could ye no put the puir bird out its misery?'

At first they thought he was going to burst with fury but when he saw the quizzical chicken Cadogan saw how ridiculous he had appeared, grinned, then roared with laughter.

'Watson! Take this away. Put an end to it for its damned impertinence. You men,' he addressed the defaulters, 'get back to your ranks – and don't be caught again.'

Spontaneously the whole battalion cheered him. It was as though he was the head of their family. Cadogan turned to Ingram, his face all smiles.

'And now, Mr Ingram, may we proceed to Alba?'

Alba was on the very right of the British line, but its bridge was the only one over the now deep-flowing river, and it was here that the brunt of the French attack was expected to fall. For Wellington had decided to make his stand here, along the Tormes, while the river maintained its present level. At last the entire French army was concentrated. Jourdan and Soult and King Joseph were all present with their troops and in total they were twenty thousand stronger than the British and Portuguese under Wellington. And the only place where they could advance while the river was in spate was here in the south by the bridge at Alba de Tormes.

But the city's ancient walls were crumbled, the gates ruined by neglect, and Howard had to set his brigade at barricading the breaches against the impending attack. Urgently the officers drove their men to close the gaps and secure the town. Late into the night they laboured in a torchlit diabolism of dust and debris, where men with torn hands ripped timbers from the houses, filled bassinets with rubble, cursed as the ramparts grew from their toil.

In time it was done and they could rest, finding billets among the abandoned houses, for most of the townsfolk had fled. On the walls only the pickets remained, keeping their vigil through the night. To the east they could see the watch-fires of the cavalry and knew that beyond them lay the French. On the hills behind the river were the camp-fires of the remainder of Hill's force and to the north the glow of bivouacs marked where the allied army lay along the bank in a line that extended for twenty miles. But it was here at Alba that the blow would fall.

It was shortly after dawn that it became obvious that the French were advancing. There was shooting to be heard from the hills in the east, sporadic at first, but getting closer as Long's vedettes were forced back by the enemy skirmishers. From the walls anxious officers watched the light dragoons darting among the trees. A detachment broke from the woodland and swung round to cover a ravine. A trumpet called and they charged off again, going out of sight behind a rise.

'Look, there go the Fourteenth,' Cadogan exclaimed.

'They're in trouble though. Look at that, sir,' said Ingram, pointing. The Colonel swung his telescope round.

'Hm. Lancers. That'll be the Seventh Polish again. They're old friends. There are dragoons further back. That's a different division, isn't it?'

'Soult's brother's got dragoons in his division, sir. I thought the lancers were with Perreymond. And Digeon's division are all dragoons.'

'That's what I thought. Send a message to General Howard telling him we've identified two separate cavalry divisions. I think this is the real thing this time. We'd better have the companies on stand-by take up their positions.'

Now the British dragoons were scurrying back in the face of the overwhelming odds. It was not their task to stand and fight; that fell to the three battalions waiting in Alba. The bugles of the 71st mingled with the drums of the two other regiments, summoning their men to their posts. Each battalion manned an equal section of the wall with half of its companies and the remainder in reserve.

'Have my bugles and the pipes join me, Mr Ingram.' Cadogan stepped back from the bastion to cast his eye along the wall. 'You've explained to Captain Hall about that traverse?'

'Yes, sir, but it's awkward getting to it. There may be difficulty in sending down reliefs.'

'Very well. Ah there you are, Pipes. Do you hear the Gordons? They're playing "Cock o' the North" already. What do you think of that, Clark?'

'Och, they're the grand pipers over there, Colonel, but . . .'

'They weren't at Vimiera, eh?' Clark had distinguished himself at Vimiera in 1808. 'Are you fit, man?'

'Och, we're not in bad fettle, Colonel. We'll maybe manage to find a tune for the lads.'

But all Clark's piping did not summon the French upon them that morning and the patient soldiers waited as the enemy drove Long's cavalry across the bridge and then sat in vedette challenging counterattack. Then, about one o'clock, the defenders watched the French artillery move into position on the hill. There were three batteries and to the watching men they seemed to take an infinite time to set themselves up and lay the guns.

'Twelve-pounders I think, sir, and they've a howitzer detachment,' Ingram reported. He felt a horror at the sight of those ugly snub-barrelled howitzers. Round shot was bad enough, and those twelve-pounders were heavy guns, but Ingram feared the exploding shells which the howitzers threw. There was no shelter from the random chance of their flying fragments.

'Aye, it's going to be a hot afternoon,' Cadogan said calmly, and somehow Ingram felt safer.

At two o'clock the bombardment began.

It was terrible to stand there and endure the cannonade. The hurtling balls came smashing into the walls, throwing up splinters and dust and ricocheting down the narrow streets. Ingram clearly saw one strike a boulder not far below him and split into two halves which went careering on their lethal way. The shells whistled overhead, leaving a trail of smoke from their fuses, and fell into the town. They landed on the roofs, in the streets and alleyways, and among the men on the ramparts. And then they burst. Not far away a house collapsed into the street in a debris of stone and broken furniture.

'I think we'll have a stroll along the line,' said the Colonel.

They set off with the pipers marching behind and as they moved along the walls the Colonel paused frequently for an encouraging word with his men.

'All well, Thomson? You'll get your chance to win another prize for musketry today, I dare say. Well, young MacGregor, you've not seen anything like this before, something to tell your mother, eh? And you, McGuinness, feeling better now we've got the frogs down our sights?'

Despite the cannonade there were as yet few casualties; a few minor scratches and a couple of wounded. The Gordons were having a more trying time; Ingram could see the wounded being carried away. Hall came up to them and saluted.

'They're not achieving much with all this noise, sir.'

'No. Still, I dare say you're glad enough that Mrs Hall is safe in Salamanca now. I'm concerned about that traverse. Can you get reliefs down there all right?'

'The ladder's exposed, sir, but it should be all right. It enfilades the ravine beautifully. You'll see the frogs have brought their skirmishers forward.'

The men were firing now in sporadic bursts as the enemy's light infantry moved forward in twos and threes. Cadogan nodded and turned away and the two officers moved to follow him.

'Are you all right, George?' Hall looked eager and excited and Ingram envied his friend's courage, but then Hall surprised him. 'You're damned cool anyway. This damned bombardment's getting my goat.'

'Captain Hall, sir!' One of his sergeants, shouting urgently. 'It is the volty-joors, sir, they . . . '

He did not finish for a round shot came through the embrasure behind him and struck his head. Hall and Ingram were splattered with his hot brains. Ingram thought he was going to vomit, but there was no time, for Cadogan had pushed back to the parapet and was bellowing orders.

'They're advancing! Bugler! Load and present!'

At the insistent bugle call the desultory firing ceased and men who had discharged their muskets hurried to reload. The last high note of the bugle brought three hundred muskets up to bear upon the advancing enemy. The men selected their targets and trained on the little figures. Still Cadogan was silent. The French were no more than a hundred yards from the wall, sniping at their heads from a ditch, and the balls whipped about them, cracking wickedly as they darted past. Someone fell with a clatter as his musket dropped from his hands. He screamed once in shock and pain, then made no other sound than a disciplined sobbing.

An officer rose from the ditch and drew his sword. Ingram saw that his blue trousers were worn and tattered and his calves were bare. His epaulettes were shabby and his yellow plume bedraggled, but his face was that of a hard-bitten soldier with the black moustache neatly trimmed. Around his neck hung a medal on a red ribbon. He shouted to his men and they rose as one, a mass of blue and yellow and red, and among them were pioneers with their axes and scaling ladders.

'Fire!'

The volley ripped out in flame and smoke and instantly the view was obscured. Immediately the men grounded their muskets and were busy with ramrods and deftly handled cartridges. Some of them had filled their caps with cartridges and placed them on the parapet before them, an old soldier's trick to save rummaging in their cartridge boxes.

'Check your locks!'

The smoke was clearing now in the limp air and Ingram peered anxiously through the swirling clouds.

'Present!'

The voltigeurs had suffered badly and there were gaps in their blue line and behind them ranks of bodies sprawled on the muddy ground. A leg kicked and Ingram saw the naked calf, identified the tarnished epaulettes he had seen before. Then the leg flopped down again and was still. Yet the enemy did not waver but approached the wall.

'Fire!'

Again the smoke blotted out everything. Ingram stepped back from the wall to look along the line. Hall was pacing the rampart watching his men. Somewhere nearby a shell exploded. His ears were ringing from the din. A soldier looked up from loading and grinned at him.

'It's like shooting pigs, sir.'

The Colonel's steady voice called again, 'Present!'

The scene was different now with the blue forms littered below the walls. The voltigeurs were trying to withdraw in order but here and there a man panicked and ran ahead. An elderly sergeant was among them gesticulating, trying to make them turn but they had learned the deadliness of those steady volleys. The pioneers had fled, abandoning their ladders, and one poor wretch lay trapped with the rungs over his legs, trying in vain to free himself.

'Fire!'

Cadogan turned to Ingram and smiled. It was more a grimace.

'That should hold them for a while. They took too many losses to try that again in a hurry.'

They looked out through the embrasure and saw through the haze that the French were back in the ditch.

'We'll have them out of there. Give them another, lads!'

That fourth volley broke what spirit the voltigeurs had left and the smoke lifted to reveal them streaming back to the ravine. The flanking fire from the traverse caught them there and they were away again with the old sergeant's curses carrying loud across to the British lines.

'Well done, Seventy-first! These fellows won't be back for more! Fire at will, lads.' The Colonel waved his hat to acknowledge the men's cheers and then stepped carefully over the dead sergeant and called Hall to him. 'I didn't realise how effective that traverse is. They're using the ravine it covers as an approach. I think I'll have your entire company down there, Captain. Mr Ingram, we'll extend Captain Reed's company to close the gap.'

Now the cannonade had begun again, and this time the guns were concentrating on one of the barricaded gaps in the wall. The kilted Gordons were scrambling from the place as their Colonel wisely evacuated them. A ball smashed one of the supporting timbers and the breaking beam cast rubble from the parapet. A boulder thrown up in a vicious arc dropped horribly on one of the highlanders. Another ball overshot and bounced behind the wall until, its force spent, it rolled almost amiably along the street beside Ingram, where it came to harmless rest.

There was support at last for the isolated garrison, for the British batteries behind the river had opened fire and the French cavalry, thus endangered, withdrew. The enemy could not now approach from the flanks without first enduring a withering fire. Yet this could not protect the walls and in time the Gordons' barricade was breached by the terrible pounding of round shot and shell.

The French infantry could be seen massing for the attack.

The first warning came from a sudden volley by Hall's company firing into the ravine, and then there were enemy skirmishers darting from boulder to boulder over the open ground. The unpleasant buzzing of bullets was about their ears again and it took all Ingram's self control to prevent himself from ducking behind the wall. There was little for him to do but stand patiently beside the Colonel and wait. The men at least could fire and reload, fire and reload, until their weapons were hot in their hands and their shoulders ached.

There were more French pouring from the ravine, and they formed into a rough column before advancing. A mounted officer appeared and rode at their head, and Ingram wondered what use his horse would be against those high walls. A drummer boy in red and yellow dropped beside the horse and tumbled over his silenced drum. And the skirmishers increased their fire as the column came remorselessly on.

'A diversion I imagine, Mr Ingram. The real trouble will be over at the breach. The Gordons will be busy enough, I dare say.'

The Colonel looked back at the column before nodding to his bugler. Again the strident notes summoned the men to attend only to the Colonel's orders. As the muskets came up in one long, even line, the French in the forward ranks wavered in knowledge of what was going to befall. Then the volley spat its death into the close-packed men.

But the skirmishers had not stopped firing. A musket ball hit the wall before Ingram and another hit a cap perched there not five yards away. The cap with its load of cartridges wobbled for a moment and its owner reached to steady it. But he was too late and it toppled over on the French side of the wall. Before Ingram could stop him the man laid down his musket and leapt on to the parapet.

'Cadwell! Get back to your post, man.'

'I'll no be a minute, sir,' the soldier cried without looking round and he leapt into space. His neighbour looked at Ingram round-eyed in surprise and gaped for a moment before they both leapt forward to the embrasure and peered anxiously down. It was twenty feet to the ground and they were sure that Cadwell must have shattered both his legs.

Around them another volley roared out and Ingram fanned impotently at the smoke which blinded him from the injured man. But Cadwell was not injured and was scurrying around collecting his cartridges and placing them in his box. He picked up his cap and looked ruefully at the bullet-hole through the crown. The French had seen him and were glad to have such an easy target and soon their bullets were spitting into the ground around him and spattering on the wall behind him. Without concern he turned and raised his cap to them, then placed it on his head and faced the wall. It was a miracle that he was not hit.

'Cadwell, you fool! Get back here at once! Do you hear?' Ingram shouted in fury at the man's slowness. The private looked up, nodded and walked casually over to where a crack had riven the wall years before. With deliberate movements he began to climb, and all the time the French bullets chipped into the wall around him. Yet he reached the top unhurt and those who had watched him gave a ragged cheer before the cursing sergeants recalled them to their duty. He came running up to Ingram, his face in excited grin, his clothes tattered with bullet holes.

'They couldnae hit a byre door, sir.'

'You're a damned fool! Get back to your post.'

The main attack on the breach had commenced and two companies of the Gordons were hurried from the reserve to repel the assailants. With bayonets fixed they halted in steady line to greet the blue wave pouring into the breach. The fusillade was sharp and terrible and the mass of blue halted in its fury. The two companies rose and advanced up the mound of rubble, their pipers in the van, and met the French with cold steel. And like a tide the enemy ebbed away, coursing in so many rivulets from the dyke.

'Oh, splendid, Ninety-second, splendid,' Cadogan rejoiced. 'Just like the drill book.'

The shouting and screaming died away and before their own section the diversionary column slipped back, leaving only the skirmishers to harry and distract. The guns reopened fire and the smoke-grimed defenders settled down to endure another cannonade, while the winter sky gathered its mantle of evening cloud.

Soult tried one more assault before dusk set in, throwing his light infantry forward to die against the unyielding walls. They died in the breach and on the open ground; they fell in the ravines and in the ditches and filled the gullies with their corpses. Wherever they stood the angry bullets plucked their random victims, and in the end, before the night cast its cold blanket around them, the French fell back and left their comrades to the crows. And as the light faded from the sky the guns fell silent.

There were troops moving on the bridge, moving in disciplined silence, treading carefully that no listening enemy could hear their approach, but the men guarding the walls could detect the murmur of their coming and derive comfort from it. Hamilton's Portuguese brigade were marching in to reinforce the tiny garrison and every man learned the news as it flew from mouth to mouth and felt less isolated, less alone, in the knowledge.

Yet despite the terrible bombardment there had been few casualties and Ingram was surprised when Corporal MacLeod brought the company returns to him where he sat in the lamp-lit room which had become his office.

'There's a form number nine, sir. That's the first of those that we've had since Almarez.'

Form number nine was the casualty return and Ingram looked at it sadly for a moment before turning his attention to the returns from each company.

'There's four men dead, sir, including Sergeant Stewart, and just the six wounded.'

'Only four dead? I thought there'd be many more.'

'I believe Cadwell told you that they could not hit a sheiling, sir.'

'A byre door, he said, Corporal.' Ingram smiled and raised his eyes significantly to where a shot-hole gaped near a corner of the room.

MacLeod grinned. 'Och who'd do that to a nice house like this, sir? These French are the very devil. I'll get you a blanket, sir, you'll be cold without your coat.'

Neither mentioned, though both knew, that at that very moment Ramon was devoted to clearing Ingram's coat of the late Sergeant Stewart's brains. The corporal shook his head sadly.

'Aye. The surgeon will send the hospital tickets over directly, sir, but, och, I can fill them in myself for you to sign. There's the weekly return still wanting to be done, but you'd be at it all night if you started. God knows what we've lost on the march, sir.'

'Thank you, Corporal,' Ingram sighed wearily; there was no end to his forms and returns. 'I'd better make a start.'

He worked for several hours with scarcely a break. The Colonel called in to see him twice and signed some papers, and Ramon thoughtfully brought him some food. It had not been much and now the congealed plate lay empty amidst the papers littering his table. The guns were firing again as they had been occasionally through the night. He rubbed his eyes and rose to look into the next room. There was no one there and he remembered that he had sent MacLeod to bed an hour before. He wondered if he could find some coffee somewhere and thought maliciously of rousing Ramon from his slumber. He remembered that he had told the servant he would not be required again, and swore softly. It would be too selfish to disturb the boy. Instead he decided to take a stroll in the night air, and he picked up MacLeod's blanket and wrapped it round him.

There was a ceilidh going on somewhere for he could hear the pipes and laughing voices. Morale was high after the day's easy victory. Ingram wondered what the morrow would bring. Another casualty return, he was certain. His footsteps carried him towards Hall's billet and when he saw a light he entered gladly. Hugh MacKenzie was there with Hall and waved airily to him.

'Weel it's oor hard-workit adjutant. Come awa ben, George, and gie us your crack.'

'Do you have such a thing as a cup of coffee?'

'Damnation, man, whaur wad ye find coffee in a siege? We hae herbal tea if ye hae stomach for't. Harry here wad droon his sorrows in it; he's pining for his Kate.'

A shell exploded nearby causing dust to fall from the ceiling. One lump landed in Hall's cup with a plop. He looked unseeing at his spoilt drink before speaking.

'I'm damned glad she's not here. Not like your nephew's wife. Peggy's still here. What's Maxwell feeling like now? Anything can happen.'

Another explosion brought the sound of a collapsing building. Ingram was surprised at the intensity of his friend's expression and realised for the first time how nasty it must have been in that exposed traverse. He noted the ugly stains were still on Hall's coat and Hall, seeing his stare, said:

'Sergeant Stewart adored her, you know. He was a great help to us both. God, George, if I could only see her for a couple of minutes.'

'God's love, Harry.' MacKenzie teased, 'it's no a week syne ye hae been pairted.'

But Ingram found that he understood Hall's mood and was surprised to realise that he was thinking of the proud Doña Margarita, from whom he had parted two days before.

She was still on his mind later as he walked along the rampart checking the watchful sentinels. Fox was on duty there and started at his approach.

'You keep a late watch.' There was a sharpness in his voice.

'I've God knows how many returns to complete.'

'Well, you're short of some of your precious mules. That last shell landed on the stables.'

'Christ Almighty! How many?'

'I don't know. They've saved some of them, but it exploded inside and brought the roof down. It's a job for latrine orderlies. God knows if there was anyone inside, but a couple of Portuguese were killed at the door.'

Suddenly Ingram felt very tired and knew that he could not face returning to his plethora of forms. He would go back to his office and tidy up before turning in, but would do no more.

'Perhaps a shell will drop on them,' said Fox consolingly as he wished him goodnight, but something in his friend's voice made Ingram stop.

'Are you all right?'

'Aye,' and the tone forbade comment.

Ingram nodded. A man's fears were private. He made to move away but Fox caught his arm and pressed something into his hand.

'Look after this for me.' It was a watch.

'What the devil?'

'It was a gift from my mother. See she gets it.'

Ingram understood. It was not unusual.

'It'll be all right – you'll see,' he encouraged.

'No.'

There was a certainty different from the false premonitions of others, past, and Ingram was chilled by it.

'No one can know a thing like that,' he murmured.

'Oh, but I do. I know. Me, Cadogan, Hall. Cother'll be wounded and most of the others, but you'll be safe.'

Death had settled on Fox and Ingram felt its cold breath.

'Perhaps . . .'

But Fox had turned away and wanted to be alone.

The garrison stood to before daybreak and tensely waited for the dawn assault. But as the grey light grew into day no attack came and only the guns continued their onslaught. It was not till mid-morning that the French infantry succeeded in moving into position and when they came forward the defenders were ready for them. The rifles of the Portuguese caçadores took a terrible toll and the relentless British volleys again forced the enemy back in ruin. This time General Howard ordered his light infantry out in sally to sweep the enemy away. The 71st went forward with the other light companies and as they advanced Ingram in the rear saw Fox watching him from the flank of his company. His eyes were dead and his face pale and he turned from Ingram without knowing him. Sensing death at hand Ingram sought the others whom Fox had named, Cadogan on his charger in the van, Hall at the head of his company. The bugles were sounding 'skirmish order' now and Ingram swallowed in despair as the battalion went into action. It was a sharp little skirmish but effective and the French melted away under their fire. It was only minutes before the recall summoned them back to the walls.

'That was well done, very well done,' the Colonel declared, 'and not a single casualty.'

Ingram could not trust himself to speak, but Cother was there.

'Aye, Colonel, we're gey weel suited here gin we maun hold yon brig till Damnation.' The major snapped his fingers in the air. 'That for Johnny Soult.'

'I doubt if we'll have to. The river has dropped considerably since yesterday. I imagine Joseph Buonoparte will try to ford further north.'

Ingram nodded agreement. The French would have learned by now that there was no progress to be made at Alba. Cother spoke, reflecting the thought.

'You're right enough. Look at them the now battering away with round shot and shell and no a chiel the waur of it.'

The three men looked east towards the active batteries on the hill, but their eyes were caught by the smoke of a shell as it dropped among a cluster of their men. A bugler tried to get his foot to the smouldering fuse but he was too slow and, terribly, the little group of soldiers dissolved into a red cloud of torn flesh and spraying blood. They barely felt the shock-wave hit them, nor heard the blast, but stood appalled, watching the ragged, bloody tissue and bone fall in ugly pattern around the place. And the bugler, by chance surviving and thrown back from his vanished legs, began to scream.

'Jesus,' said Cother softly.

Ingram shuddered. Yet these were the last men to die in the affair at Alba de Tormes. Already the French guns were limbering up as the enemy prepared to slip away. Ingram was able to excuse himself and move down the line in search of his friend. They had not spoken since; the distance was too great. Fox was with his company and watched expressionlessly as Ingram approached. It was embarrassing.

'Your watch.'

'Aye.' He took it and slipped it into his fob pocket, then grimaced. 'Somewhat silly, that.'

'These things happen.' Ingram looked over the corpse-strewn fields. 'You had me worried, don't you know.'

'Christ. You were worried . . . ' Fox began and then grinned. 'It's one occasion, Mr Adjutant, when I'm mighty glad that it was you who was right.'

There was no distance between them after all.

It was several hours later that General Howard entered the room where the Colonel was in conference with Ingram and the quartermaster.

'Sit down, gentlemen,' Howard waved them back into their chairs and turned to Cadogan. 'Our job here's done, Henry, the river's fordable. We're falling back before the enemy can turn the northern flank. Miranda's staying here with his Spanish battalion – they'll be able to hold the bridge as long as is needed. The rest of us will pull out tonight.'

'Very good, sir. I think we can manage that all right, Mr Ingram?'

'Yes indeed, sir.' There was nothing else he could say though he worried desperately about the transport problem. They had been talking about the dead mules when the General entered.

Howard placed his cocked hat on the table. 'This is my last march with the brigade, Henry. The Guards are brigaded and waiting for me now. It's been a long time.'

'Nearly two years, sir.'

'They're giving you the brigade, Henry, you knew that. Take good care of them. I know they're in good hands.'

In the November darkness the brigades marched out of Alba de Tormes and left Miranda's Spaniards as a tiny garrison. Howard marched with his brigade through the night and in the morning he said goodbye and rode away to take command of the Guards Brigade. And Cadogan took over and led them on their road. It was later that they learned that Cother had received his brevet to lieutenant-colonel.

At Salamanca Wellington made another stand in a last effort to avoid a withdrawal to Portugal. His line extended along the old positions of the July battle and the men bivouacked among the unburied skeletons of the slain. The French refused the challenge and simply marched round to turn the flank and, thus out-manoeuvred, Wellington ordered his army to withdraw again. As the weather deteriorated, the British army began another miserable retreat to Portugal.

6

In appalling weather the allied army strove to escape the French. Knee-deep in mud the soldiers marched, in a misery of exhaustion and disease. Dysentery and typhoid ravaged their ranks; and fatigue, for they slept without shelter from the incessant rain. The commissariat had broken down and supplies ceased to appear. In his headquarters Wellington raged at his incompetent Quarter-master General, then turned his wrath upon his starving troops who, to still their famine, were slaughtering the peasants' swine. The French harried constantly and women and children who lagged behind fell, with the weakened stragglers, to the hands of the enemy. Here and there by the roadside lay the corpses of men defeated by it all.

To Ingram it was a special nightmare, for Doña Margarita had remained in the regimental train and their rearguard functions placed her in peril. Though his duties kept him from her she would not go ahead but stayed with Catherine Hall and the other wives, isolated by the barrier of language. Ingram saw his anxiety reflected in the gaunt face of Hall, his mind ever troubled by the danger to his wife. Then one sharp skirmish caused a rapid withdrawal and several of the soldiers' families were caught by its suddenness and left behind. Hall became adamant in insisting on Catherine's immediate departure and Ingram took the opportunity to hurry the ladies away to safety. It became possible to pause during desperate fighting and look over to his friend and smile in sympathy of relief. The retreat continued.

As they neared Portugal the pursuit slackened and fell away and at last the battered army could seek winter quarters among the towns and villages of the frontier. Cadogan's brigade was billeted in Coria amidst the mountain passes, and there the 71st was able to rest and take stock of its condition.

Ingram was immediately swamped in a morass of requisitions and returns. There were endless conferences with the Colonel and departmental heads, and the company officers with their prodigious demands. And disorder on the march had fathered indiscipline and every day bore its miscreants before justice. Patiently Corporal MacLeod toiled without complaint, chasing trivial problems from Ingram, while Ramon fed him and, at the end of each long day, helped him to bed.

In time the wives rejoined them, but Doña Margarita did not come and Ingram knew a disappointment which surprised him. Catherine Hall's eyes were gentle as she handed him the letter.

'I do not know where she has gone.'

The missive was short and gave no clue to her whereabouts. 'I am safe now,' he read, 'and owe you my thanks. Perhaps we may meet again.'

There was little solace in the warmth of her words. With the whole world engulfed in war it was unlikely that he would ever see her again. Ingram put the letter aside and buried himself in his discarded hospital returns. Dysentery had found more victims than all their fighting. Officers were not spared and the thinned mess was overworked and irritable, unreasonable anger another cross for Ingram to bear.

Each afternoon he reported to Colonel Cother to discuss the matters requiring attention but on one occasion it was Cadogan who was there to interview him.

'Ah, there you are, Mr Ingram. Sit you down.' The Colonel looked at him thoughtfully.

'Maxwell MacKenzie's majority has been confirmed at long last, I'm pleased to tell you. That means that his captaincy is vacant and available for purchase.'

Ingram sighed inwardly. They were going to burden him with the auction.

'As you know, Alasdair Laurie of the second battalion is the senior subaltern, but I understand that he does not wish to accept the captaincy.'

That was a delicate way of saying that old Laurie could not afford the purchase price and was doomed to eke out his existence training recruits in Dumbarton Castle. Ingram decided to protest that he was too busy to organise the auction of another officer's commission.

'I am authorised by Major MacKenzie to offer his captaincy to you at the regulation price without auction. Like myself he is concerned for the good of the regiment.'

Ingram was dumbfounded. There were many officers within the regiment waiting for the vacancy and perhaps outsiders anxious to purchase in. An auction would have brought MacKenzie a good price. Yet Ingram knew that he would be hard pressed to raise the regulation £1,500.

'Sir, I appreciate this, I . . . the kindness . . . but I don't . . .'

'Think about it very carefully. It is not often that a vacancy is offered at regulation price; normally that privilege extends only to the senior man of the appropriate rank. Dammit George, you're a good officer, one of the best I have. I want to see you with more responsibility. We don't want you selling out or buying into another regiment.'

'I wouldn't do that, sir,' declared Ingram in the warm glow of the astonishing things which the Colonel had said.

'Well, there you are.' Cadogan leaned back in his chair and placed his hands on the table. 'You'll want time to consider it, I appreciate that, of course. No doubt you'll have to review your arrangements but, if it's at all possible, I want you to have this captaincy. You might let me know as soon as you can.'

Ingram left the building in turmoil. He knew it would be useless to return to his office so he began to walk through the rain towards the town wall. The rain was almost pleasant and he found it invigorating, stimulating his cluttered mind. His brain began to work, classifying his thoughts, ordering them into priorities.

The Colonel had given him time to decide upon the captaincy but he already knew the answer. He revised the facts carefully. He could not hope to auction his present commission; there were few enough men willing to serve as subalterns in the Peninsula. Indeed he might have a long wait to obtain the regulation price, a third of what he needed. He had a small income from rents, but that with his lieutenant's pay was just sufficient to maintain him, with a little left over to help the family. His own parcel of land was entailed so he could neither dispose of it nor raise money on a bond, even if a creditor could be found after his father's financial collapse. His brother was the only member of the family with any available funds, but they had not communicated in the five years since Donald Ingram had ranked with his father's other creditors. That left Ingram's own few savings and possessions. There was not enough security in the latter to make up the necessary sum.

He leaned on the parapet of the wall and gazed moodily down the valley. It was shameful to have to refuse the generosity that had been offered, to spurn the compliment that had been paid. He sighed in frustration. His thirtieth birthday was two days hence and he wondered if he would still be a lieutenant at forty; or fifty, like old Laurie rotting in his dank billet in Dumbarton Castle.

The chill was in his bones and he shivered. It was an effort to wrench himself from his self-pity. He would speak to the Colonel at the first opportunity and then to Major MacKenzie to thank him for his consideration – or charity, he sneered at himself. He drew himself erect and turned to retrace his footsteps. Cadogan would understand, he hoped; the present atmosphere was entirely friendly.

However, when Ingram returned he found Cadogan in changed mood. Black furrows of anger scarred his face and an unfamiliar rasp was in his voice.

'The captaincy? Yes. We'll speak of it later. I wish to address all the officers, Mr Ingram. Kindly summon them to the mess.'

The officers assembled in muted curiosity, puzzled by the Colonel's sudden wrath. Fox caught Ingram's sleeve and whispered.

'We've done well; what's wrong? We're nearly back to strength.'

Cadogan stood up and produced a letter from his pocket which he tapped with his fingers as he looked round at them, and a respectful silence fell over the worried officers.

'Gentlemen, I have here a general order from the Commander-in-Chief which has just come to my hand. I will be obliged if you will do me the courtesy of permitting me to read it without interruption.'

They listened as Cadogan began to read Wellington's letter. The first few sentences were routine but the second paragraph drew their attention to the state of discipline in the army, implying that it had been far worse than the circumstances justified. It was true, the listeners reflected, that there had been too many stragglers, too much drunkenness and pilfering, but the men had gone for days without food or shelter.

'It must be obvious,' Cadogan read, 'the officers lost all control over their men. Irregularities and outrages of all description were committed with impunity; and losses . . .'

The officers were stirring restlessly, glancing at each other in annoyance. This was most unfair; there had been regiments where discipline had broken down, everyone knew that, but the 71st had behaved well. The same was true of the whole brigade. It was the bad characters who had caused any trouble and those who had been caught had been disciplined. Now Wellington was complaining of short marches and long halts.

'He didn't have to walk in the mud,' someone growled and Ingram, hearing, remembered the men slumping exhausted at the end of each wretched day. But still the letter went on.

'I have no hesitation in attributing these evils to the habitual inattention of the officers of the regiments to their duty . . .'

'No!' Captain Walker was on his feet protesting, and a rumble of agreement rose from his fellows. 'That's a damnable statement, sir. You know it is false.'

Cadogan looked at him coldly and waited until, discountenanced, Walker resumed his seat. The catalogue of complaint went on. Every one of their privations and losses was being attributed to the regimental officers. And now the letter was lamenting 'the facility and celerity with which the French soldiers cooked, in comparison with those of our army'.

'Give us decent pots and let us burn the house timbers and then we'll do as well,' Ingram heard Fox grumble.

Now they were being exhorted to avoid depriving their soldiers of food when everyone knew that the guilt lay with the Quartermaster General. They seethed in outrage. But the epistolary diatribe was ending. A final emphatic sentence called on them to attend to their duties, and then Cadogan was silent.

For a moment no one spoke but then the murmur of resentment began. Cother rose defiantly.

'Sir! Ye ken that's no reasonable.'

Cadogan looked at the new lieutenant-colonel and his expression was grim and stern.

'I will not comment, Colonel Cother, but to say this, that if the Commander-in-Chief is not satisfied with the Seventy-first then we must all take note – not least myself, for I can find no complaint. Indeed, I would state that you have all worked wonders to achieve what you have in the few days we have been at Coria.'

Despite their Colonel's words the letter created a mood of open resentment which somehow conveyed itself to the men. It was the same throughout the brigade and the town echoed to the complaints of conscientious men against their unjust master. They would continue to follow Wellington, such was their duty, but what admiration they may have had was quenched by their grievance. No love and little personal loyalty was due to this aloof peer who protected the incompetents around him and indiscriminately blamed his soldiers for the faults of a few. Ingram's lost captaincy magnified his bitterness and he found himself hating the man, envious of those privileges by which he had gained a colonelcy after a mere seven years' service. Generalissimo – no wonder Biarroco resented being placed under his command.

The anger was in them all. Major MacKenzie expressed it one morning after inspection. He stumped into the office shaking the rain from his cape and when he removed his sodden cap rain cascaded from its crown. He grinned in satisfaction.

'They are beginning to look like soldiers again. Oh, they're the skinny ones, all wasted away, poor devils, but they stand to their drill like soldiers. We'll just have to fatten them up over the winter if that damned peer is to make skeletons of them again. Aye, and lay the blame on us. He would be better spent at finding tents, aye, and a new quartermaster. Or advancing worthy officers.' He smiled sympathetically at Ingram.

His uncle, too, had his grumble.

'There's a pay chest arriving this forenoon,' he announced.

'So there'll be drunks in plenty, Hugh,' Ingram observed.

'Aye, and wha'd blame them. Three months they hae waited and there'll no be enough in yon kist. It's nae wonder there's discontent, aye, and boozing whan they do hae siller.'

The paymaster paused and watched him with wise eyes.

'I hear ye refused oor Maxwell's captaincy,' he said suddenly.

'I appreciate his kindness but . . . ' Ingram would not confess the reason.

'Aye, but ye lack the price. Man, it is writ on your face. Ach, Maxwell was fair disappointed – he'd his heart set on gieing ye it. Now, gang easy wi' your pride, George, I ken fine what it's like. Ye'll mind I'd tae sell oot myself and am only here noo by the grace that na ither body wad hae the job. It wasna charity if that's what's fashing ye and nane wad think it. Maxwell had the regiment in mind, and ye'd hae done the same yourself, I ken. It's time ye'd a company for ye're gey suited for it but if ye've no the funds then there's an end tae it and it's best forgot. Ye can console yourself with the kenning that ye're weel regarded.'

'That's what galls me.'

'The army's filled wi' able men that canna get on for want o' a bittie siller. But yon's the way o' it and it's just tae be tholed and bide till there's casualties and vacancies for them that's favoured.'

'Aye, like enough,' Ingram conceded. It was an exception to the purchase system that promotion on merit was available to vacancies caused by casualties in action.

'Ye ken fine. Your chance'll come. There maun be casualties in this battalion, my soul on that. There's a wheen o' fechting yet afore the French are oot o' Spain.'

But in the meantime the condition of the battalion was improving and gradually life became ordered again with little more to do than organise the pickets and work-parties and complete the routine forms. Invalids were returning from the hospitals already and the ranks at drill grew longer every day. The men were eating well and in good shelter, and slowly they began to lose the wasted look which the rigours of the retreat had cast over them. Morale restored itself and the disciplinary problems faded away. Later in the winter there would be boredom to overcome, but for the present it was enough to rest well nourished and dance to the pipes in the evenings.

Sometimes on these occasions the officers would go along from their quarters and Ingram was impressed to note the ease with which the local population joined the fun. There were fandangoes danced in the firelight and years afterwards he would recall the skirts flying against the flames, the feet crackling in time with the castanets. The soldiers were quick to test the hearts of the village girls and Ingram foresaw that there would be the usual problems with anxious mothers and the proud Spanish men.

Fox had managed to buy a horse and it became their custom to pass afternoons riding in the foothills of the Sierra. It exhilarated Ingram, freed from his claustrophobic office, to urge his French charger across the terraces and feel the rain driving against his face. Then to return to dry clothes and a warming drink before dinner.

Other more significant improvements began to appear. The long-awaited cooking-tins materialised, handy pots light enough to be carried by the individual. The despised iron kettles were dispatched with relief. A rumour began that bell tents were to be issued, and astonished everyone by proving correct. The new shako which had been issued to the rest of the army was received at last by Hill's corps and the heavy stovepipe was seen no more. It seemed to Ingram that Whitehall was beginning to understand the reality of campaigning.

He was standing by the window one afternoon when Fox came in with the riding-cloaks to liberate him from his desk. He saw the adorned cap in Ingram's hand and frowned.

'What's that?'

'This, my dear Humphrey, is my light infantry cap. My new uniform has arrived. It's been on order for months.'

'Good Lord! I must say, I thought your current rags suited you admirably. Let me see.'

He was examining it when Corporal MacLeod came in to collect the returns for the post and, seeing him, Fox set the new cap at a jaunty angle on Ingram's head.

'What do you think of Mr Ingram's new hat, Corporal?'

MacLeod eyed Ingram with deliberation. 'Och, it just suits you fine, sir. We'll be having all the ladies of Spain chapping on the door after you.'

'Get out of here, Corporal.' Ingram removed the thing.

'I'll just away and give these to the courier, sir.' MacLeod, unabashed, left the room.

'I suppose it'll make you look a bit more reputable. Pretty target for the frogs.'

'Target yourself. Look at you. A disgrace to the profession. No wonder you thought the frogs were after you.'

Fox looked startled. 'Do you know, that's a thought that hasn't occurred to me since yon night in Avila. Nasty that, but I do believe I'm going to come through in one piece.'

'Touch wood.'

'Come on, time's getting on; it must be almost two o'clock.' Fox drew out his watch, inspected it, nodded, and then, seeing Ingram's shocked stare, put the timepiece away with a nervous laugh.

'Silly superstition. Come on. I'll wager a certain lady inspired the new uniform.'

Ingram looked at Fox with suspicion; he had been wondering what Doña Margarita would think.

She was brought sharply to mind on the following day when the battalion received orders to prepare for a move to Puerto de Baños.

Among the assorted papers was a general order requiring the immediate apprehension of Biarroco by anyone who saw him. Ingram was badly upset, and hoped that his friend would keep his distance.

That same morning he was summoned by Colonel Cadogan. This was unusual for, though he retained nominal command, Cadogan's duties as brigadier had devolved the administrative command to Cother. In the circumstances Ingram felt certain that Wellington had found duty for him again, and he determined to refuse. Both colonels were in the room when he entered and he had a moment's nervous rehearsal of his objections. But Cadogan did not want to talk about Biarroco at all.

'Ah, there you are, Mr Ingram. Come in and sit you down.

'Have you been in Plasencia? No? Well, it's a big town and as you know it's an important road junction. There's unlikely to be a permanent garrison, however, and our brigade is going to be further up the road in the villages at the head of the pass. Obviously Plasencia is the key to our communications and it falls within the brigade area so I want to have a town major there who speaks good Spanish and whom I can trust. I want you to accept the appointment.'

'Thank you, sir,' said Ingram; it was a splendid opportunity and tempting to accept. He would be his own master, running the military administration of the town, making his own decisions. Yet he was comfortable in the battalion, despite his paper drudgery, and his friends were here. Above all there were his duties as adjutant and he could not let Cother down. He swallowed. 'I would prefer to remain with the battalion.'

'You're a damned fool if you do.'

'Dinna worry about us, Mr Ingram,' Cother interceded. 'We'll miss ye, I ken that, but there are able men who could be grand adjutants on the foundations you've laid. Ye'd be daft to refuse, man.'

'Normally it would be a captain's appointment,' Cadogan said, 'but we can do no more about that at present. You would, of course, have the normal staff. It is mainly administrative work, for which I know you are well able, but it has in addition some of the responsibilities of independent command. I want you there behind me in Plasencia because I can think of no officer in the brigade better suited to hold the position. I trust you will accept.'

There was a rasp in Cadogan's voice which denied the alternative of refusal. In a moment they would be ordering him to go. Moreover, the responsibility appealed to him.

'Sir, Colonel Cother has indicated his consent, and that was my sole concern. I am very grateful, grateful to you both.'

'That's settled then. Good. Now your adjutant is an ensign from the Fiftieth. A bright young fellow called Penderleigh. Then there's the assistant provost marshal and the commissary. . . . '

They began a discussion of his new duties and Ingram had to borrow pen and paper to note the various points which the Colonel emphasised. The staff orderlies had been drawn from the 50th Foot and Ingram had one request to make.

'I'd like to take Corporal MacLeod with me, sir.'

Cadogan looked at the lieutenant-colonel and Cother shook his head.

'No no. Ye maun make do with what you've got from the staff there. I'll no part with MacLeod; I cannot do with the both of you away.'

'There you are then, Mr Ingram. You must manage without the phenomenal Corporal MacLeod. I'd be happy if you left in the morning. The sooner I know you're in Plasencia the easier I'll feel about troop movements. I'll have your orders delivered to your quarters this evening. In the meantime you might prepare to hand over your present duties.'

It was not till after dinner that he broke the news to his friends in the mess. Hall was delighted for him.

'That's splendid, George, splendid. It might just as well be promotion.'

'Hey, Vandeleur, pass up the port,' Fox called, 'we'll celebrate this. We'll have no more trouble over damned public mules.'

'Let's make a party of it,' someone cried, 'as good an excuse as any.'

'Not I,' his neighbour grumbled, 'I've got the morning pickets.'

'Hey, Ingram! You'll be sure we have good billets when we pass through Plasencia.'

'Does anyone know when we're moving?'

'The Colonel's said nothing to me,' Ingram observed.

'Please God it's not before the New Year.'

'There's a ceilidh you'll miss, Ingram.'

A captain scowled. 'Och, Lord Wellington will find some duty for us. Can't have officers celebrating Hogmanay, don't you know.'

Hall declined the decanter passed by his neighbour. 'No thank you, Reed, no port for me. I'm joining my wife. Would you two care to accompany me?'

'That would be pleasant.' Ingram watched the shrinking decanter. 'Things could get out of hand in here.'

'Aye,' teased Fox, 'and no doubt you'll be riding at the crack of dawn.'

It was a short walk to the dilapidated building where the Halls were billeted and a friendly light beckoned them in from the gloom. Catherine Hall welcomed them with her customary charm.

'Come in, gentlemen, how pleasant to have time to gather again. Sit down, do, and Harry will open the brandy.'

Hall spoke from the corner where he was collecting the glasses.

'George is leaving us in the morning to be town major of Plasencia.'

'My congratulations, Mr Ingram. We will miss you. You must be very satisfied. It is normally a captain's appointment, is it not?'

'Aye, well, these things can be arranged, ma'am,' Fox said innocently.

Ingram eyed him in surprise, wondering how much he knew.

'Let us trust so.' Hall raised his glass. 'Here's success to you, George.'

Ingram looked around the cosy little living room, cluttered with the Halls' bits and pieces. They were lucky to afford such a comfortable billet with its tired furniture. There would be a bedroom beyond and he had a moment's bitter pang as he thought of the squalid room where he and Fox had hammocks slung, and Ramon slept in the straw, oblivious to the rats scampering over him. He could expect little better in Plasencia.

His eye settled on a portmanteau where a letter lay white against the worn wood. The only mail he received was complaint of the family's poverty.

'I see you've had word from home,' and he kept the sadness from his voice.

'Why, yes, it arrived only today. Harry's father is thinking of putting sheep on the hills but I doubt if the men of Appin would like that.'

'Aye, it'll be a bad thing if father's tenants have to be removed for sheep. Look at those here in the regiment. Can you imagine how Sergeant Stewart's widow would look after the children without her bit croft?'

'Sheep, eh?' Fox murmured. 'Aye, things are changing at home. Reed's had a letter from his factor wanting to sell twenty acres for a bleach field at Paisley. It's good arable land, and bonny forbye. I know it well.'

'He should hold out. It might help to purchase Cother's majority,' Ingram half jested at his private difficulties.

'He'd have to win in an auction,' said Fox sourly; 'we're not all privileged by favour.'

The room shrank around Ingram. Fox was actually jealous, antagonised by the neglect of his three months' seniority. In the brittle silence Ingram realised that the Halls also knew. His financial embarrassment was public knowledge. Every officer in the battalion must be sneering at him, and every subaltern hating him for the preference he had been shown. He looked in misery at his friends and saw sympathy in Catherine Hall. But it was her husband who spoke.

'If there's an auction, Walker'll win. He'll beat me, Reed, Pidgeon, and all the rest. We will all have to live with that and you'll just have to live with the fact that none of the pair of you has the price of MacKenzie's captaincy.'

'Aye,' growled Fox.

'That's a thought to keep you warm in Puerto de Baños,' Ingram avenged.

'Well, you'll be all right in Plasencia, won't you now? God, I hate mountain villages.'

Hall intervened again: 'Someone's got to watch the pass. The Fiftieth are going to be in Bejar – now that is a miserable place. I remember Puerto de Baños as a pleasant enough town.'

'It is a spa, is it not?' Catherine lightened the mood. 'Mr Ingram, I'm sure you must envy us. Let Harry refill your glass.'

'Make it a big one, Harry, and mine too.' Fox was grinning. 'The man's away tomorrow, damn his eyes.'

It was at dawn that Ingram passed through the drowsy picket and set off, with Ramon at his side, to ride the eighteen miles to Plasencia. When he stopped on the brow of a hill to look back and take his farewell of the battalion, he heard the pipe-drones stir the chill morning with the first notes of the reveille.

7

It was not till after dusk that they rode into Plasencia and inquired of the Spanish picket the way to the town major's office. The soldier looked at them without interest and pointed casually down the street. They nudged their mounts forward, uncertain which building the sentry had indicated in the darkness, and had actually passed it when Ramon, looking over his shoulder, saw a rifleman step into the street. Ingram hailed the soldier and the man stopped and saluted smartly.

'This here's the place, sir; as I've just come out of.'

Even in the gloom Ingram could see that it was a distinguished building, elegant with carved galleries at the windows and the inevitable coat of arms over the door. He dismounted and, leaving Ramon with the animals, passed through the portico and entered the candlelit hall. His boots clashed on the tiled floor and the orderly lounging at a table looked up casually before identifying his rank and snapping to attention. Ingram noted that he was wearing the black facings of the 50th.

'Where's the adjutant?'

'The officers is all at their dinner just now, sir. If you'd care to wait in the office . . .'

'No, I'll join them.' The thought of food stirred him for he had eaten nothing since breakfast.

'Well, sir, I don't know. . . .' The soldier was uncertain, wanting to protect his officers from intrusion.

'I am the town major. Now show me the way and have someone attend to my servant.'

'Yes, sir. Of course, sir. Begging your pardon, sir, but we wasn't expecting you till tomorrow.'

'That's all right.'

The private was eyeing him curiously but recalled himself

and led Ingram up the staircase to a door on the landing.

'In here, sir. If you'd care to give me your hat and cloak, sir.' He opened the door. 'I'll look after your servant now, sir.'

There were three officers sitting round the polished table and they looked up in annoyance at Ingram's entry.

'I regret disturbing you at dinner, gentlemen, but I have just this minute arrived. I am Ingram, the town major.'

Their expressions changed instantly and they rose at once. The youngest had a pleasant smile as he extended his hand.

'How do you do, sir. Penderleigh, ensign, Fiftieth Foot. We were not expecting you to arrive tonight.'

This must be his adjutant, the bright young man of whom Cadogan had spoken. He would be no more than twenty, and his eyes were eager under the tangle of fair hair. Ingram took his hand. 'I look forward to working with you, Mr Penderleigh.'

He took his letter of authority from his pocket and opened it. 'You are hereby appointed . . .' Ingram read aloud the brief sentences and then put the letter away. Penderleigh smiled again and turned to indicate his colleagues.

'Mr Stoneman, assistant provost marshal.'

Stoneman's handclasp was firm. He was tall and broad-shouldered and approaching middle age. Ingram guessed that he had received his commission and present appointment after long service as a senior warrant officer.

'What were you doing before this, Mr Stoneman?'

'I was in the old Fifty-seventh, sir.'

'The "Diehards" eh? Then you'd be at Albuera.'

'That's it, sir. I was sergeant of the grenadier company then.'

Ingram turned to the third man and Penderleigh introduced them.

'This is Mr Schumacher, the commissary, sir.'

The commissary clicked his heels and bowed.

'It will be an honour to serve you, sir.' His accent was distinctly German.

'King's German Legion?' Ingram wondered.

'No, sir,' Schumacher smiled. 'I am a poor Bavarian who was fortunate to receive his present appointment from your King George. I have been here so long that I wonder if the German Legion exists at all.'

Ingram cast his eye over the litter of plates and dishes on the table and Penderleigh intercepted his glance.

'We were just finishing our meal, but I'll have the cook prepare something for you, sir, if you wish.'

'I'd appreciate that, Mr Penderleigh. I've been in the saddle since dawn.'

It was a good meal that appeared eventually, a hot soup rich with corn, and pork with crusted pie and succulent potatoes and lightly fried onions. There was apple sauce too and a white wine Ingram had not tasted before. And a fine tart to follow, laced with brandy. He ate with pleasure, scarcely talking in his hunger, but listening while Penderleigh and his colleagues outlined the situation in the town, noting what each of them said about their respective duties. It appeared that his adjutant had only held his appointment for a fortnight and clearly relied heavily on his two elders. Schumacher had been here since the spring and obviously had the local supply system well in hand. Ingram was impressed, too, by Stoneman's matter-of-fact contributions to the conversation. It was gratifying that his staff seemed efficient and appeared to co-operate happily with one another.

He pushed his plate aside and reached for his glass.

'An excellent meal, Mr Penderleigh.'

'Oh, we eat well enough, sir, Schumacher sees to that.'

'I try to give satisfaction.' The German smiled. 'I can generally manage to scavenge something from the countryside.'

'You're not alone there, what with the Avilans taking their quota.' Stoneman turned to explain. 'There is a gang of guerrilleros – bandits more like – who keep raiding the villages.'

'It is a damn nuisance for me,' said Schumacher. 'They seem to wait until the quotas are gathered.'

'Avilans?' Ingram mused. 'When was their last raid?'

'Last week, sir. We hadn't had any trouble for about two months before that. Schumacher and I call them Avilans after their leader.'

'El Abulense? Have you heard of a man called José Perez?'

'He's the henchman. A ruthless devil who's put the fear of God into the villagers, but El Abulense's the leader all right.'

'Not now he's not, Mr Stoneman. I saw him killed outside Madrid some two months ago.' Ingram recalled the scene vividly. He remembered having heard that the bandits were well outside their normal beat at the time.

'Well, that's a coincidence and no mistake, sir.' Stoneman paused. 'Mind you, the villagers were still talking about El Abulense last week.'

'I dare say he's part of folklore now. From what I saw he deserves that much for keeping José Perez in hand.'

'He is a murderous devil that one, sir, as you'll know, if you've met him.' Schumacher sipped his wine. 'It seems that we are stuck with him.'

'I fear so, gentlemen. Unfortunately, it's a civil and not a military matter. I appreciate the difficulties it must cause you, Mr Schumacher, but really it is not our problem.'

'Well,' Stoneman hesitated, 'we have reason to believe that they're giving refuge to deserters. We've lost a few men from detachments in the town already this winter, sir.'

'You've sent in reports, of course? Then no doubt headquarters will deal with the matter.'

It was a disturbing problem and the coincidence worried him. He had striking recollection of the man who had defied Biarroco and himself. Still, there was nothing he could do about it and he was beginning to feel weary. He yawned and Penderleigh was instantly solicitous.

'I've taken the liberty of having your gear moved into your room, sir. If you'd care, I'll show you up.'

'Thank you. If you gentlemen will excuse me. You can show me around in the morning.'

'This way, sir,' said Penderleigh. 'I believe your servant is already settled in.'

Ramon was unpacking Ingram's few possessions in the room when Penderleigh showed him in, and he looked up with a grin at Ingram's gasp. The bedchamber was sumptuous, carpeted and draped, with a wardrobe and dressing-table and even a writing-desk. And it was blissful to sink into the soft bed and turn over to sleep as Ramon doused the oil lamp and quietly slipped away. After weeks of lying on the wet ground or in a hammock it was surprising how quickly sleep overwhelmed him.

In the morning Penderleigh showed Ingram his office and the new town major settled down to assess the task before him. It was satisfactory that his staff had prepared reports to assist him, and as he examined the assorted files Ingram felt justified in his earlier impression of efficiency. Penderleigh had everything in order – detailed troops movements, requisitions, general orders. An indulgent glance at the latter revealed the reference to Biarroco properly indexed in its place. Someone had trained the ensign well. But one problem required immediate attention; he rose and walked through to the boy's room.

'Mr Penderleigh, I see from the reports that we've only an approved accommodation establishment for two hundred men.'

'That's right, sir. I'm afraid that up till now we've been relying on non-approved billets. There hasn't been time to inspect all the applications.'

'But even with the applications here we'll be a hundred short of battalion strength. The Seventy-first is due in a few days. Get your hat, Mr Penderleigh. We'll start the inspections right away. You ought to know your way around the town by now.'

At the first house to which Penderleigh took him they were greeted by a surly old Spaniard whose face broke into a leering grin when Ingram explained their business. He led them upstairs to show them the rooms that he could make available for troops. Ingram scowled when he saw the squalor in the place; the stench of vermin was strong. But they could put ten men in here – he would have to remember to ask Schumacher how many palliasses were available. Clearly it was too much to expect furniture.

As Penderleigh took notes the old man pulled at his sleeve and muttered something about payment, and to Ingram's surprise the ensign replied in perfect Castilian.

'Payment? You're sure we're taking it, aren't you? These rooms are filthy. They'd have to be cleaned.'

'Oh, señor, of course I'll clean them for the fine young soldiers, and I a poor old man.'

Ingram smiled to himself, and as they left he said to Penderleigh, 'I didn't appreciate that you spoke fluent Spanish, Mr Penderleigh.'

'I was fortunate in my education, sir. My tutor was a scholar from Burgos. I flatter myself it's nearly as good as yours.'

'One of the advantages of a classical education. I have a degree in humanities for my pains. It has been of assistance. And I find the people interesting to talk to. My Portuguese is bad, though; so my servant keeps telling me.'

It was a pleasant morning that they passed, wandering through the town, visiting the houses on their list, talking to the townspeople. By lunch time they had found adequate accommodation for sixty men and Ingram was satisfied when they returned to his headquarters.

There was a small fat man waiting for them in the hall and he rose self-importantly when they entered. Penderleigh made the introductions. 'Mr George Ingram, Lieutenant, Seventy-first Highland Light Infantry; Don Miguel Esteban Talante y Rodriguez, Mayor of Plasencia.'

The little mayor bowed grotesquely over his layers of belly. 'It is an honour to welcome you to our noble city, señor.'

'I am fortunate indeed to be posted here and to make the acquaintance of its distinguished mayor.'

'The citizens of Plasencia are conscious of the compliment paid by Count Wellington in sending such a renowned officer to serve among them.'

'I am indebted to the citizens, señor; my duties have already taken me among them and I have never known such dignity and courtesy.'

That was stretching things a bit after spending the morning among the more surly and grasping of the townsfolk and for a moment he thought he had gone too far. Talante's eyes glinted beadily.

'You have already communicated with the people? This would doubtless concern the provision of accommodation for the soldiers?'

Ingram inclined his head, smiling to himself at the man's too apparent anxiety. He would be wanting to control these matters himself, of course, extracting for his own pocket a proportion of the fees paid. It would seem quite unreasonable to him that the army should deal directly with the landlords. Ingram guessed that the same procedure would apply to the supply of food and wondered what arrangements Schumacher had made. He supposed that the commissary employed his own indirect methods and imagined that Schumacher had reached some mutually advantageous agreement with the mayor.

'A number of the townspeople have asked me to represent them in this matter,' Talante said. 'I am sure you will appreciate the opportunity this affords. As you will have seen this morning, many of the houses offered privately are quite intolerable.'

Ingram would be damned before he played into the man's hands and paid more than he need, but he simply said, 'Some of the properties did not quite conform to our requirements, but many did. You will understand that we require a substantial number of billets and any list which would avoid compulsory billeting would be most helpful.'

The mayor nodded in satisfaction. 'There is another matter with which I hesitate to trouble you. I know that your duties must make great demands, but doubtless you will be well able to solve this one trivial problem without difficulty. There has, in the past, been controversy over the price and availability of wine and spirits in certain establishments in the town and the tradespeople are anxious that the matter be resolved before the major troop movements take place.'

'Ah,' said Ingram, knowing that they had reached the really difficult problem. 'Perhaps, señor, you would care to come into my office and take a glass of wine. Mr Penderleigh, kindly ask Mr Stoneman to be good enough to join us. Have the orderly bring wine and glasses – oh, and let me have the report on stabling. I'll take the opportunity to get that one straightened out as well.'

It was a prolonged discussion which followed, handicapped by Stoneman's appalling Spanish and the consequent interruptions for translation. According to the assistant provost marshal, there had indeed been trouble over drink in the past and he was anxious to place a number of premises out of bounds to the troops. Talante, on the other hand, welcomed this source of revenue and the lavish claims that ensued.

In the end they reached an initial agreement on which they could work for the present, and it took only a few minutes more to deal with the question of stabling and ensure that this would receive the mayor's attention. The little man rose to go.

'Lieutenant Ingram, in a few days it will be Christmas Day. My wife and I are giving a reception in the Ayuntamiento for the civic dignitaries and we would be greatly honoured if you and your staff could find a moment to spare from your duties in which to grace us with your presence.'

'You are too kind, señor. It will give us the greatest pleasure to attend.'

Ingram sighed inwardly at the thought of the dreary collection of local politicians, merchants and landowners with whom he would have to ingratiate himself. He cocked an eye at Stoneman, passively unaware of the invitation that had been accepted on his behalf, and wondered if the ex-grenadier would find some pressing disciplinary matter to preclude his attendance. Oblivious, the little mayor waddled happily down the street.

The 71st arrived on Christmas Eve and by dint of frenzied activity, and assistance from the advance party under Major Mackenzie, accommodation was available for every man. There were two hours of seemingly blind confusion while the hurried arrangements were put to the test and the soldiers were marched off to the company areas and allocated their billets. Twice, there were furious arguments between the officers, where rushed work had led to the doubling up of men at one of the perimeters, but these matters were soon resolved, and even Schumacher's terrible, German oaths subsided when Gavin, the quartermaster, eventually accepted that his requisitioned supplies had been delivered. At last, Cother announced that he was satisfied and Ingram was well content. In future, they would have these initial difficulties resolved.

It was rather fun pompously to invite Fox and Hall as guests to his little mess, to introduce them to his colleagues and offer the splendid dinner prepared by Schumacher's Bavarian cook. A chance remark led Hall and Fox to look at each other in surprise and then Fox exclaimed:

'Of course! You won't have heard – Boney's ruined. He's lost the Grand Army.'

Ingram and his staff gaped in puzzlement and Fox explained himself.

'Boney issued a proclamation in early November admitting the Grand Army was destroyed. Think of it – that was before Alba de Tormes.'

Penderleigh nodded. He could remember Alba well enough; his company commander had been wounded there.

'A great victory for the Russians,' Hall declared. 'An army of half a million bayonets destroyed.'

'A great victory for the winter,' Schumacher amended. 'Jesus Christ – half a million men.'

They sat for a silent moment contemplating what the German had said. Every one of them tried to visualise the enemy soldiers perishing in the cold, but it was impossible to imagine a disaster so great that it could overwhelm half a million men. The world had never known so mighty an army as the Grand Army and its destruction was too dreadful for them to comprehend, but as they sat there they felt humbled in the knowledge of the tragedy which had befallen their terrible enemy. It was Stoneman who spoke first.

'Boney must be short of troops now.'

'Do you think he'll pull out of Spain?' Penderleigh asked eagerly.

'There's no sign of it,' said Hall, 'otherwise I do not suppose we would be marching tomorrow to defend the pass. Still, I doubt he'll have any alternative if he is going to defend France.'

Fox nodded. 'The frogs'll have to go back. They must be about the only troops Boney's got.'

It was extraordinary to consider that the protracted war in the Peninsula could be ended by events in the unknown wastes of the Russian steppe. Their eyes glistened with excitement but again Schumacher broke the spell.

'No. I think they will not depart. Napoleon Bonaparte will raise fresh armies. He will scavenge his garrisons for every spare man, and he will drag from their homes boys of fourteen and weary old men to serve as conscripts who will die without complaint.'

They were appalled by the bitterness in his voice and could find nothing to say, but Stoneman was his friend and knew him well.

'Damn you for a German hope-not. Rise, man, and give us a toast to cheer us.'

Schumacher rose to his feet and smiled self-consciously at his outburst. 'I will not ask you to drink to the destruction of the Grand Army for too many of my poor, misled countrymen were with it. But drink, gentlemen, to this dreadful blow which has fallen on the vile tyrant, and may the next year bring an end to him and restore the world to peace.'

They growled their approbation and drained their glasses. As Fox filled his again, he cried, 'I'll give you a better one for hopeful officers – a bloody war and a sickly season.'

'Dammit Humphrey, you're after my epaulette,' Hall protested, for it was the traditional toast of promotion-hungry officers.

'That's Ingram's privilege,' grumbled Fox, but Hall was quick to silence him.

'Wheesht, man, and fill your glass. I drink to peace. It is a better omen at Yuletide.'

Ingram grimaced, but not at Fox's jealousy. He had remembered the mayor's reception on the morrow.

Ramon made a final adjustment to Ingram's crimson sash, then grunted with satisfaction. He stood up and handed Ingram his best cap and kid gloves and his hand twitched in one final correction to the sword belt. Ingram tucked the hat under his arm and pulled the gloves over his hands and then, with a curt nod to his servant, he went downstairs.

The others were waiting there, Penderleigh in his smart

regimentals with the tall plume of his hand-held shako tickling his chin, Schumacher wooden-faced in his plain scarlet coat, and Stoneman. Stoneman put them all to shame. He was immaculately turned out and he must have kept a rigorous eye on his batman to create the perfectly pressed coat, the pure white of his pipe-clayed belts, the dazzle of his buttons and plates, and those glistening boots. Ingram suddenly realised that the assistant provost marshal was actually looking forward to the reception.

There was a liveried footman to greet them at the Ayuntamiento and a pompous major-domo to make a sorry apology of their names as he announced them. The fat little mayor was there to welcome them and introduce them to his large, drab wife. There were all the functionaries to meet, and the self-important people of the town, and here and there was the odd face or voice that drew Ingram's interest. Schumacher had friends in this company, managing with a handful of Spanish words and eloquent gestures to convey the continuance of old liaisons. Penderleigh had engaged himself with the family of the prettiest girl present, and Stoneman was in laborious communication with a group of venerable drinkers. Ingram readdressed himself to the landowner who had caught his attention.

'Of course, we cannot be certain that Joseph Bonaparte will be in a position to provide any extra troops, but with the Grand Army destroyed . . . '

But here was the mayor waddling over to draw him away again.

'Permit me to present . . . '

'Señor Ingram and I have already met,' said Doña Margarita.

His head swam in confusion at finding her here and he tried clumsily to find something conventional to say as he made his deep bow.

'It is a quite unexpected pleasure to meet you again, señora.'

The little mayor was bobbing with curiosity and the lady deigned to explain.

'Lieutenant Ingram had the gallantry to escort me to safety when Avila fell. It was a sad journey made tolerable only by his presence.'

'The pleasure was mine, señora, as it is to find you here in Plasencia. Your letter gave no indication, but I imagined you had withdrawn to Portugal.'

'It is my regret that circumstances were such that I could say no more than I did. I had no wish to leave my own country and you will understand, señor, that I was anxious to be as close as possible to my home.'

'Doña Margarita is anxious . . . ' The mayor began, but she caught his eye with her old haughty coldness and he tailed off nervously. Ingram wondered what was being hidden from him and hazarded a guess.

'Have you had word from your brother-in-law?'

She eyed him with the disturbing wariness he remembered so well.

'Do you inquire after his health or are you on duty again?'

'There is a general order for his arrest,' Ingram admitted, 'but I assure you I asked out of concern. You know that I have the highest regard for Major Biarroco and it is my sincere wish to see him well and safe before the world is too greatly aged.'

Her eyes became soft again and she was almost contrite.

'Forgive me, Lieutenant, I will never forget your kindness during the retreat. It is difficult at a time when so many remember imagined slights to find the hand of genuine friendship.'

Ingram inclined his head in acknowledgement and noted that Talante was beaming as though the warmth between them was a reflection on his hospitality. 'Perhaps . . . ' Ingram began, and then stopped. It would be as well if he did not know whether or not Biarroco was in the vicinity.

But the woman seemed to have understood him.

'I will tell Marcelliano of your kind wishes. I know that he holds you in esteem, and he has asked after you.'

He was moved by her words and the trust conferred by them, for there could now be no doubt that Biarroco was in communication with her.

'You will understand, señora, that the recent general order places him in danger. Like any British officer, if I were to see him it would be my duty to take appropriate action.'

'I am well acquainted with your high sense of duty, Señor Ingram, and regret the impertinence which prompted my comments on an earlier, less happy occasion. It is your fortune to serve honest men and to your credit that you serve them so loyally.' She paused and then teased, 'I fear that I must not talk of Marcelliano lest your loyalties are too severely tried.'

Talante was muttering something, trying to intervene with some pleasantry or other, to separate them and drag Ingram off to meet another tedious contractor. But he did not want to be parted from her and tried desperately to find some neutral topic for conversation.

'Perhaps you would permit me to introduce my officers . . .'

'I should be most privileged.' She smiled engagingly at the dismayed mayor, quite disarming him, before turning away with Ingram in acknowledgement of their little conspiracy.

Stoneman was the most conveniently placed and flushed with pleasure to be introduced to so grand a lady. It was significant that his cronies slipped discreetly away, and he struggled with his embarrassment to mumble a few conventionalities in his appalling Spanish. But the assistant provost marshal's Spanish was good enough to recognise her name, and he cocked an eyebrow before speaking in English.

'Biarroco? That's a coincidence, sir. Now in general orders . . . '

'It was Major Biarroco whom I saw kill El Abulense. We were on duty together at the time. Doña Margarita is his brother's widow.'

'I see, sir,' said Stoneman evenly. 'Well, let's hope he doesn't turn up here.'

Inwardly Ingram cursed the man's lack of tact; the whole business was embarrassing. Doña Margarita was awaiting a translation but it was difficult to find suitable phrases.

Fortunately Schumacher appeared at that moment and was not the lady related to the wife of a friend? And it was a relief to trace the complexities of the Menorez-Cabezon side of her family, away from the sensitivities of the Biarrocos, although in the end Ingram felt some satisfaction that Schumacher's friend's wife was not, after all, a relation.

In the corner of his eye he saw Penderleigh disengaged from his pretty girl, and he took the opportunity to draw Doña Margarita away before the conversation again touched an awkward subject. The young ensign was all grace and charm and smiled easily when the lady complimented him on his Spanish.

'It is my good fortune, señora, in that it enables me to discourse with you.'

Ingram was amused to note that the girl's family were drifting back to rejoin him now that he was in such distinguished company, and there was another round of formal introductions and elaborate compliments. Yet Doña Margarita was in light-hearted mood and was content to stay beside him while he moved round the assembly under the careful shepherding of Talante and his wife. The mayor was in ecstasy at the success of the evening and Ingram was so enjoying himself that he could even jest lightly with the bumptious little man. This pleasantry was rewarded for when they were alone for a moment Doña Margarita had a comment to make.

'Don Miguel is a kind man, is he not? It is good of him to offer me a place under his roof. Of course, he is not of important family, and his achievements have made him somewhat officious, but he is a man of merit nonetheless and he is generosity personified.'

Ingram agreed tactfully. It had been thoughtful of Talante to invite him and his officers, and his soul sang with gratitude for the meeting with Doña Margarita. He reflected ironically on his earlier disgruntlement at the prospect of the evening. And he was blissfully unaware of the eye that Schumacher cocked in his direction and Stoneman's wise old wink.

Now the company was thinning and it was time to tear Penderleigh away from his pretty señorita and gather the others together to take their leave. And at the door he could rejoice at Señora de Talante's invitation to call, and note the warmth in Doña Margarita's eye as she wished him goodnight.

8

It had been a beautiful day, sharp and clear, with the mountain air refreshing after the recent rain. From his bedroom window Ingram could see the snow on the nearby tops glow pink in the setting sun. He paused to gaze at the dark banks of cloud creeping in with the night. High in the sky an early star danced in the frosty air. The lights were lit now in the town, and the smoke from the fires drifted into the growing darkness. Over there at the Talantes' house Doña Margarita would be sitting by the window where he had left her, watching the deepening shadows in the valley. The firelight would be darting round her as it was round him, and he became aware that behind him Ramon had banked up the crackling logs and was waiting for him to indicate that he was ready to change.

The afternoon had been a considerable success. Señora de Talante had welcomed him with astonishing warmth, and it had been pleasant to let her escort him into the chamber where Margarita – he realised that in his own thoughts he had discarded the 'Doña'. He grinned to himself. It was like thinking of Catherine Hall as Kate and yet maintaining the formal mode of address.

She had been quite charming as they sat together in the midst of the Talante women and talked in light fashion of the matters of immediate moment; the deportment of such and such a lady, the gallantry of young Penderleigh, the profound responsibilities of the mayor. It was a matter of concern whether the snows would block the passes and cut them off from news of Castile, and Ingram, cocking an eye, wondered if Biarroco was near at hand. Someone remarked that the winter would be hard in Avila with the French at every hand. How could an army be maintained by the poor people? There was an embarrassed silence for the British army too was present, but Señora de Talante quickly remarked that the pigs were fattening, and that was another fascinating topic of conversation. And Ingram endured it happily, for Margarita's dark eyes were kind and friendly.

He turned away from the window, unclasping his cloak, which he handed to Ramon. Then he started to undo the buttons on his best uniform coat. There was hot water waiting and he could have a leisurely wash before donning his undress uniform. It would be a busy evening, for a large draft of the 50th was due to arrive on its way to join the battalion at Bejar. Remembering the afternoon's conversation, Ingram reflected that there was still no news from the passes, and considered that it would be well to detain the draft here in Plasencia until he was sure that the road to Bejar was open.

He undid his shirt and nodded to Ramon, who poured the steaming kettle into the basin, but as Ingram approached the wash-stand he was interrupted by a knock on the door. At his response an orderly entered.

'Mr Penderleigh's compliments, sir, and that's the draft coming in now.'

'Damn and blast. Very good, I'll be down immediately.'

He had to forgo his relaxed ablutions and made do with the quickest splash before slipping into his tunic and hurrying for the door while pulling his sword belt into place. It was Ramon who remembered his gorget and fumbled to fasten it round his neck while he fumed with impatience. He could not possibly go on duty without the burnished symbol of authority, but he was anxious to get downstairs and confirm that all was in order. Already he was imagining matters left unattended, and cursing himself for his self-indulgent afternoon.

When he came hastening down the staircase he found one of his sergeants in the hall with the orderlies who were to act as guides already forming up.

'Where's Mr Penderleigh?'

'Outside, sir, with the other gentlemen.'

They were standing in a little group on the steps in the beam of light cast from the open doors, and Ingram saw that Penderleigh was in deep discussion with the officers commanding the detachment. Schumacher nodded at his arrival.

'There's a hundred and fifty of them, sir. That's thirty more than we were expecting.'

'You'd better attend to the extra supplies needed – and you'll have to dig out the extra palliasses. Mr Stoneman, have a couple of orderlies stand by as guides to the extra billets once I've got them worked out. Mr Penderleigh!'

Penderleigh turned and led the two strange officers up the steps to him.

'May I present these friends from my regiment, sir. Captain D'Alby, Lieutenant Willard; Lieutenant Ingram of the Seventy-first.'

'Your servant, gentlemen. You made a quick march. I regret the present confusion, but we were informed that your draft was only one hundred and twenty strong. Perhaps if you'd accompany me to the office, Mr Penderleigh and I will be able to allocate the additional billets in a few minutes.'

'Splendid! I hope you've a fire in your office,' D'Alby declared, nudging Penderleigh. 'Perhaps young Jack here can find us a glass of brandy. Willard, you'd better have the sergeant stand the men at ease.'

It was a simple enough matter to select the extra quarters and advise the landlords of their unexpected guests. Schumacher bustled in with a requisition to sign and hurried off to superintend his well rehearsed arrangements. In the hall Stoneman was instructing the last of the guides. It only remained to have D'Alby and Willard shown to their billet a few doors down the street.

Ingram stopped them for a final word. 'I trust you find your quarters comfortable, gentlemen. I think you would be well advised to rest here for a day or two. I have reason to believe that the pass is blocked and am presently awaiting a report on the condition of the road.'

'Dammit, we'll stay put until you know then. No good ever came from trudging around in the snow, eh young Jack? Come on, Willard, I want to get my head down. It's been a damned long day.'

To Ingram's astonishment, the two officers bade them good-night and left for their quarters without making any attempt to look to the troops in their care. But Ingram wanted to ensure that his arrangements were satisfactory.

'Come on, Mr Penderleigh, I want to inspect the billets.'

Penderleigh nodded and picked up his shako. He made no comment on the conduct of his two regimental colleagues.

Coronado, the captain of the Spanish town guard, was in the hall and he bowed to them as they came out of the office. It was his custom at this time of evening to join Schumacher and Stoneman over a glass of brandy in an endeavour to improve his shocking

English. Ingram often wondered how they could endure the broken conversations, but they seemed to get on well enough. As he knew his colleagues were busy for the moment, he suggested that Coronado make himself at home in the warmth of the mess, and the Spaniard thanked him gracefully. The incident gave Ingram an idea.

'If this draft is detained by the weather we'll have your friends to dinner in the mess tomorrow night.'

Penderleigh beamed his gratitude. 'I'd appreciate that, sir. Captain D'Alby's been awfully good to me; I was in his company until he was wounded at Alba.'

The ace of hearts fluttered briefly over the table, extinguishing D'Alby's king. Willard inclined his head.

'Well led, young Jack.'

Ingram looked round them, at Willard smug and already counting his winnings, at Penderleigh smiling at the unexpected compliment, and at D'Alby, already flushed with his port and uncaring whether he won or lost. But Ingram had decided that he could only afford to lose another hand. He eyed D'Alby thoughtfully, resenting his carelessness, the ease with which he could squander his stakes, untroubled by his partner's losses.

Ingram spread his assorted nines and sixes, and picked out the ace of trumps – his only trump – which he placed on the table, then swept the cards towards him.

D'Alby guffawed at Willard's chagrin before turning to Ingram.

'There you are – the rest are ours,' and he placed the surviving master cards on the table.

'That's rubber – and at a shilling a trick.'

Ingram glowered resentfully. The rubber would have been lost if he had not held the ace. He was irritated by the other's too apparent wealth as he sat there, beaming, in his beautifully tailored coat with its easily purchased captain's epaulette. The memory of his own lost captaincy was aggravating and it annoyed him, too, that he had allowed himself to be drawn into this folly. Schumacher and Stoneman had had the wisdom to retire discreetly.

He drew his share of the winnings towards him, and wondered if he could reasonably excuse himself. But D'Alby was grinning across the table at him.

'This is fun – eh, Ingram?'

He assented, cursing the pride which bade him remain. Penderleigh began to deal, but D'Alby was addressing them all.

'The stakes are damned low, let's up them to a crown a trick and five guineas on the rubber.'

Penderleigh smiled in benign acceptance, and Ingram was appalled. His mind went blank in panic as he wondered how to protest in dignity when his own adjutant agreed so easily, while he could not afford to lose at these stakes. Then Willard demurred.

'Gentlemen, you'd have my horse from me, would you?'

'Yes! And your sword, too!' cried D'Alby. 'Dammit man, young Jack here will support you.'

For the first time Ingram saw the worry flash briefly on Penderleigh's face. He decided to intervene.

'Captain D'Alby, I myself would prefer not to play at such stakes.'

'Come on, man, Penderleigh'll look after you.'

'I most certainly will not impose my obligations on my junior.'

'Damn me, Ingram, would you spoil our evening?'

'I trust not, Captain, since I am your host. Neither Willard nor I, nor, I imagine, Penderleigh . . . '

'Damn you for a Scotch Presbyterian – and a pauper to boot!'

Ingram struggled to control his growing fury.

'The former, sir, I take as a compliment which I will permit to cancel the second, in view of your unfortunate condition.'

The insult took a moment to sink in, but then D'Alby was on his feet clinging to the table in rage.

'You surly Scotch bastard, you'd dare . . . '

'I'll thank you to control your tongue, sir. The drink bids it give offence.'

'It's you who give offence, sir! You damned Scotch church-mouse . . . '

'For God's sake, D'Alby, sit down.' There was anxiety in Willard's voice, as he rose with Penderleigh.

Ingram remained seated, his eyes on D'Alby's, willing him to some folly as he listened to the meaningless outpourings. The enraged captain was looking around now for some object which, in his fury, he could cast across the table.

'Please, sir, please sit down.' It was Penderleigh speaking, his voice distinct and authoritative. He had D'Alby by the arm. Suddenly the drunken man took notice and stopped. He seemed to bring himself into focus and looked around stupidly.

'Please, sir, will you sit down.'

'No, I will not. I shall depart forthwith. Are you two "dirty shirts" coming?'

Willard made to join him.

'Penderleigh?'

The lad looked confused. In the circumstances it was difficult for him to refuse the appeal in his regiment's nickname, but clearly he did not want to go. Ingram acted at once.

'Mr Penderleigh has duties to attend to. I require his presence here.'

'Damn your eyes, sir.'

'And yours, sir. Goodnight.'

While Penderleigh escorted them downstairs, Ingram breathed out slowly, and poured himself a glass of brandy. His anger had evaporated in the satisfaction of provoking D'Alby into making a complete ass of himself. He grinned ruefully. If there had been any devilment in the other two it would have almost inevitably led to a duel, and he had no doubt that Fox would find the story amusing. It would be embarrassing to meet D'Alby in the morning.

He rose and carried his glass over to the fireplace, and stirred the hot embers with his boot. He was standing there when Penderleigh returned.

'I'm most dreadfully sorry, sir, I don't know how you controlled yourself. I . . .'

'That's all right, Jack,' he said, feeling the Christian name to be appropriate for the first time. 'It was I who invited them, was it not? The French would be delighted if British officers sought satisfaction on every occasion a few thoughtless words were spoken in drink.'

Penderleigh nodded seriously. 'I was very glad of your assistance – I didn't want to get involved. It's all most upsetting; Captain D'Alby is a very fine officer.'

'I'm sure he is. The incident is best forgotten.' Suddenly he felt very tired. 'I'm going to get some sleep now. You'd be advised to do the same.'

'Oh, I don't think I could sleep yet. I'll go out and walk around for a bit. It's a beautiful, frosty night.'

'Well, don't let your mind prey on it. These things happen to us all.'

Someone was knocking at the gates of hell – no, at his bedroom door. They could knock till eternity. His bed was warm and soft, and he snuggled down in the blankets. Kate Hall was laughing at him with her brown eyes, but no, it was Margarita, galloping away with him in the snow, fleeing from the fair-haired man who might be a deserter. Someone was shooting at them. No. It was knocking. Let them knock. The fire was out and the room was cold. But there were flames as his eyes opened. Candles.

'For God's sake, sir, you must come. There's trouble with the dagos.'

It was Stoneman, with Ramon holding the light.

'What's wrong?' He was awake now, the bedclothes thrown aside. The room was very cold.

'I don't know, sir. The guard's been called out and there was a shot just then.'

He was pulling on his trousers. 'Where is this?'

'Just down the road. You can just hear the rumpus – it looks quite serious.'

Now his coat was on, over his nightshirt, and he was scrambling for his boots. It was funny to note that Stoneman, too, was still in his nightshirt, the neck just visible under the open collar of his scarlet coat. He took his sword from Ramon.

'Where's Penderleigh?'

'No idea, sir. He's not in his room.'

'Come on then. Let's find out what's happening.'

At the foot of the stairs they found a corporal with half a dozen men, armed with fixed bayonets.

'Where are the rest of the men, Corporal?'

'Falling in, sir. They'll be down directly. The guard's gone up the road, sir, with the sergeant and Mr Penderleigh.'

'Right. Becket, Davis, fetch lanterns and have them lighted. Corporal, keep two men here and assemble the others as they arrive. Send someone to call Mr Schumacher with my compliments, and ask him to take charge here. I want all weapons loaded, but God help the man who fires without orders. You others come with me.'

It was difficult to determine what was happening when they stepped into the darkness of the street, but there was a frenzy of activity not a hundred yards away. Ingram, with a sinking heart, realised that it appeared to be centred on the house where D'Alby and Willard were quartered. There were lanterns there, and he could see the uniforms of the town guard as they milled around. A sudden flash was followed by the familiar sharp crack of a shot.

'Christ Almighty!' Stoneman muttered as they hurried down the street.

Ingram could see that the Spanish militia were forming into a line, and beyond them he observed the scarlet coats of Penderleigh's guard. The Spaniards raised their muskets in readiness and it was obvious that the British were hopelessly outnumbered. He drew his sword and pushed through the Spanish ranks.

'Stop this madness!' he bellowed in Spanish. 'What is this folly? Put up your arms!'

He turned on Penderleigh and saw that the British soldiers also had their muskets at the present. There were civilians crowded around and he saw D'Alby slumped against the wall. Willard was there too, sword in hand.

'What the devil d'you think you're doing, Penderleigh? Ground your arms before someone is hurt.'

But D'Alby was struggling to his feet.

'You men! Stay as you are! I'm the senior officer here – we'll not give way to these damned dagos.'

Ingram turned round desperately to make sure that the Spanish line was still steady, and to his relief saw Coronado striding towards him.

'What in God's name is the meaning of this, Captain? Why do Spanish soldiers threaten my men?'

'In the name of Christ it is your soldiers who have caused this affair. It is they who have prevented my guard from carrying out their duties. I must ask you to withdraw your men.'

'That I will do when I have had a satisfactory explanation of this disgraceful incident, but I refuse to take any action until your men have lowered their weapons.'

'I insist that your soldiers stand down before I take any such action, Lieutenant. These fellows have intervened between my men and their prisoners, and I warn you that I regard the matter as a serious breach of discipline, for which I hold you responsible.'

'Stand aside, Ingram, and we'll give those bastards a belly of lead!' It was D'Alby who was shouting and Ingram turned on him in fury.

'Hold your tongue, sir! These troops are under my command. Sergeant! Order arms!'

'Sir!' The sergeant was wooden-faced at the confrontation between his superiors. He turned with precision to face the little line of red. 'Guard – order arms!'

Ingram tried not to reveal the considerable relief he experienced when the muskets were snapped smartly to the ground. It would have been natural for these men to obey D'Alby, a captain in their own battalion and the senior officer present, and Ingram was gratified by their loyalty to him, and the sergeant's sound common sense.

D'Alby was screaming something at him but that could be ignored; there was more urgent business than D'Alby's drunken abuse.

'Mr Penderleigh, come here if you please.' He turned back to Coronado. 'Now, Captain, will you lower your weapons?'

Stoneman had pushed through the militia now with the other men behind him, and he nodded grimly to his friend Coronado, as the line of Spanish muskets were shouldered at that officer's command. Penderleigh scowled angrily at the Spaniard, and Ingram, intercepting the look, glowered at the ensign.

'Well, sir, what explanation do you have for your conduct? Captain Coronado advised me that you interceded between his guard and some prisoners.'

'By God, I did, sir,' Penderleigh replied hotly. 'That damned lieutenant of his was about to arrest Captain D'Alby and Mr Willard.'

'You didn't tell me that these prisoners were British officers,' Ingram accused Coronado. 'By what authority was your lieutenant arresting them?'

'This town guard will arrest anyone who conducts himself as they did. These so-called gentlemen discharged their pistols at their landlord for some imagined complaint, and then when he sought apology they threw the unfortunate man down the stairs and cast him from his own house. When my guard arrived they were throwing furniture from the house at him.'

'That in no way justified the violence of your guard, señor,' Penderleigh interrupted, to Ingram's annoyance. Coronado snapped his fingers.

'And then this young whippersnapper comes charging down the street with bayonets fixed, and I have to call out my entire guard to control the situation.'

'I'd scarcely call it control,' Penderleigh jibed.

'That's enough, Penderleigh,' snapped Ingram. 'You will return to the office this instant and prepare me a report on the matter.'

'But . . .'

'Go forthwith! Do you realise that every soldier in the garrison has been called out by your folly? You will present my apologies to Mr Schumacher for disturbing his sleep and advise him that he may stand down the remainder of our unfortunate men.'

Penderleigh's face was working in a mixture of misery and rage.

'Yes, sir,' he saluted, and pushed unhappily through the Spaniards to make his lonely way up the street.

Ingram turned back to Coronado. It was an extremely delicate situation; it would be humiliating and deeply resented by the men if he were to meekly hand the two offenders over to the Spaniards. Yet he could see no alternative. Already the civilians were crowding round with complaints, and Ingram recognised the unlucky landlord, voluble in protest. It was difficult to know what to say, and as he paused it was Coronado who spoke.

'You have had your explanation, Señor Ingram. Will you now withdraw your men and let us proceed with our duty?'

Ingram looked at Stoneman standing silent and perplexed by the conversation in Spanish. He would not understand if Ingram suddenly gave the orders for a withdrawal, abandoning D'Alby and Willard to their fate. Nor would the men. They would not listen to any explanation but would simply be aware that the two officers were languishing in a Spanish gaol until the high command decided what to do with them. And what could he do about that draft of a hundred and fifty men if it were deprived of its officers?

'These officers are required for military duties,' he began firmly, but Coronado was in no mood for conciliation.

'I don't care if they're required to bed with the Empress Josephine. I'm putting them out of harm's way.'

'Psst!' It was the Spanish lieutenant who drew their attention to the problem. D'Alby was using his rank and position to influence the sergeant and the other men. They had been with him for years – seen action together. The rest of the officers were strangers by comparison. Ingram saw his opportunity at once.

'Mr Stoneman, take your men and place Captain D'Alby and Mr Willard under arrest.'

Stoneman's jaw fell open in astonishment for he had understood little of what had been said. But he was quick to pull himself together and he could see quite clearly which parties were causing the trouble.

'Yes, sir,' he snapped, and with the practice of years in the ranks he led his party forward so quickly that the two officers were in custody before anyone realised what was happening.

While Coronado was still taken by surprise, Ingram spoke.

'You saw that these officers were suborning my men, Captain Coronado. I regret that I had immediately to place them in the custody of the assistant provost marshal. You will understand that their new offence is far more serious than their earlier drunken escapade. If you will clear the way I will now withdraw my guard together with the prisoners in custody.'

Coronado's face went through a gamut of expressions from amazement to comprehension to fury. Their roles had been neatly reversed. His lieutenant had not succeeded in effecting the arrest and now the men were in British custody. Were he to intervene he would be in the same unwarranted position as had been Penderleigh, the more serious as he would be removing prisoners quite properly under the custody of the assistant provost marshal. He could expect the most severe censure for such interference.

'By the Son of the Virgin, Ingram, I'll protest to the Adjutant-General about this. You had better be very sure those two drunkards are court-martialled for this night's work.'

'If you would now give way, Captain? I assure you that I profoundly regret everything that has passed tonight and consider that my uniform has been discredited by the whole affair.'

Coronado grunted and waved to his line to open before stumping away in anger. Ingram nodded across to Stoneman, and led his troops through the gap. D'Alby was silent now, he and Willard realising the gravity of their position. It was a sombre little procession that marched the few yards up the road to Ingram's headquarters.

Ingram dismissed the guard and led the officers into his office, closing the door behind him. Penderleigh looked up in anxiety as Ingram turned to D'Alby and Willard.

'Well, gentlemen, you've got us into a damned serious situation.'

Willard began to speak, but D'Alby motioned him to silence before speaking himself.

'Mr Ingram, I am grateful to you for saving us from a Spanish gaol, but you will understand that I feel it would be better if we were to discuss the complexities of the matter in the morning. I do not think I could . . . At present I . . . I regret . . .'

His voice tailed off in a weary slur, despite his new-found dignity. It would be hopeless to get any sense from him until he was sober.

'Mr Stoneman will escort you to a room upstairs where you will oblige me by confining yourselves until I request your attendance in the morning. You will appreciate that you must remain under arrest until I have clarified the position.'

They left, hanging their heads, under Stoneman's silent escort.

'Well, Penderleigh?'

'I had to intervene, sir, the Spaniards were threatening them.'

'Will you understand that these officers were behaving in a most violent fashion. Their assault on the landlord more than justified the actions of the town guard. If they had any complaint about their accommodation they should have made it here, but no, they behaved in the dreadful fashion which they did. And you, sir, had no business to interfere. And your impropriety forced me into the position where, for disciplinary purposes, I had to arrest them both. Court-martial will now be difficult to avoid – and in my present opinion would be well justified.'

Penderleigh thrust a sheet of paper into his hand with a scowl.

'There is your report, Mr Ingram. If you have no further duties for me, sir, I shall retire.'

As the ensign strode from the room Ingram realised for the first time the embarrassing nature of his own position. D'Alby was his senior who earlier that evening had given such offence that many a man would have provoked a duel. However meritorious Ingram's self-control had been, his subsequent arrest of that officer and his friend, and their ensuing court martial, would be bound to be misunderstood by the army. He would be dishonoured and held in contempt by even his closest comrades. On the other hand, were he to release the officers, Coronado's report would lead to a full investigation and he would be seen to have failed in his duty even if the dictates of discipline did not necessitate court martial.

Stoneman came into the office and shook his head sadly.

'I left a sentry in the corridor in case they try to start things again.'

'Thank you. Er – you will no doubt be recording the arrest?'

Stoneman met him with steady eyes that were full of understanding. As assistant provost marshal the matter, strictly, was in his hands. If he made record of the incident a report would require to be submitted to Division, and to the Provost Marshal himself at Wellington's headquarters. It would not be possible to release the officers without a general order to that effect.

'If I detain them, Mr Ingram, who will command their draft?'

That was an important point, for a hundred and fifty soldiers could not be moved to their urgent destination without competent officers. There was Penderleigh, of course, but Ingram required his adjutant's services. It was a convenient escape that Stoneman offered. If Coronado could be restrained from protesting to the Adjutant-General the whole business could be dealt with quite satisfactorily by reporting the incident to the Colonel of the 50th. That would adequately solve the interrelated problems of discipline and honour.

'Thank you, Mr Stoneman. I think the matter may now be conveniently left till the morning.'

It was Talante who was the first angry petitioner on the following morning, bustling in with voluble complaint, protesting at the offence to his civic guard. Ingram had spent a sleepless night planning the conversation.

'I have already apologised to Captain Coronado for the disgraceful incident. I intend to see him today to explain more fully my reasons for acting as I did. At the time the breach of military discipline appeared so serious that I had to place the matter in the hands of the assistant provost marshal.'

'But you imposed on the jurisdiction of the militia.'

'That was not my intention. I had to act as I did to prevent these officers from commanding my men to open fire. Many Spanish lives were saved in consequence.'

Talante gaped in surprise. It had not occurred to him from Coronado's account that the British soldiers could have inflicted casualties on the overwhelmingly superior town guard.

'My intervention, Don Miguel, avoided an incident which would have made Plasencia the source of bitter division between our two nations.'

'It was your men who caused the trouble!'

'It was caused by two drunken officers who are now in my custody. Captain Coronado behaved perfectly properly and I will brook no criticism of him; but between you and me he could have behaved with more tact.'

That was unfair, as was his omission of Penderleigh's part in the proceedings, but the mayor rose to the bait of the flattering confidentiality.

'You think that he could have handled the matter differently?'

'Tell me, Don Miguel, would Spanish soldiers stand meekly by when foreigners tried to arrest their officers?'

'They would die first,' stated the little civilian.

'Precisely,' said Ingram.

'Ah,' said the mayor as realisation dawned. 'How fortunate that you were there, señor; there might have been appalling bloodshed. Clearly Captain Coronado behaved with gross insensitivity.'

'Oh no, señor, he behaved quite properly and his anger was entirely justified.'

'Then he should have kept his emotions under control. Why, he is angry yet! I shall have to explain to him how matters stand.'

'Hm. I imagine that his anger concerns the fate of the two prisoners. He requested me to ensure that they were court-martialled.'

'That's none of his business; it's not within his jurisdiction.'

'Quite. But he would impinge on my discretion; he indicated that he would submit a complaint to the Adjutant-General.'

The mayor positively bristled with indignation. 'He'll do no such thing. That would greatly damage the good will which exists between the army and the people of this city.'

'That is a point which might well be made to him. He is a proud officer who would be quite justified in making his protest.'

Talante smiled with self-satisfaction. 'I will be able to persuade him otherwise.'

Ingram was relieved to think that some subtlety would be used. Coronado would be more furious than ever if he heard Ingram's account of the events. But the mayor was looking at him intently.

'It would be interesting to know just how you do propose to deal with the miscreants, Señor Ingram.'

There could be only one answer, for the whole town would shortly witness D'Alby and Willard at the head of their draft as it marched out from its billets. To vacillate would indicate bad faith.

'As I explained to Captain Coronado last night, these officers have important duties to attend to which will necessitate their release. I shall, of course, be lodging a full report of their conduct.'

'Quite, quite. Military necessity is the supreme judge.' He fixed Ingram with a steady eye. 'It is good that we can be so frank.'

With a shock Ingram realised that the little man knew perfectly well that Ingram had been outmanoeuvring him and had virtually collaborated to that end in order to establish that their relationship was now that of confidants. He felt foolish and crude in the face of such subtlety, and he wondered what the new relationship would cost him.

9

Schumacher threw his papers down on the desk.

'That's the third time they've raided that village this winter. Now they're away with all my pigs.'

Ingram laid down his quill with a sigh. The commissary was being driven to despair by the Avilan bandits. They had long since stopped regarding the gang as guerrilleros.

'Did they drive off all the pigs?'

'Oh, they didn't drive them off – that would have been too tiresome. They waited until the beasts were slaughtered and then rode in and helped themselves. We arrived half an hour after they'd gone. They only took what had been killed.'

'So there are pigs left?'

'Just enough for the villagers' own needs. You know how it is; they'll butcher the animals that are left to make their sausages for the year. You won't get another pig out of that village.'

Ingram nodded and rose to his feet. He walked over to the fire.

'You were only half an hour behind them?'

'Yes – it was beautifully timed. That's the fourth occasion I've just missed them.'

'It's very strange that they always seem to get there just before us.'

'Yes, isn't it,' said the German. 'Their intelligence is very good. These fellows really understand how we work.'

Penderleigh, standing by the window, turned to Stoneman.

'That would bear out your ideas about where the deserters are going.'

'They're getting help out there somewhere. We'd have caught more of them otherwise.'

There was always a steady trickle of men who dared the appalling penalties to desert, even from the best regiments. These were, of course, the worst elements, the dregs from the gaols, the less trustworthy Irish, the unruly, and the malcontents. Few, very few, managed to make good their escape, and the majority were caught to die on the gallows. Yet here in the mountains, despite the cruel winter, men were disappearing as if into thin air.

'Do you think deserters would settle in with a gang of bandits?' Ingram asked.

Schumacher grinned ruefully. 'Well, the way these bandits are picking up our supplies they're eating better than anyone here.'

'But even if they are taking in the deserters that doesn't explain their detailed knowledge of your arrangements,' Ingram mused. 'They'd know the system, but not the timing of your convoys.'

'Perhaps . . .' Penderleigh began and then hesitated, unsure of himself. Ingram looked at the boy intently; since the D'Alby incident he seemed afraid to commit himself.

'Go on,' said Ingram gently.

'Well, they do seem to be behaving well towards the villagers – leaving them their own pigs, only taking what we've requisitioned – perhaps they're getting help from the people themselves.'

'Ach, no peasant will befriend a thief,' Schumacher scorned. 'The villages have all lost from the payments we'd have made.'

But Ingram was more thoughtful, and impressed that the ensign's sensitivity and knowledge of the Spaniard could have revealed to him an important clue. 'There may be much in what Mr Penderleigh says. Bandits would normally have no regard for the villagers. I remember myself, in Pinto, seeing . . .'

He broke off as the contradiction occurred to him. The bandits he had seen in Pinto that day with Biarroco were the same gang as that causing the present trouble. It was an extraordinary reversal of conduct.

'How much do we know about this José Perez?'

'Ah . . .' Schumacher hesitated. 'That's another thing I must raise. We're not just dealing with José Perez. The villagers said that El Abulense was leading the bandits today.'

'That's impossible; the man is dead.'

'So you've told us, sir, and Major Biarroco killed him,' Stoneman intervened, 'but here's Schumacher saying the villagers saw him today. And Coronado was grumbling about him just the other night.'

'But I can assure you I saw him lying dead, and José Perez took over without question. He struck me as a ruthless man – and a disciplined one. Are you positive that you are not thinking of him?'

'The villagers certainly were not,' Schumacher affirmed. 'They know José Perez well enough.'

'And I made the same point to Coronado, but he's certain José Perez is still number two. Coronado's no fool and after what Schumacher says I'm sure he's right.' The assistant provost marshal was adamant.

'Is it possible there is a new El Abulense?' Ingram wondered. 'What do we know about the gang?'

Schumacher picked at his ear. 'Well, they've been around for a long time. They were a thorn in my flesh all summer and then disappeared to join the guerrilleros swarming round Madrid, which is when you saw them. Then in late November they were back, apparently with El Abulense, and they've been causing havoc since.'

'Were they always so considerate to the people, so disciplined?' Penderleigh was quite right to emphasise that point, Ingram thought.

'Now that hadn't occurred to me before.' Schumacher pointed with a wax-stained finger. 'That's new – it's really only since the army moved into winter quarters. And they're far better organised than they were.'

'Aye, they've changed since I saw them at Pinto.' Ingram walked back slowly to his desk and sat down. 'Their leader, whoever he is, has clearly installed discipline and order.'

'And he's gathering strength,' noted the commissary. 'Not just deserters, but his bands are growing. One hears rumours.'

'Coronado said it was as though he was a military man,' Stoneman ventured.

'That is possible enough,' said Ingram thoughtfully. 'It would fit what we know. So we must surmise that there is a new El Abulense, another Avilan, and that he is a man of extraordinary ability.'

'He'd have to be if he's getting help from the villages.' Stoneman held Ingram's eye. 'Biarroco's an Avilan, isn't he?'

Ingram nodded. The disturbing coincidence had occurred to him and with it came recollections of Biarroco's friends and the fair-haired man among them. But Penderleigh had a further contribution to make.

'Could these people be paying the villagers? What do you think, Schumacher?'

'Oh, I dare say they could. The peasants don't give much away, but they didn't look too upset this morning. Yet you'd hardly expect bandits to carry a military chest. They'd need assistance; perhaps they've got a paymaster here in Plasencia.'

Penderleigh smiled. 'You can hardly call them bandits if they are making payment.'

'But harbouring deserters,' growled the assistant provost marshal.

'And taking requisitioned supplies,' the commissary grumbled.

'Quite,' said Ingram, 'and I don't like the idea of a private army being raised in this area, whoever they are, military chest or no. I find your thought about the paymaster disturbing, Schumacher, to say nothing of the leakage of intelligence about our supply system.'

They were all watching him now, nodding in grave agreement, wondering what he was going to do.

'I fear this is a matter for Division, but first I want to consult the civil authorities.' He rose. 'I'll go now and see what Talante has to say.'

He was on his way to the Ayuntamiento, striding purposefully through the rain, when he had to step aside in the busy street to make way for a horse litter. Some sick officer was being brought down from the mountains to attempt recovery in the military hospital. He glanced at the face lest he knew the man. It was D'Alby.

The invalid smiled weakly. His face was drawn and skeletal, and he was sweating with pain.

'Here I am, back to trouble you again, Ingram.' It was no more than a hoarse croak.

'I'm sorry to see you so ill, Captain. What troubles you?'

'My wound, my wound. My horse fell on me in the snow. My old Alba wound is open again. It never was right, I was always in pain, but now' – he reached out a trembling hand – 'it bleeds, Ingram, my whole side bleeds.'

Ingram took the waving hand and pressed it, feeling its coldness. The man must have been dreadfully hurt.

'You'll be all right now. Surgeon Goss is an able man.'

'I'm sorry, so sorry about what happened. I drank to ease the pain. So very sorry, ashamed.'

'That's all right. It doesn't matter now.'

'Never thanked you properly. Could've been a court-martial. Grateful.'

'You'll tire yourself. You'll be in bed in a few minutes.'

'Grateful. And young Penderleigh. Give my regards.'

The litter moved on its painful, jolting way, and Ingram, disturbed by the incident, had to re-order his thoughts for his interview with the mayor.

For such a fussy little man Talante listened to Ingram's narrative with remarkable equanimity. His opening observation was not inspiring.

'Oh, indeed there are many bandits, señor, and guerrilleros too, but I fail to see what concern that is of mine.'

Ingram tried again, patiently. 'It must be of concern to the local junta that the villages are persistently being raided for their produce.'

'If there had been complaints from the villages no doubt the junta would be taking a more serious view.'

Ingram started. 'Have there been no complaints from the villages?'

'I am aware of none.'

Surely Talante would have been well aware if the peasant population to the east was grumbling under the oppression of persistent outlawry. It gave credence to the theory that the village people were receiving payment.

'If the villagers were being paid . . . '

'Then there would be no cause for civil complaint.'

'Don Miguel, these people are harbouring deserters and intercepting army supplies. But, apart from the military question, it surely worries you that there is a growing band of freebooters to the east of this city.'

The mayor eyed him blandly. 'On what do you base this assumption? The loss of a few pigs, your failure to take deserters?'

Ingram could not understand; it was inconceivable that this shrewd man was so ignorant of the local situation. He leaned forward in emphasis. 'I have already explained this to you. There is no doubt that this group exists, that it is under strong leadership and that it is growing in strength. In dealing with the problem I look for your co-operation.'

'You shall have that, of course,' Talante conceded with a smile. 'However, I do not see where I can help. Even if you are right the whole affair is outside my jurisdiction.'

'Hm. Plasencia is well placed to be the centre of their excellent intelligence network. And if we assume that the villages are being paid, then El Abulense will require a paymaster. This city is the ideal base for such a person.'

'Oh, come, Lieutenant, this is preposterous. A robber band who do not rob. A mystical leader. Spies in our midst. These are fantasies, señor.'

It was a curious position to adopt now that his jurisdiction had been established. Clearly his offer of co-operation was meaningless. Yet this was a man who was jealous of his responsibilities. His attitude could be seen as deliberate obstruction. The suspicion, once planted, took seed; the mayor knew far more than he was admitting. The possible explanation took root in Ingram's mind and his skin prickled at its implications.

'Señor, I do not find your remarks constructive. I am now satisfied that the paymaster is in this city.'

'Mere speculation! Really, señor, do you seriously believe that if such a person, a paymaster, exists, he is living among us here in Plasencia?' The mayor smiled benignly, ridiculing him.

'I think she is.'

Talante tried hard, very hard, to conceal his surprise, but it took him a moment to recover. When he spoke it was with slow caution.

'Just what do you imply, Lieutenant?'

It might all be coincidence: the men at Avila; the deserters; Margarita's presence; the mayor's attitude. Ingram willed that hope from his mind. Biarroco was a man of remarkable qualities. Talante was watching for his reply.

'I mean, señor, that I believe you have good reason to obstruct my investigation.'

The mayor spread his hands, then placed them on his knees. He leaned his tubby little body forward and the chair creaked sharply. He looked steadily into Ingram's eyes.

'There are matters in Spain which the most sympathetic friend cannot understand. It would be well to leave alone.'

'Don Miguel, I have tried to explain that a grave situation is developing with the threat of wholesale brigandage. Already our supply system is breaking down. Do you condone these outrages?'

'There have been no outrages. Your army has failed to receive the quotas from the villages for the simple reason that another party has purchased the produce in advance. I quite agree that this would indicate that there is being gathered a substantial Spanish force, supplied by the Spanish people.'

'A gang of outlaws and deserters!' exclaimed Ingram in exasperation.

'Guerrilleros, señor. That is surely the case.'

'Led by a man who is proscribed by the junta? I should have thought you would have been more responsible of your duties as mayor.'

Talante looked at him with interest. 'You know who their leader is? But you mentioned a lady.'

Taken aback, Ingram hesitated and Talante seized the initiative.

'No doubt that is a military secret for the present. I quite understand. But I trust that our relationship will permit you to discuss the matter freely on some future occasion. I shall, of course, be delighted to render such advice or assistance as may be within my competence.'

Ingram grunted. Further conversation would have proved fruitless. He was anxious now to raise the matter with Margarita and casually mentioned his intention to call on her.

'I have no doubt your visit will please her,' said the mayor, but there was constraint in his voice. In that moment Ingram felt certain that his suspicions were justified.

The darkening shades of the evening were around her where she sat in the great windows which opened on to the balcony. Only firelight spluttered against the gloom, but now a servant was lighting the lamp on the table where Talante's sister sat at her needlework. Despite the cosy glow the room was cold and draughty.

'I do not wish to close the shutters until the last of the evening light is gone. The hills are so lovely in the dusk.' Margarita smiled at him. They had welcomed him with smiles, a brightness in their dull afternoon.

Rain spattered against the window as they gazed across the fading valley. In time he suggested that they might be alone. 'There is a matter of duty in which you may be able to assist.'

'Indeed? I would not have thought you ever needed assistance in your duty,' she teased, but turning to Talante's sister she said, 'Josefa, you would greatly oblige me by leaving us in privacy.'

Scandalised that they were to be unchaperoned, the woman left without question; it confirmed Ingram's opinion that Margarita was a much-honoured guest in this house.

'And what is this problem that causes you to seek the aid of a mere woman?'

Ingram told her of the Avilan bandits, narrating the mystery of El Abulense, outlining the disorders which were plaguing him, and finally explaining the action he would have to take. She listened in silence and when he had finished said:

'I can see the difficulties this must be causing you, but why do you seek help from me?'

'I rather think you know.'

'I do not understand.' Caution was within her.

'There is a substantial coincidence, is there not? We have an Avilan of undoubted military skill leading a gang of bandits and deserters, a private army operating in this area. At the same time you are here and clearly in contact with Major Biarroco, who is therefore near at hand.'

'Coincidence?' Her eyes were hard now, in anger. 'Why, you're playing the policeman again. Really, it would be simpler if you concentrated on your duty and did not try to implicate Marcelliano in this business.'

'He is implicated, as I'm sure you know, for I believe you are his paymaster.'

'This is intolerable!' She stood up with all the icy hauteur which he remembered so well from their first meeting. He had hoped that their relationship had progressed beyond such hostility. 'Does your impertinence have no bounds, señor, that you can allege . . .'

'Señora, I am confident that you are quite aware that my allegations are well founded. You must understand that it is my unhappy duty to refer the matter to divisional headquarters, and that without reference to yourself. The army does not tolerate brigandage on its supply system.'

'Brigandage! When a loyal man . . .' she stopped in annoyance at her angry exclamation. Then, realising that she had confirmed what Ingram already knew, she challenged, 'So, Lieutenant, you regard Marcelliano as a brigand – a common thief! And I am his accomplice!'

'Doña Margarita, you cannot be unaware of the high regard in which I hold you both. I would never imply dishonour to your house.' He tried again to force her comprehension. 'The fact remains that Major Biarroco is proscribed, is operating illegally in this area, is appropriating my supplies, and is receiving assistance from yourself.'

'And what does your precious duty bid you do now, señor? Summon the militia and have us carried off to the gallows?'

That was precisely the fate which would befall Biarroco if Ingram instituted a cavalry operation which achieved his arrest. It was to avoid the whole beastly business that he was conducting this difficult interview. 'I am here out of consideration of our friendship, which I hold dear. I urge you to bring this outlawry to an end before . . . My duty is to request cavalry assistance to clear this territory.'

'Then no doubt you will do your duty. I seem to recall that you contrived to protect your honour when you came to arrest Marcelliano in Avila.'

The insult struck him with almost physical hurt. His motives in coming to her were seen as duplicity, the contemptible action of a man too weak to do his duty without first excusing his part in it.

'That is most unfair,' he managed to say.

She looked at him with hostility and saw the crumpled hurt on his face which the shards of broken pride could not conceal. She saw the wound which she had inflicted and the anxiety for them which had made it so terrible and she realised its cause and knew that he was their friend.

She wanted to express her regret, to apologise, but her pride would not permit it. In frustration she turned away from him, where he stood, not understanding, and gazed bleakly from the window. Pent up within her the strain of months was fighting to be free, gathering in force until it was released.

'Oh, Ingram! What is to become of us?'

He did not comprehend at first.

'What . . . ? I . . . '

But now she knew why she could trust him.

'You. Me.' She paused, leaving a question unasked. 'Marcelliano. What will become of him? If he is found by the junta he will be hanged. The French would hang him. If you do . . . If your army arrest him . . . '

'He will be handed over to the Spanish authorities,' concluded Ingram quietly. He was heartsick to see the tears glistening in her eyes, to witness her misery.

'He has no friends but those around him. And you.' She spoke with such tragedy that Ingram accepted the trust in her voice without then being affected by it, although later it would gladden him. She fought to keep the tears from her face. 'I owe him everything: he has been a true brother to me. And now I have betrayed him – to you. And you – you must . . . '

Her dignity was gone and she fell weeping on his shoulder. Soft she was in his arms and her body was hot as it shook with her sobs. He wanted to comfort her then, to seek oblivion together, but all the things that were in his mind to say were overwhelmed by his sense of duty which nagged its way to the fore.

'If only he would move away – prey on the villages in French control. And turn out our deserters.'

She shook her head against his shoulder, then turned to look at him.

'He cannot do that. The villagers there would be persecuted and the French . . . It's too dangerous.'

'It'll be damned dangerous for him here when I bring in the dragoons.'

'Not you.' She threw her face against him again. 'Dear God, not you.'

Ingram sought another escape. 'Can't he go to Andalusia or somewhere?'

'They would hang him there.' The bitterness rang clear in her voice as she broke away from him. 'He has to stay here. Avila . . . '

She was standing proudly facing him, as though contemptuous of his weak solution. Her face was strong but he could see that again she was angry for betraying something. Already, he imagined, she was regretting the weakness of her collapse. He felt the old fear of making a fool of himself, too self-conscious to approach her. Somehow his clumsiness had spoilt it all. He could find no words.

She waited for him to speak, for long seconds she waited, but he did not, nor did he move. Her pride took control of her.

'I regret, señor, my embarrassing behaviour. No doubt you wish to attend to your duty.'

The bitterness of the words provoked Ingram to exasperation where other emotions had failed to match his uncertainty. 'For God's sake, woman, do you think I take pleasure in this? Do you think I enjoy seeing you weep?' He seized her by the arms, bruising her. 'Don't you understand that I . . . ' He stopped short, afraid to commit the ultimate folly.

She looked into his eyes and softly she said, 'Yes. I understand.'

In the clarity of her bright eyes he saw that she knew that he loved her. He felt trusted and powerless.

He eased his cruel grip and held her gently, feeling her warmth through the thin black silk. Her eyes were darkness waiting for his soft words. But he felt the trap closing round him and wrenched his mind back to their mutual problem.

'Cannot he be persuaded to disband his men?' he asked. She had expected different words and the hurt showed in her eyes, but he did not comprehend and tried, blindly, to explain. 'He would be safer, then, with only a few trusted comrades. In time his conduct – er, his proscription – would be forgotten. The armies of Spain need their best officers.'

She looked at him calmly, and half smiled. Her husband, too, had placed his duty before all else. Like his troublesome brother with his strange ideas. But not for them this unfeeling loyalty to high command.

'My friend, my dear friend,' she amended, 'Marcelliano will never disband his little army. He has great things to achieve. And his men must eat. It would be sad if British and Spanish soldiers were to kill each other over a few pigs.'

'But dammit, they are not Spanish soldiers!' He released her arms in irritation. 'They are British deserters and murdering thieves. He'll not achieve much with a gang like that.'

'Enough to save your life,' she replied with kind irony and, when he did not reply, she said, 'Marcelliano will not be stopped. If you must do your duty, I will understand. I will think no less of you.'

'For God's sake, stop him raiding our supplies.'

'Perhaps other arrangements could be made, but that will be difficult to manage. There are many men to feed.'

'Are all these supplies essential? How many men does he have?' Five hundred would be a moderate estimate, perhaps twice, three times that number. Enough to create a major distraction, loose and undirected. But these men had a purpose – a minor campaign, then. 'Good God! What is this thing that he is trying to achieve?'

'I thought we were talking about bandits and deserters.'

'Deserters? Yes, by God. Look, he's got to stop taking our deserters. Every malcontent in the ranks knows that he can run to the mountains and hide away from his sergeant. Whatever Marcelliano seeks to achieve these people are useless to him. They are the sweepings of gaols and gutters. Vermin to provide bodies to fill the ranks and die that better men might live, but too craven to endure their place. He would be better without them.'

'And would your army?'

A boy cast his shadow over his memory, a lad of sixteen from the Gallowgate slums. He had hidden himself away, a frightened child, persecuted by a vicious corporal. Ingram's defence had saved him from the gallows, but the lash had twisted his spine, and Ingram, seeing him later, had wished that his plea had not been so convincing and that the lad had hanged. But there was no room for sentiment.

'Deserters must hang. Marcelliano must know this.'

'I rather think he does,' she replied and Ingram cursed his thoughtless tongue.

'I did not mean . . .'

'I know you did not. And it is not your heart that speaks so contemptuously of unfortunate men. Now they have a leader and follow him loyally.'

'They are scoundrels and Marcelliano knows it if you do not. He would do better to throw them out.'

'That he will never do. He needs every man and does not betray those who follow him.'

'What the devil is he up to?'

'He and his men will be safe in the mountains,' she decided, ignoring his question. 'You may feel free to do your duty.'

'Well that's damned decent of you!'

She laughed and, stepping towards him, took his hand and quelled his indignation. He felt it all bubble up within him and had to struggle to control himself. Her sympathy with him bade her release his fingers.

'And now, if you will excuse me, señora . . .' He bowed and made to leave, but she stopped him with her gentle voice.

'Whatever you do, señor, I know that you will act with honour.'

He turned away in confusion and hurried down the stairs. It was only when he was in the street that it occurred to him to wonder whether or not he need reveal Biarroco's identity as El Abulense. He cast the thought from his mind. Clearly the leadership of a force of such size was essential intelligence. Yet he was all too aware that the knowledge had been confirmed in intimate circumstances.

'What the devil can I do?' he asked plaintively of a laden mule. But the mule just stared at him in boredom.

10

Ingram drummed his fingers on the desk and scowled at his completed report. He had worked late into the night at drafting it and missed breakfast to write out the fair copy which now lay in accusation, awaiting his signature. The temptation to delete reference to Biarroco was still with him; at least he had contrived to avoid any mention of Margarita. He drew the document towards him and in ultimate decision dipped his quill in the ink-well. At that moment the door handle squeaked.

Penderleigh was apologetic as he entered the room.

'It's this letter, sir; a personal one to you. It came in with the post last night. I'm sorry. I would have remembered sooner but . . .'

Ingram had been so preoccupied that the letter might have been tendered before now without his remembering.

'That's all right, Mr Penderleigh. You've attended to the rest of the mail?'

He took the letter and nodded dismissal. It was pleasant to recognise Fox's hand in the superscription. He welcomed the distraction and, looking ironically at the discarded quill, still in his silver ink-pot, he saw for the first time the sunlight on his desk. The foul weather had broken at last. Gratefully he slipped his pocket-knife through Fox's seal.

But the letter contained none of his friend's usual wit for it told of the death of Fox's mother, and Ingram was saddened, remembering her with affection. It was terrible to read of the guilt that she should have died alone in the dank old house at Paisley, to know that Fox was alone in the world and that the tireless flow of correspondence was ended. Ingram wondered how his own people were; there had been no word for months. Wearily he decided he would write again, but first he would reply to Fox, he thought, folding the letter and placing it on his desk.

He rose and walked to the window and was there when Penderleigh returned, shako in hand.

'I thought I'd inspect that magazine now, sir, and take an early lunch. Then, if you've no objection, I'll go riding in the afternoon. It's a lovely day.'

It was a happy thought. He longed to be away from the accumulating misery on his desk, out from the stuffy offices and their dismal tasks. He could feel the power of the horse under him, the rush of the wind in his face, could relish the bruising of softened limbs. In a sudden mood of abandon he made up his mind.

'That's an excellent idea, Mr Penderleigh. I'll join you, if I may. And I'll come down to the magazine now; I want a look for myself. Why, we can be mounted by one o'clock and still be back in time for me to clear this damned business from my desk.'

It was interesting to reflect that none of his staff knew the outcome of his meetings on the previous day. Well, their curiosity could wait. There would be time in the afternoon to put everything in order.

But the inspection took longer than they had expected, with an irascible warrant officer detailing a long list of complaint and excuse. Both officers were in irritable mood when they returned to headquarters, curtly acknowledging the sentry's salute as they entered the building.

'You'd better do those requisitions now, Mr Penderleigh – I'll have to write a damned report on this before lunch. Yes! What do you want?'

The orderly thus addressed flinched in his effort to attract attention.

'Well, sir, beggin' your pardon, sir . . . '

'What is it?'

'It's the mayor, sir, says he wants to see you. He's in the ante room, sir.'

'God, that's all I need: Talante.'

'Yes, sir. Sorry, sir.' The soldier was abject in apology.

'It's not your fault, Becket. It can't be helped.'

'No, sir. Thank you, sir.'

Ingram felt some of his good humour revive and caught Penderleigh's flashing grin as he disappeared into the office.

'Very well, Becket. I'll see Don Miguel now.'

The little mayor was his customary self with all the courteous hedging before he approached the subject in his mind.

'You will no doubt have been devoting much thought to our conversation yesterday.'

'No doubt.'

'Doña Margarita advised me of her conversation with you.'

'Then she doubtless told you of the action I am about to take.' Ingram looked coldly at the man's hard eyes. 'It would be unfortunate if I could not mention your co-operation in the matter.'

'Hm. Particularly as I am in a position to arrange a meeting with the man in question. He is anxious to meet you.'

'Since when did the mayor of Plasencia run errands for a discredited brigand?' asked Ingram spitefully.

Talante inclined his head gently, not allowing the insult to wound him. His smile was, for a moment, ironic. Then he spoke in quiet earnest.

'There are ideas afoot in Spain which need the talents of every man. Major Biarroco will never be discredited in my eyes.'

'You are speaking treason, Talante.'

Ingram had hoped to frighten the man with thoughts of the garotte, but to his surprise the fat, greedy little magistrate met him with steady eyes, revealing a mettle that Ingram had never suspected.

'Do you wish to meet him?'

It was a difficult question to answer, for Ingram felt himself being drawn into the vortex of Spanish politics. Whitehall would show no mercy towards an officer who fell into so confused a pit. But his curiosity was aroused, greater even than his torn loyalties.

'Where is he?'

'Come. He is at my house.'

Ingram was appalled.

'Here? In Plasencia?'

'He has been here for two days, señor. Come with me. It is better that you speak with him.'

The mayor led him from the headquarters, bustled him through the muddy streets, and ushered him into his home.

'If you wait here for a moment, señor, Major Biarroco will join you.'

Talante slipped away leaving Ingram alone in the stark anteroom. He paced fretfully up and down, his eye on the door, half in dread of Biarroco's imminent presence. The man seemed so very much more powerful, more dangerous than the amiable renegade he remembered. It was a fitting room for such a meeting, with its bare white walls, the heavy wooden chairs on the tiled, naked floor. In one corner a little madonna, by her grace, emphasised the confines of the walls. He was looking at this when the door opened behind him.

'Ah, Ingram, my friend, it is well met.'

His grin was infectious, his pleasure obvious.

'Well met, Biarroco.'

'Ha-ha, we've still to drink wine in Avila – but Talante has a good cellar. Hey! Miguel! Let's have a bottle of that Rioja, you rascal.'

He looked at Ingram and took him by the shoulders and the Scot could feel the stocky strength in his grip.

'By God, you're looking better than when last I saw you.' It was an apposite reminder. 'The mountain air suits you Scotsmen well enough, eh?'

'Well enough,' said Ingram cautiously.

'By Santa Teresa, you're damned reserved.' His eyes glinted with amusement. 'So, we're on different sides again? Dammit, I understand; it can be no other way. But we'll not let it stand between us. Hey! Miguel! Where's that wine?'

Talante came scurrying in, bearing the tray himself.

'You see, I bring it in person, without servants.'

But there were only two glasses, and the mayor left them alone at once.

'Miguel is a very sensitive man.' Biarroco looked up from pouring the wine. 'He understands things better than people imagine. He has power, too, and influence.'

It might have been a warning, Ingram thought, as he accepted his glass. Talante clearly could be a dangerous enemy.

'I'll give you a toast. Friendship.' Biarroco drained his glass and stooped to refill it. 'Ah, Ingram, it is sad, is it not, that the world will not leave us peace to ride together again.'

'Damn me, why blame the world, Biarroco? My poor fellows are going hungry on account of you.' He hoped he had found the right note of banter.

Biarroco laughed gaily. 'Then they should join me! My lads eat well enough. Here – your glass needs filling.'

Ingram submitted and wondered if the Spaniard was set to find which of them could last the pace. It was a tempting game which two might play.

'Biarroco, how many British soldiers have you got up in those mountains of yours?'

'There's room for more; I'm short of good officers. I don't suppose . . . No, I didn't think so.'

'Just what the devil are you up to?'

'Ah, I thought we'd come to that.' Biarroco placed the bottle on the floor and beckoned Ingram to a seat. 'Tell me, why is Spain at war with the Emperor Napoleon?'

How could Ingram answer? The country was obsessed with hatred for the French. The meanest hamlet had its martyrs, its atrocities. All Spain had been ground under the imperial boot but the will of the people could not be quenched in blood, and Frenchmen died in terrible number and circumstance to prove it. But why did this death happen and go on happening? Because the Bourbons had been deposed?

'You don't think so, Ingram; no more do I. God, yes, it was the catalyst that started it. Remember the Dos de Mayo. Can you imagine the people of the conquistadores, the people who rid Christendom of the Moors, submitting to foreign rule? If we have to have kings, we'll have our own kings and no others. But these miserable Bourbons, Ferdinand, or Carlos who meekly delivered his crown to Napoleon. And the others in Cadiz, in America even. They keep themselves safe enough while the soil of Spain grows green from their lieges' blood.'

'That is their duty, to preserve the dynasty.'

'Dynasty! Good God, do not talk to me of dynasty! The Emperor I served for my king thinks much of dynasty, and now his army lies dead in Russia. My own commander, Murat, is King of Naples and dreaming, no doubt, of dynasty. How many thousand more must perish for the sake of dynasty? Perhaps we Spaniards are fighting about dynasty, but I tell you, Ingram, I see a hundred years of war in Spain if dynasty returns.'

'Good God! You're a republican.' It was a shocking thing to discover.

'In France a man would meet the guillotine for such a crime,' Biarroco grinned.

'The garotte in Spain,' replied Ingram evenly.

'Or hanged in England.'

'In Scotland, you'd be hanged, drawn and quartered.'

'Ah, now that really presents a challenge. But did you hear what happened to the republicans in Cadiz?'

Ingram could imagine and hurried to avoid that interesting subject. 'But what bearing has this . . . ?'

'Tell me, what do you think of our Spanish armies?'

'They do well enough,' said Ingram to avoid offence.

'Man, do you take me for a fool? I was on Murat's staff. They are rabble and you know it.'

Ingram inclined his head in embarrassment and wondered if it would be too impolite to reach for the bottle on the floor. The whole conversation was proving exceedingly uncomfortable. But Biarroco was in full flood.

'The Spanish soldier can fight like a lion, but without training, without leaders, he is useless. Brave, perhaps, but useless. Remember the armies which have disappeared, just run away. That is the fault of the generals. But the guerrillero, he has no generals, nor cares for juntas. He fights for his land, his woman, or his hate.'

'That's probably very true,' said Ingram, wondering where all this was leading.

'What is the guerrillero going to gain from this war? The restoration of the Bourbons? The scourging of the French? No, my friend, he is going to get more. He is going to win freedom.'

Ingram's mind was chilled. Suddenly all the pieces began to fit together. Ballesteros's abortive coup in Andalusia, Biarroco's years with the radical French, his proscription by a worried junta, the importance attached to his arrest, the assistance from the villages and the constantly growing body of armed men around him. He was talking about seizing power for the people, about leading a revolution, about plunging Spain into further years of bloodshed; into civil war.

'Christ Almighty,' he said, in awed undertone.

'With his assistance,' the other affirmed calmly. 'Look, Ingram, when I was with the French I saw what freedom can mean, what reform can achieve. But it takes a strong hand to lead it. Now is the time to prepare.'

'Good God Almighty, man, this is treason. You are arming yourself for a war against the junta, against the King.'

'But not against the people of Spain. Whom will they follow? The gelding Ferdinand and his squabbling tribe, or the men who have fought to rid the country of oppression?'

'You're mad. You're bloody well mad.' Ingram was in a fever of anxiety. 'You'll bring years of bloodshed in your trail and in the end the garotte for you and those with you.' A fresh thought came to him. 'What of Margarita? Will you drag her into this madness?'

Biarroco's eyes hardened as they cast upon him, and Ingram felt his soul being searched. Then the Spaniard softened and shook his head sadly.

'So it is like that, is it? Ah, my friend, I suspected as much. I fear that yours is a difficult road, for both of you. Margarita does her own bidding. She believes as I believe.'

'She believes in you!' Ingram's voice was raised. 'She follows because you lead. For God's sake, do you not see? Do you wish her to die on the garotte? Cannot Talante carry out her duties?'

'He has other matters on his hands.'

It was incredible. Here he was talking to a self-confessed traitor, a republican rebel, and passionately discussing his staff arrangements. But he knew that matters had gone too far for him now to turn a Nelson's eye.

'Look, Biarroco, you do not understand. I am obliged to refer this to the Adjutant-General. You will be hunted down like a dog. You and your followers. I regret for our friendship – and for Margarita . . . what you have told me leaves no room for sentiment. You have left me no option.'

'Of course I have not. That is why I have told you. You were having me hunted in any event but must have hated yourself. Now, perhaps, you will not, and perhaps, also, you will understand.'

Ingram suddenly understood and felt a great disburdenment. There was still room for affection in their opposition. He knew a warmth for the wiry Spaniard and almost found himself wishing the man success. But his worry for Margarita was paramount.

'Keep her out of it, Biarroco, for otherwise I will have to advise her arrest.'

The searching eye sought his mind again and then the voice was hushed. 'Santa Teresa, you really meant that.'

'Now do you comprehend?' Ingram asked harshly.

'She is all that they have left me with, Ingram. She is my sister, my only family.'

'She is much to me,' he retorted.

'Then we have one interest at least in common.' Biarroco rose suddenly from his chair and picked up the bottle. 'Here, my friend, to our common concern.' He cocked an eye sharply. 'You are a determined man. I wish . . . but you are too loyal a heart to join me. I am impressed. Margarita will terminate her duties.'

'Thank God.' The relief washed his mind clean.

'And now you will be free to hunt me with an easy mind,' said

Biarroco, exactly reflecting Ingram's thoughts. 'Come, Ingram, she will wish to see you.'

He led the way into the room beyond and Margarita was sitting there, to welcome them. There were two men standing in conversation with her, but Ingram ignored them, unseeing in the beam of her smile.

'It is most pleasing to see you together,' she said.

Biarroco laughed merrily. 'Yes, we are still friends, you see, despite it all.'

'I can see that you have managed to form some agreement.'

'Oh, that we have. You are right, my dear. Ingram here is a real man, a good soldier. He is going to hunt me to the death.'

It was said with gay acceptance, but one of the men hissed sharply and Ingram, noticing him for the first time, recognised his little guide of Avila, Fernando, still carrying his lethal dagger. But Margarita's voice commanded his attention.

'Surely this cannot be true, Jorge. Have you not understood what Marcelliano is seeking for Spain?'

'Oh, he understands all right,' Biarroco affirmed. 'Well enough to ensure that you, at least, are spared from my deeds.'

'What do you mean?' Her voice was harsh.

'Your work here is too dangerous. You are relieved of your duties.'

She stood in fury and turned on Ingram with blazing eyes. 'So this is what your friendship means. You worry for my safety, mistrust my strength, my courage. Let me assure you, señor, that I ask for nothing more than to wreak my vengeance on the French. That, and to build a Spain worthy of Luciano's death. I do not know with what treachery you have persuaded Marcelliano to do this to me, but you have deprived me of all purpose.'

She strode past him to the door, which she opened before turning back to him.

'I thank you, señor, for your consideration.'

The bitterness of her voice hung in the room long after the door closed behind her.

'Hombre, the lady dislikes your friendship, it seems.'

It was the second guerrillero who had spoken, and when Ingram whipped round to retaliate he realised that this too was a man he had seen before. He saw the fair hair and skin, the heavy bones, the blue eyes and he remembered the same face challenging his humanity in that bloodstained field near Avila.

'We have met before,' Ingram said coldly.

'It was an honour to be of assistance to you, señor.'

There was a strange quality about the man's speech, a sharpness of vowel, which betrayed him as surely as his face.

'And which regiment did you desert?' Ingram asked in English.

The man looked at him in cynicism and replied in Spanish. 'I am sorry, señor, what did you say?'

Ingram turned to Biarroco. 'I asked this man which regiment he deserted.'

'Eduardo? Why, he is an Avilan like myself. He and Fernando never leave my side.'

'He is a British deserter.'

'No, hombre,' the man smiled calmly. 'No one can say I am anything but a Spaniard.'

'I can, Eduardo. I hear you speak. Where is your home? London? Kent?'

The man grinned. 'Why, you've been listening to your own men for too long. I see the old 'dirty shirts' are the garrison here.'

The man's bold use of the 50th's nickname broke Ingram's patience.

'Biarroco, I won't stay any longer under the same roof as this deserter and his damned impertinence. By rights I should summon the guard now and have the whole gang of you arrested.' Fernando hissed and reached for his knife, but Biarroco motioned him still, as Ingram continued. 'I give you till dawn tomorrow to get out of town and God help you if you set foot here again.'

'Won't you stop to finish the bottle?'

'Go to hell,' but Ingram stopped at the door. 'Perhaps we'll get that drink in Avila some day. I hope so. Good luck, Marcelliano.'

'God go with you, Jorge.'

In the hall Talante was waiting to pester him. Ingram scowled darkly when the mayor addressed him.

'I understand you have your duty to perform, señor.'

'That is my intention.'

'Hm. It is unfortunate, perhaps, what one slight misjudgement can cause. Captain Coronado advises me that a certain Captain D'Alby is in town again. I doubt if I can prevent an official investigation.'

'What the devil do you mean?'

'It might have been better if the matter had been dealt with normally. As it is, I imagine there will be questions asked; no doubt the authorities will want explanations, scapegoats.'

Ingram was enraged by the thinly veiled threat and waved a furious finger under the mayor's nose.

'Now look'ee here, Talante, I have you marked. You're playing at treason, señor, and would compound it with blackmail. I do not know how far you are committed to this thing but you must be aware that it will end on the garotte. So I'll thank you to bear that in mind and not tell me how to do my duty.'

'It is a pity that you will not see reason.'

'You can go to the devil, señor.'

Ingram pushed past the shocked manservant and stormed out of the house. He strode across the square, trying to control the fury within him, feeling his lips working in his rage.

'Damnation,' he said loudly, 'damnation to hell!'

It was no help to see the people stare and whisper their curiosity.

The sentry at the portico saw his humour as he saluted and rolled a wary eye to the soldiers lounging in the street. The orderly felt his temper and tried to recover his sleepy thoughts. Twice in one day was more than a bloke should expect.

'Well, answer me, Becket, damn you. Where the devil's Mr Penderleigh?'

'G-gone ridin', I think, sir.'

'God dammit to hell.'

'Yes, sir.' That exactly expressed Becket's thoughts.

'Where are the other officers?'

'In the mess, I believe, sir.'

Ingram tried to recover his dignity but his impatience was too great and he took the stairs two at a time. Schumacher and Stoneman were sitting by the fire, over their wine, and they nodded casually at his entry. It was extraordinary to realise that for them it was a perfectly normal, tedious day.

'Has Penderleigh been away long?'

'About ten minutes. He waited for you but it didn't look as if you'd be back.' Schumacher waved his arm towards the table. 'Do you want some lunch?'

'Ragout of pork,' Stoneman recommended.

Ingram swore.

'A bad afternoon, one gathers,' said Schumacher.

'Talante can be poisonous,' said Stoneman equably. 'Coronado says so, anyway. Try some of Schumacher's hock, sir, that'll set you to rights.'

'It's brandy I need.' Ingram helped himself and washed some of the poison from his mouth. 'I am sorry, gentlemen, for my humour just now. I have been dabbling in politics. A soldier should stick to his own trade.'

'If he's left in peace to get on with it,' said Schumacher.

'The dagos are damnably tricky,' Stoneman murmured.

It was wonderfully comforting to sit in their ordinary company as if nothing untoward had happened, to take time to co-ordinate his thoughts, to console himself that even if Margarita despised him she was safe. Then, when he was ready, he told them what had passed. He spoke of Ballesteros, and of the junta, of his friendship with Biarroco and of Avila. He told them of the growing force being mustered and of its purpose. He did not mention the woman and did not know that they saw the omission and understood it.

Schumacher gazed thoughtfully into the fire. 'It is all so familiar,' he said heavily, 'this dream of freedom.'

Stoneman snapped his fingers. 'That's too much philosophy for me. But I was right about the deserters. The army will have to act now.'

'Oh, it will act all right. And the junta, I dare say. But there's a lot we can do here in Plasencia. I want Coronado brought in on this.' Ingram paused. 'How has he been since that affair over D'Alby?'

'Old Coronado's not a man to bear a grudge,' affirmed Stoneman.

'That is as well. D'Alby's in hospital here; I'll be going down to see him later.'

'Yes,' said Schumacher, 'we will need everyone's hand to stop this thing from growing, whatever the personal cost.'

But it was Penderleigh who caught Ingram's heart later in the afternoon as he prepared to ride to Coria with the report for Hill.

'The lady, sir, is she out of it all?'

'I believe she is now.'

'I'm glad. Had she still been paymaster I'm sure they would have hanged her. It must have cost you a great deal, sir.'

They were words which would come back to him in the bustle of the arriving detachment, which echoed over the thoughtful dinner table and reflected in Ramon's sympathetic eyes, and which stirred in his mind during the chill, wakeful night.

11

The young year was growing older and the trees were bringing forth their leaves. February was gone and March, too, was passing in peace. The peasant folk watched the weather and prayed for a good year. For them the restful winter was over; for the waiting armies the season of war was approaching.

Officers returned from leave to talk of the delights of Lisbon or tell the news just out from home, and colleagues who had wintered in the cantonments listened with envy and reflected grimly that summer would afford no one rest. In every camp the regiments drilled and waited to test their manoeuvres in the field. Here and there along the front armed probes were made, assessments bringing nothing but, perhaps, a little intelligence, costing nothing except a few lives, small affairs to be quickly forgotten. They gave no sign that the disaster in Russia had caused the French to slacken their grip on Spain.

As the army stirred from hibernation and flexed stiff muscles, the pulse that was Plasencia throbbed in flood with hurrying drafts and cluttered transport. Every day brought troops seeking billets, convoys of waggons, bustling mule-trains, and changed orders, unforeseen requisitions. And every day Ingram and his staff had afresh to free the town from congestion, find needed stores from emptying magazines, keep the army's life-blood flowing. In the midst of it all there were reports to read, from the mountains, where the hunt for Biarroco was bloody and unabated. There was little joy for Ingram in pondering the butchery he had released and still Margarita refused to see him. He knew her movements, however, for Coronado had his spies in the mayor's household.

Coronado had proved to be not only loyal but an able and understanding officer whose co-operation was unstinting. He had virtually carried the matter from Ingram's burdened shoulders; it was, after all, a Spanish affair, and his pride demanded a Spanish solution. Yet his pride caused other tensions because he had lost face and was bitter in his hostility towards D'Alby. For D'Alby, in the latter stages of his convalescence, was spending most of his time in their company, ever ready to assist when there was some task which might otherwise go undone. Between them, Coronado and D'Alby did much to ease Ingram in his labours.

Cadogan returned from England late in the month and stopped in the town for a while before going on to join the main body of the brigade. He seemed well satisfied with Ingram's administration and it was comforting to hear his praise. But Cadogan was anxious to go on to the mountains and be with his command again. It would not be long before the army was on the march once more.

'Boney pulled out some troops during the winter, our old friends the Seventh Lancers among them, but it's only recently that there's been any significant change. Now Soult's on the march back to France and the Old Guard are going home as well. It seems the frogs have abandoned southern Spain, but they're concentrating in the north. All the troops in La Mancha have been moved up to Avila. There's bound to be hard fighting before we get back to last year's position.' Cadogan threw the end of his cigar into the fire. They were alone in the mess, for the others had discreetly retired to an early bed.

'It will be another month or more before the weather is dry enough to move, but you'll be kept busy enough, I've no doubt. The Commander-in-Chief wants to strike north and take one of the Basque ports; until then we'll have to keep the roads to Lisbon open.'

'I understand, sir,' said Ingram despondently. He was to be left behind in Plasencia while the battalion went to war.

'I shouldn't think you'll be here too long, Mr Ingram, but in the immediate future you're more use in Plasencia than with the old Seventy-first. I've got you earmarked for a company and Colonel Cother is in agreement, but at the moment you'd be supernumerary, and I don't want to replace the new adjutant. Still, you'll get your chance. I rather fear that there will be vacancies enough in this season's campaigning.'

'Dead men's shoes, sir.' Ingram thought of Hall and all his other friends, but it would be fatuous to say that he hoped that an opportunity for his advancement would not arise.

Cadogan grunted.

'I hear you've been having trouble with your friend Biarroco.'

'I had to request assistance, sir.'

'Hm. General Hill is most concerned about the situation. He is anxious that you know that he expects you to give the Spanish authorities your fullest co-operation.'

Ingram wondered if he was thought lacking in determination to stop Biarroco, but then realised that he was being urged to involve himself in Spanish politics. The matter required clarification.

'Am I being ordered to involve my command in circumstances that could be of purely Spanish interest?'

'Clearly the General can issue no such order. It is a difficult situation and I wish it had not arisen. But I have confidence in you to deal with it properly.'

'Sir, I must know where I stand. The mayor here is implicated. It may be that action will need to be taken against the civil authorities. Am I to be a party to such action?'

'Hm. You will understand the grave political embarrassment that could ensue. The extent of your co-operation must be dependent on the probable consequences. It is well appreciated that the situation is sensitive and you are given discretion to act accordingly. You must judge the circumstances for yourself, and take what action you consider would best serve to terminate Biarroco's activities. If I can assist at all let me know at once. You may rely on my fullest support whatever happens.'

'Thank you, sir. I understand,' Ingram said unhappily. The officer who embarrassed the Army by interference in Spanish politics would never be forgiven by Wellington. It was a thought that kept him awake long into the night. There was the faintest hope that nothing would happen to spoil the delicate political balance in the town.

That hope was doomed to disappointment.

Just two days after Cadogan's visit Ingram was toiling at his desk when he was disturbed by a commotion outside. He heard Stoneman calling for the guard and D'Alby's voice raised in impatience.

'Quickly, sir, quickly. Lest the fellow be gone.'

Half pleased at the distraction, Ingram laid aside his quill and sanded the wet ink before rising to investigate. He was mildly annoyed to hear D'Alby giving orders to his officers. In the hall the corporal was telling off the guard and checking their weapons, and he was surprised to note that Stoneman had a pistol stuck in his belt.

'What's going on here?' he asked sharply.

Stoneman made to reply but D'Alby, standing impatiently at the main door, spoke first.

'We're after a deserter, Mr Ingram, a man from my own company. Recognised him right away – though he's been on the run since October. Damned fellow had the cheek to swagger right past me as if he was a dago like the rest of the crew he's with. They went into a bodega off the Calle Sancho Polo.'

Ingram felt tension grow within him, a feeling that matters were about to come to a head. Surely only the deserters with Biarroco could mingle so easily with Spaniards.

'I'd like a look at this fellow when you bring him in, Mr Stoneman. And beware how you handle his Spanish friends.'

'I'll do that, sir, but it seems to me that his mates might not be dagos, but deserters like himself.'

'Come on, for God's sake,' cried D'Alby. 'The birds might fly.'

They clattered down the steps into the street, leaving Ingram alone with only the duty orderly watching him curiously.

'Is Mr Penderleigh in his office?'

'Yes, sir.'

But he found that he could not voice his suspicions to the young ensign and for a moment stood silent at the door while Penderleigh gazed back at him wondering what was the matter. On an impulse Ingram said, 'I'd be obliged if you'd seek out Captain Coronado with my compliments and ask him if he would be kind enough to advise me on an urgent and delicate matter.'

He returned to his own office, leaving the ensign to puzzle the thing out for himself as he gathered his shako and sword and set off on the errand.

Ingram stood at his desk and frowned at the work he had so lightly abandoned. He could not concentrate now, with the important possibility of the presence of Biarroco's men in the town. Yet Stoneman could be right and D'Alby's deserter have nothing to do with the Avilans, in which case a suitable explanation had best be found for the impetuous message to Coronado.

He sighed in heavy humour at himself. The affair would be no better resolved if he allowed himself to fret and he forced himself to sit down and drew his diary towards him. It was a complex business to adjust troop movements through the town. Artillery, cavalry, line and light infantry, baggage carts and mule columns, all moved at different speeds. When the offensive began congestion in the town would be worse than ever, without this careful planning to ensure the best use of the available roads. Reluctantly he reached for his quill.

'Where the devil has Stoneman got to?'

It would be difficult if Coronado arrived before the provost marshal's party returned successful. The Spaniard was too strait-laced to favour a trivial summons by Ingram.

In the end he was engrossed in his calculations and did not hear them arrive until Stoneman knocked at his door and entered with D'Alby.

'We've got him, sir.'

'Was there any trouble?'

'Enough. Davis and Wainwright were wounded and there's a couple of the dagos dead. It could have been worse – the lads did well.'

From Stoneman's bland description Ingram had a vision of the desperate struggle in the confines of the bodega. Clearly the Spaniards had not readily yielded their companion.

'Let's have him in here, then.'

The man's arms were pinioned behind his back as the escort pushed him into the room, and one side of his face was bruised and broken, but his blue eyes retained their defiance.

'So, Eduardo,' said Ingram in Spanish, 'Avila is not your home.'

It was almost a relief to have his suspicions justified, to need no excuse for disturbing Coronado. But he would now have to interfere in Spanish affairs.

'Ned Armit.' said D'Alby. 'One of my sergeants.'

'One of Biarroco's lieutenants,' supplemented Ingram.

'Damn your eyes, Mister Lieutenant, and yours, Captain D'Alby.' He spat on the floor between them. The corporal made to strike him but Ingram intervened. 'You would not come to Plasencia alone. Where is Major Biarroco?'

'He is safe, Lieutenant. As his friend you should be glad.'

'Keep a civil tongue in your head,' Stoneman snarled.

But D'Alby had realised the significance of what had passed and said, 'Armit, tell us where he is. It will go better with you.'

'I will never betray Don Marcelliano.'

The corporal drove the butt of his musket hard into the man's ribs.

'Speak civil, Sarn't Ned,' he said with relish. 'I've waited for this.'

'Stop that!' D'Alby barked. 'I won't . . .'

He was interrupted by the entry of Penderleigh and Coronado.

'Armit!' Penderleigh exclaimed.

'Why, Mr Penderleigh, a pleasure to meet you, sir.' The man tried to bow.

'Take him away, Corporal,' snapped Stoneman.

'Wait!' said Coronado. 'This man is known to me.'

Ingram met the Captain's gaze. 'He is a British deserter.'

'Perhaps. But he rides with José Perez. His name is Eduardo Valdes.'

'He is a deserter, Captain, from Captain D'Alby's company.'

'Indeed?' Coronado looked coldly at D'Alby and then at Ingram. 'You requested my advice?'

'Yes. Carry on, Corporal.' He waited till the prisoner had been led away. 'Captain Coronado, that man's presence in Plasencia causes me to believe that Major Biarroco is visiting Don Miguel Talante.'

'They would not dare to meet.'

'What else would cause that deserter to risk returning here?'

Coronado's eyes narrowed. 'Señor Ingram, we have unhappily reached a point where we must deal with blatant treason. I must speak with you alone.'

'I do not think that will be necessary, Captain. I feel that we will require the co-operation of every officer available.'

For a moment Ingram thought that the Spaniard would not agree, for he looked hostilely at D'Alby. Yet D'Alby could understand nothing of what was being said; Stoneman too was lost, though Penderleigh looked keen and excited. Coronado shrugged heavily.

'Señor, it may prove to be my duty to arrest Don Miguel.'

'That is what I feared.'

'My men . . .' – the Spaniard hesitated – ' . . . my officers I can trust, but my men . . . '

Ingram nodded. He had spent many hours visualising this situation. Coronado's officers would understand and would be loyal, but his men, volunteer militia from the town, could well be reluctant to act against their respected and powerful mayor. This was precisely what Hill and Cadogan had envisaged.

'My command is at your disposal, Captain,' he said.

He saw the relief in Coronado's face and realised that had he phrased his offer of support in another fashion the Spaniard's pride would have compelled refusal.

'Mr Penderleigh, have the men fall in. Ordinary day dress with full arms. Load with ball. A corporal's guard to remain here with Mr Schumacher. Mr Stoneman, you come with us. Captain D'Alby?'

'I'm at your disposal, Mr Ingram.' He had not the faintest idea what was happening, but was eager to take part even though he was placing himself under Ingram's command.

It took only a moment to arrange for Coronado to throw a cordon round Talante's house. The Spaniard nodded.

'When you arrive, Señor Ingram, we will enter together, with your men. I am most grateful. And now, if you will excuse me, I will make my dispositions.'

The meeting quickly broke up as they hurried to arm themselves. Ingram found Ramon waiting in his room and slipped the proffered sword belt over his shoulder.

'Here is your pistol, señor, it is loaded and primed.' The Portuguese servant eyed him curiously. 'It is Major Biarroco whom you seek?'

'Word travels quickly.'

'Be careful, señor. He is your friend, but he is very dangerous and very powerful.'

'That's enough of that.' Ingram slipped the pistol in his belt and picked up his hat.

There was a bustle in the hallway as the soldiers hurried to make ready. In the street the sergeant waited impatiently for his men to fall in.

'You, Wilmot! Fasten your top button. And that man larking there! Straighten your crossbelts and get fell in.'

Schumacher was at the office door to receive his instructions and there was Stoneman, proud and grim. D'Alby too had his sword and pistols, and Penderleigh was coming downstairs as Ingram stepped outside. The sergeant snapped to a noisy halt and saluted.

'Detachment on parade! Present and correct. Loaded with ball ammunition. Sir!'

'Thank you, Sergeant. Detail two men to each officer as escort when I require it, then follow us to Señor Talante's house.'

As they marched through the watching streets Ingram outlined the situation to his colleagues. It was Penderleigh whose sensitivity found Ingram's open wound.

'Doña Margarita, sir. Is she involved?'

'I wish to God I knew,' said Ingram unhappily. He had no doubt that the prisoners of this day's work would die on the garotte.

'Perhaps I could look to her,' the boy ventured.

'I'd appreciate that, Mr Penderleigh.' He would be as gentle as anyone, tactful and sympathetic. 'I'd appreciate it, thank you, Jack.'

Coronado was waiting in the square.

'I've got my cordon round the building. There's been no movement. I'll come in with you – that'll keep us both right; we'd better do this in the name of the Regency. Young Llobregad can look after things outside.'

D'Alby took a detachment to cover the rear and side exits while Ingram and the others faced the ornate portal.

'Open in the name of the King's Regents!'

But no one came and they had to force into the hall. Henrique, the manservant, challenged with his eyes, but fled before the fixed bayonets and somewhere a woman screamed.

Ingram looked around in momentary perplexity. It was impossible to guess in which suite their quarries would have gathered. Coronado's voice was harsh, urging him to commence the search, and he responded.

'Mr Stoneman, clear the ground floor; Penderleigh, come with me. Escorts, Sergeant!'

Then Talante was at the head of the stairs.

'Captain Coronado! Lieutenant Ingram! What dares this intrusion?'

Coronado took the responsibility of reply.

'We seek the renegade Biarroco, whom we believe you shelter.'

'Indeed, Captain? If it were so your intrusion would be barely excusable. As it is . . .'

A shot blasted the close confines of the hallway. The shock of it stunned them all and for a moment Ingram felt blind panic. Coronado was tumbling forward, in a slow painful arc, to crash full length on his face. He coughed once and then the blood flooded over the floor and Ingram knew that he was dead. There was an instant of brittle silence before the sickening crunch as Wilmot smashed the butler's skull.

'The murdering bastard!' the sergeant declared.

Talante whipped round and darted across the landing.

'Come on, Penderleigh!' Ingram yelled, drawing his sword as he leapt up the stairs. He felt the anger crush his mind, the fury urging him on, aware of the pack of baying men behind him united in their sudden rage.

The door facing them was open. Biarroco stood inside, eyeing them with almost gentle irony.

'So, Ingram, you've caught me at last.'

'By God, Biarroco, you . . . Are you aware that a good man lies dead downstairs?' He kicked his way into the room, Penderleigh at his shoulder, the others crowding behind.

'Captain Coronado had no business to force in as he did.'

It was Talante who spoke, breathless and defiant, from the corner. Ingram swung his blade. It quivered, deadly in his hand.

'You bastard. That was cold-blooded murder.'

'Your soldier killed Henrique.'

Ingram raged forward. But Biarroco spoke and his voice lashed across their insanity.

'Stop this folly! Is there to be more bloodshed? Gentlemen, put up your swords. There is no need. Talante and I are at your mercy.'

Ingram turned round, and felt his reason return, though the anger still burned and gave edge to his voice.

'How many men are with you?'

Biarroco smiled his charming, easy smile. 'I will not betray my men.'

'You have done so since you began your course of treason. I have no quarrel with your men, only with the deserters.'

'Have you taken Eduardo, then?'

'His presence betrayed yours. But how many are here? Or do you wish me to have the house turned out?'

'There is only Fernando,' said Talante, breaking his now sullen silence.

'And Margarita,' said Biarroco evenly.

'Jesus, Marcelliano,' Ingram heard the despair in his voice. 'You swore she would not be involved in this.'

'Ah, Jorge, she is a headstrong woman.'

Biarroco's eye was steady in its sadness and Ingram knew that there was no hope of saving her. The bitterness of his achievement was overwhelming. Then Penderleigh spoke.

'I am confident that Major Biarroco means that Doña Margarita would have no part in the conspiracy.'

Biarroco's eyes did not flicker. For a moment no one would endanger the silence, then Talante sighed.

'Doña Margarita is innocent. The treason was mine.'

And Ingram's heart went out to the mayor in his misery and he blessed Penderleigh for his loyalty and understanding. Together they would keep Margarita from the scaffold.

'She is through here.' Biarroco indicated the room beyond. 'Perhaps if you gentlemen would put up your swords . . .'

There was a disturbance on the stair and here was D'Alby hurrying into the room.

'I see old Coronado's a dead 'un. The word's got out to his men. Llobregad can't keep them together. Bloody dagos. You'd better get these characters out quickly. The locals are being stirred up.'

'Wait,' said Ingram, sheathing his sword and allowing Biarroco to usher him into the next room. The Spaniard stopped him at the door.

'Jorge, whatever happens, swear to me that you will take care of her.'

'I swear it.' He was distracted, worried by D'Alby's words, though the Spaniards could not have understood. Behind him, D'Alby pushed through the door, and Penderleigh, who moved guardedly over to the window.

She was standing by the table with Fernando and she scowled bleakly at him. Biarroco laughed loudly.

'Come, my dear, this should be a happy occasion. I am leaving you in your dear Jorge's care.'

'Señor Ingram will do me the honour of removing himself from my presence,' she said in defiance. 'If I am not to be arrested he has no reason to offend me with his friendship.'

'He does his duty,' Biarroco snapped. 'For an officer there is no greater law.'

She opened her mouth to reply but no words came and she sat slowly on the high-backed chair.

'You will now please leave me alone.'

Her anguished dignity bade them turn away, save Ingram, who watched in piteous fellow-suffering.

A silvery sliver flicked across the room and then Fernando hurled a chair at the window.

'Quickly, señor! Jump!'

Ingram saw that Penderleigh was pinned to the frame with Fernando's knife through his throat.

He pulled at his pistol but already Biarroco was leaping through the shattered glass and the little lieutenant was at his back. Then Talante pushed Ingram aside and ran forward. D'Alby's pistol was out and cocked and as the stout little mayor was framed against the light he fired. The shot echoed loudly in the room and the small, fat figure rolled against the broken shards and tumbled over to fall on the outhouse roof below. There were shots outside but Ingram knew that Biarroco had escaped.

'Oh Jack, oh sonny.'

D'Alby was trying to support Penderleigh's dying body. Ingram moved desperately to pull out the knife, but the hilt was covered in blood and slippy, and the blade buried deep in the window frame. He knew he was being hopelessly clumsy. Everything was moving so slowly, so very slowly, and the boy's eyes were rolling in puzzled wonder. Suddenly the knife came free, wrenching out with spurting blood and the body sagged in D'Alby's arms and Ingram saw that he was dead.

'Oh dear Jesus, what a pitiful waste,' said D'Alby in desolation.

Ingram lumbered unseeing through the soldiers crowding into the room and let the dagger slip from his limp fingers. She was facing him and her tears were for his loss.

'Oh, Jorge, he was so young, so gentle.'

And her head was on his shoulder and she weeping in his arms.

12

The duty orderly knocked and entered the room.

'That's the post, sir, just arrived. And the supply column's reported in sight.'

'Thank you,' said Ingram taking the heavy packet of mail.

For days the town had watched the army march through to concentrate in the mountains for the thrust into Castile. The clatter and jingle of the cavalry, the treading infantry with their drums, the rumbling and squealing of the guns had played their overture. Now all had passed and the British Army was pouring down every serviceable road to assail the waiting enemy. In Plasencia Ingram remained, a bearing, a lubricant, to ensure that the communication system did not break down.

He opened the packet and went through the folded papers it contained. The usual bundle of requisitions, routes and returns, but here was the one order he was awaiting.

'You are hereby directed and required to deliver up your present duties to Captain Anthony Bowmaker who is appointed town major in your stead . . . and to restore yourself to your appointed battalion with all proper dispatch.'

It was to be expected. His continued appointment had been a source of embarrassment to the administration since the ugly events of last month. He pondered, as he had done ever since, whether he was under a shadow at headquarters and shook his head in the knowledge that the Spanish outcry would almost certainly have found in him a scapegoat.

Yet it would be good to be back with the battalion again, free from the internecine Spanish politicking, free from the endless form filling. He would be a company officer like Hall and Fox, with only his soldier's duties to satisfy. He thought of their faces, of Cadogan's knowing eye, of the Halls smiling in some secret happiness, of Fox muttering over some half-forgotten complaint. It would be very good to be among them again.

With a shock he remembered Margarita. He would have to leave her here unless, a thought occurred to him, Avila was safe, in which case he would be able to escort her home without diverging too greatly from his authorised route. It was pleasant to consider. He wondered how long he would have to wait before Bowmaker, his replacement, arrived.

He wanted now to see the woman and grimaced at the conscience-nagging papers on his desk. Since Penderleigh's death he had had no one to assist him with his eternal forms. He supposed he would have to make some effort to put everything in order before he handed over to Bowmaker and took his freedom. In the meantime these matters could wait. He had to give his news to Margarita.

It was D'Alby who saw a more deadly opportunity in a diversion by Avila. It had become his custom to mess with them, morose and discontent, impatient to be away, irritably awaiting the authority to travel. He ran his finger round the pattern on the tablecloth.

'Avila, eh? I'll ride with you if I may.'

'Don't be a damned fool,' said Schumacher, 'you'll open that wound again.'

'Dammit, sir, I am no cripple. I have lain here long enough; it will be May in a week. If my regiment has forgotten me, it's time I acted.'

'Why do you wish to go to Avila?' asked Ingram, for he realised that this had set the spur to D'Alby's impatience.

'I think we will find our little knife-thrower there.' He stared across the table at Ingram. 'Would you deny that?'

Ingram shook his head. He had already reckoned the chance of finding Biarroco and his gang. It was ominous that D'Alby had uncovered his darkest dread.

'It is a possibility,' he agreed.

'I wouldn't mind an hour with that little dago, myself,' Stoneman growled.

'That's damnable justice from a provost,' Schumacher teased, but the mood did not change. They missed the young man's face too keenly.

'Permit me to come with you,' D'Alby insisted.

'Yes,' said Ingram, and his face was grim.

Bowmaker did not make Ingram's departure easy, insisting on a complete review of all the files, snubbing any proffered suggestions or explanations. But at last the final interview was over and the horses were outside, saddled and waiting.

'I need detain you no longer, Mr Ingram.'

'Thank you, sir. Then I'll say goodbye.'

Like a clumsy fool he extended his hand and then hesitated before Bowmaker's surly scowl. For the captain was one-handed and, embittered by his disability, he made no move to ease Ingram's discomfort but curtly nodded his head. Nonplussed, Ingram withdrew his hand, made to speak again but changed his mind, and like a spurned dog he left the office.

Stoneman and Schumacher were waiting in the hall, with smiles and good wishes. The German cocked his eye towards the office.

'We'll miss you. Take care of yourself – and the lady.'

'You'll get home to Bavaria some day soon. You'll see.'

'Good luck, sir. Watch out for that little dago.' Stoneman's handclasp was warm and sure.

'Goodbye.'

He took a final look round and then down the portico steps for the last time, acknowledging the sentry's salute.

'Goodbye, sir.'

'Goodbye, Becket. I'll remember you to the old Fiftieth.'

Ramon was holding his horse and the others were already mounted. He swung up into the saddle and Ramon scurried to mount. He nodded to them and Margarita smiled. D'Alby half-grinned. It was like being on holiday.

'Vamos,' said D'Alby. 'Let's rid ourselves of this damned town.'

The countryside was warm in the May sun, still bearing the green of spring, and here and there the streams yet carried water before the dry summer scorched the land. A wind stirred from the mountains and carried the white cherry blossom from the trees so that the air was filled with the delicate petals.

'See, it is snowing with flowers,' cried Margarita in delight, and D'Alby, seeing her pleasure, understood her meaning, though not her Spanish words.

'Damned like snow,' he declared. 'Same every year.'

A slow burr of red and brown crossed their path and came to rest not far ahead, with its bell-like call. The bird eyed them warily and raised its crest.

'Look there!' Ingram pointed.

'Hoopoe,' said D'Alby carelessly. 'See plenty of them round my guv'nor's estate in summer. Pretty bird though.'

But there were other sights too along their road, grim tokens of the fragility of their peace. The semi-skeletal remains of a horse, a broken gun-limber, or trees with blackened corpses yet swinging where they had been hanged in the winter. And these were as normal to them as the very milestones of the road, more true of the Spanish scenery than an unspoilt field or an unbroken village in a country where every meanest hamlet bore the scars of four years' bitter war.

They stopped that first night at Jerte, in a miserable inn where they were compelled to lie on the earthen floor, huddled among the other squabbling guests in the smoky atmosphere, for the roads were busy with people returning to their homes now that the French scourge had been lifted from their land. Yet it was cheery enough to rest there, bound together by their journey, by their weariness and by the past. And Ramon was irrepressible in his merriness as he tended to their wants.

In the welcome flush of early morning they set off once more, climbing high out of the valley of the Jerte and up over the great pass where the rutted road was broken in many places by the winter's storms. Thus they went on their way, through the mountains where Biarroco had held his sway, down into Castile, following the roads where the French had so recently marched. In the evenings they slept in the villages and were saddened by the poverty of the people.

On the fourth day they came at last to the great plateau and knew that Avila lay not far ahead. There were sights before them which bade them stop. For several miles the road had been littered with French corpses, harried from some hurrying column by the persistent guerrilleros. In time the French had turned to fight and had caught their attackers in the open field. There, at every point, the tattered bodies lay and, as the riders approached, the crows and vultures stirred uneasily from their meal.

'Do you think this was Marcelliano's band?' Margarita fretted.

Ingram had already observed the scattered rags of British scarlet and knew that it was so. She saw his expression and cried in dismay for it was clear that the French had inflicted a crushing defeat. The stench of death was appalling.

D'Alby, too, had seen the British dead and he shook his head grimly. 'Biarroco's gang. There can't be much left after this.'

They dismounted for she would seek Biarroco's body and so, while Ramon held the horses, they scavenged among the dead.

Again and again she exclaimed in sorrow for many lay who had been her friends, but still they did not find the one she sought.

Then, on the very fringe of the field of dead, Ingram found the horse. He could have mistaken it for no other, even as it lay bloated in death, and he was saddened to see the beautiful grey thus discarded.

'La Paloma.'

She spoke nervously and hesitated for one brief moment's hope before running on to search by the stinking carcase. Biarroco was not there nor anywhere in that blighted place and there was no sign, no clue to indicate his fate.

'The answer will be in Avila,' said Ingram quietly.

D'Alby was waiting by the horses.

'Our little friend doesn't seem to be here, either,' he said. 'Ask the lady how many men she thinks might have survived.'

Margarita could form no impression of numbers and shrugged unhappily.

'It is not far now to Avila. There, we shall learn.' But her voice was heavy with dread, lest the survivors had been taken by the French.

It was not till three hours later that they reached the city. The timbers of the bridge rang hollow as they approached the gate and found it closed against them. It was not the French who held the city and denied them entry, but Spanish irregulars, and there were others, taller men with fair hair, or dark, with reddened complexions who cursed to see the British officers. But when Margarita commanded them, they knew her and the gates were opened and an escort came forth.

'Biarroco's gang,' D'Alby murmured. 'They seem to be in some strength.'

Ingram nodded, watching the people gazing with curiosity as they were led through the narrow, well remembered streets. He reached across and touched Margarita's hand where it rested on the bow of her saddle.

'Marcelliano will be here,' he affirmed, and she smiled back, secure in the knowledge. Their escort was silent and made no comment and Ingram's watchful eye could detect among the guerrilleros a tenseness, a sense of grim expectancy.

They came at last to a palace by the eastern wall of the city and there dismounted and, leaving Ramon with the horses, allowed themselves to be ushered into an ante-room as though they were prisoners.

Margarita was strained by the silence for still no one had told them of Biarroco's fate. It was intolerable that she should be treated thus by his people, and yet, perhaps, understandable, for the deserters would fear identification by Ingram and D'Alby.

'How many men d'you think he's got here?' D'Alby asked suddenly.

'Say three hundred? I shouldn't think it's more.'

'Hm. That's about my own estimate. Difficult to know though. He could have another couple of thousand hidden away. Still, a few hundred is about all he'll have I suppose. Not many to defend long walls like these.'

'He's got no guns that I saw.'

'No. The frogs'll have taken care of that. He won't be able to hold out for long against our regular forces.'

'Not long,' Ingram agreed. 'It'll tie up a siege train, though.'

It was madness that Biarroco should commit himself to the defensive here, where the junta's troops would crush him; troops which were needed elsewhere. Perhaps the idea was to give the revolution a symbolic base, but Ingram could only foresee tragedy for the people of Avila.

The door opened suddenly and they turned to see Fernando standing there. He recognised both officers at once and hissed his loathing at them.

D'Alby moved back with a low growl and reached for his sword. Instantly Fernando's knife glittered in his hand as he crouched waiting for D'Alby to move again.

'Don't be a bloody fool,' said Ingram, but D'Alby's hand was on his hilt. The knife flickered in final warning.

'No!' Margarita's voice was like a lash.

The two men stood tense, watching like cats and the Spaniard did not look at her when he spoke.

'These men would hang Don Marcelliano.'

'These gentlemen are my escort. I will not have them harmed.'

They could all hear the fear in her voice and the Spaniard's eyes flickered towards her and saw that it was caused by himself.

'Doña Margarita, it is I, Fernando.'

'I took you for no other.'

She spoke with such bitterness that the little man crumpled visibly. He slipped the knife into his belt and looked at her for forgiveness. But she had none and crossed herself.

'Come with me,' he said and his voice was heavy with his misery.

But D'Alby had not understood and was still braced for revenge.

'Here! Wait!' he shouted, drawing his sword.

The Spaniard glared at him and there was death in his eyes. He hissed again and then turned on his heel and left the room.

Ingram caught D'Alby's wrist.

'For God's sake, sir, put up your sword. Do you want to fight the entire city?'

There was an irrational glaze in the captain's eyes and for the first time Ingram realised the force of the man's obsession.

'I could have had him then,' D'Alby snarled, but he sheathed his sword nonetheless.

In disharmony they followed Fernando along the corridor but as they progressed Ingram could detect a fresh lightness in Margarita's step. He half smiled to her. Marcelliano would be here, affable as ever, and they would drink in friendship. The die was cast; division would serve no purpose.

However it was not Biarroco who rose to welcome them to his chamber, but another, vaguely familiar to Ingram, Though finely dressed and clearly accustomed to command, his face had a peasant coarseness which accorded with his speech.

'Doña Margarita, gentlemen. You are Lieutenant Ingram, are you not? We met in Pinto.'

That was it, of course. This was José Perez. Ingram's mind returned to the hot October afternoon and Biarroco standing over El Abulense's corpse. He could almost smell the horses and the blood, see the ruthless ring of faces. He remembered how this man had instantly taken control, how readily the men obeyed him. These men were here now, all around him.

'Where is my brother-in-law?' Margarita's voice was harsh in anxiety.

'He is well and safe. Where he is . . .' The guerrillero shrugged. 'He has gone north to raise support. We others remain here to hold Avila.'

'And do you expect to hold the city long against an allied army?' asked Ingram sarcastically.

'We will manage as best we may. Don Marcelliano will return with many men.'

'Pray God that he does,' said Margarita. 'We have had grave losses.'

'Yes, too many. The French dragoons scattered us like chaff in the wind. There were many dead. But we took the city from them.'

D'Alby was pestering Ingram for a translation and Ingram had to wave him to silence.

'But you must be short of men for the defence.'

'I have men enough. And more than enough to deal with spies who come here uninvited.'

'That is an impertinence, señor.' Margarita was indignant. 'These gentlemen escorted me here that I might come home in safety.'

'Then their care of you may now end. Your home is well guarded. These gentlemen are now a danger to us and there are some who are uneasy to have British officers here among us.'

'They've deserted once, they can desert again,' said Ingram.

'Oh, I don't think they'll desert me.' His voice was grim, and Ingram could imagine what he would do to deserters.

'No, perhaps they would not.'

José Perez nearly smiled. 'You may sleep here tonight, but in the morning you will be gone. I will not answer for my men otherwise.'

'What's the fellow saying?' protested D'Alby.

'I'll tell you later,' said Ingram, depressed.

The chapel was just as he remembered it and he experienced the strangest sensation of rediscovery as he stood by the pillar and watched her hearing mass. When she had made her final obeisance and walked up the aisle towards him he recognised the same quiet dignity in her movements.

'Santa Teresa will be watching over you,' she said.

It offended his Presbyterian ethic but it was good to know. In the street outside she took his arm.

'And now you will be rejoining all your friends.'

'Yes.' He longed for their simple, uncomplicated faces.

'You leave a true friend here.'

'I am aware of that.' Her tranquillity moved him. It was appalling that she should be staying in Avila to face the wrathful Spanish army. 'Look, I'd like you to come north with me.'

Her fingers pressed on his arm. 'Oh, Jorge, you have been so kind. It is not possible. My place is here.'

'Margarita, the city is bound to fall. Can you imagine . . . '

'I can imagine too readily. But I am among my own people now and have no desire to be elsewhere – even with you.'

'No.' He could understand, though he was cast down by the knowledge. She heard his despondency.

'If our time were different . . . . Yes, I would follow you. But now I am needed here.'

They walked in silence through the early evening, isolated by their approaching loneliness, comforted each by the presence of the other. In other circumstances there would have been much to say, but now neither could find the words and the houses were listening to scorn the bleakness of half-expressed thoughts.

When they reached the palace courtyard she stopped and spoke at last. 'I will come no further. You will be safe now and I shall return to my home.'

'Margarita . . . '

'If you see Marcelliano in the North . . . ' she began hurriedly, but faltered.

Ingram knew that Biarroco was now risk to no one bar himself; that his conspiracy was doomed to ruin. He would take no part in the inevitable retribution.

'I will greet him as my friend,' he said.

'I am glad,' she said seriously, and he felt treachery in his heart for she did not understand. She raised her hands to her neck and slipped a little chain over her head and Ingram saw that it bore a silver crucifix. She pressed it into his hand.

'I will say prayers to Santa Teresa for you.' She smiled, 'Pray for me sometimes.'

'I will,' he affirmed with righteous resolve.

'Perhaps some day you will return.'

'Yes,' he contrived to grin. 'Marcelliano has still to entertain me at his home.'

She clasped his hands. 'Come back to look for me.'

'For God's sake get clear if the city is about to fall.'

'Goodbye, Jorge.'

'Goodbye.'

She walked away from him with all the old dignity he knew so well and as she passed through the gate he almost cried out to stop her. But he did not and without pausing or looking back she moved resolutely from his vision. Deep in thought he entered the building.

He was spared the misery of lonely reflection by D'Alby, whom he found waiting in his room. The captain eyed him sympathetically.

'You've said goodbye?'

'Yes.'

'Damned hard luck.'

'Yes.'

'Fine woman.'

'Yes.'

'I didn't think you'd let her stay here.'

'I did ask her to come away with me.' Ingram was mildly irritated.

'Oh. Damned sorry.' There was a moment's silence and Ingram realised that D'Alby had been drinking, then, 'That's the price we pay. Moving on and never a moment for those you leave behind. All the long roads, and the towns – here today, yesterday Plasencia, and before Talavera, Badajoz, Toledo. We've seen them all and left our own behind, good and bad. And tomorrow? Madrid perhaps or Burgos, but more partings, more friends gone.'

'Aye,' said Ingram, falling into the mood, 'but you don't forget them, do you? Any of them. The bad ones, the good ones. Like young Penderleigh.'

'Yes. Like poor little Jack.' He looked up and the bitterness was in his eyes. 'You know, Ingram, my guv'nor sired him. He never knew it, of course, but I . . . that boy meant a great deal to me.'

He rose and walked over to where the brandy lay on the table and Ingram saw that he was dragging his feet.

'Is your wound troubling you?'

D'Alby cocked an eye at his refilled glass. 'You mean this? All my wounds? Yes, Ingram, all my wounds are troubling me.'

'Go easy, though. Don't forget we're riding at dawn.'

'Oh yes. Ever moving on. I'd like a word with our knife-throwing friend before we go.'

'Don't be a damned fool, man.'

'Whatever you say, Ingram, whatever you say. But remember I am the senior officer.'

'I meant no disrespect, Captain.'

'Course you didn't. Dammit, we're friends, aren't we?' He extended his hand unsteadily. 'No doubt you're right enough.'

In the grey half-light of dawn they led their horses through the watching town. No one spoke to them or wished them goodbye, and only their sullen escort accompanied them to the Salamanca gate. If the city was glad to be rid of them it gave no outward sign of its pleasure.

At the gate one man waited to make his own farewell, and he

spat at their approach. It was Fernando. On the instant D'Alby was keyed to acceptance of the challenge. Ramon slipped back among the horses. Ingram caught at D'Alby's shoulder.

'For God's sake, leave it man. Do you think they'd let you near him?'

All the men around the gate, their escort and the guard, were eager for violence. Ingram felt naked before such hostility and regretted that his pistols were in his saddle holsters. Fernando hissed again.

'Hombre,' he growled as D'Alby stirred.

'D'Alby! Move on, for Christ's sake.'

'Get back! I'm going to have the bastard.'

His sword was barely free from the scabbard when the knife hit him. It hit him in the neck, just as Penderleigh had been hit. It struck him with such force that it threw him back, and as he fell he gurgled in his open throat, and it might almost have been a scream. And his sword clattered noisily on the cobbles and his shako rolled unseen beneath the feet of the crowd.

'You bloody murdering bastard, you vicious little . . .' Ingram was screaming the words in shock and rage, tugging furiously at the strap of his saddle holster. He did not remember approaching the horse, aware only of the pistols. 'Christ! I'll make you crawl . . .'

A firm hand grasped his wrist.

'Now, sir, that would be unfortunate, would it not now?' The gentle Sligo voice was calming. 'If you was to upset the fellows here. The truth is they're murdering bastards, every mother's son of them. Not that I'd let them harm a hair of your head, myself, but it would be convenient if you'd just take the trouble to be on your way.'

There were several of them grouped in a tight knot around him, some still in their British uniforms, and he saw the ruthlessness in their faces. He looked beyond them to where Fernando stood in his hatred and met his eyes in challenge, then turned to where D'Alby lay, drowned in a sea of blood.

'Well, his troubles are over, God rest him,' said the Irishman. 'You be on your way.'

Ingram nodded.

The sun in its rising found them as they approached the peasant's hut and Ingram shivered at the memory of the terrifying minutes he had spent inside. The field where the young couple had been slain was neglected and weed-ridden and he sighed in guilt. He had caused so many needless deaths.

Ramon, seeing him slumped low in his saddle, waved his arm to embrace the brilliant sky and the orange-pinks of the dawn.

'It is a fine day, señor, a day for hope. The winter is behind us in Avila. Soon, the Colonel will be glad to see you.'

And as the morning grew they urged their horses forward to new times. He would be sleeping on the rough ground again, with the welcome bivouac fires and the clear, clear stars. There would be his friends nestling round the sparking flames while the crickets sang through the night. MacKenzie would be there, yarning about old campaigns, chuckling over some half-forgotten merriment. Hall, too, serious and sympathetic and casting long, happy eyes as Kate brightened some dull moment. And Fox, hunched in some inner thought, rising in sudden, brilliant outbursts, or virulent cursing, or lying in companionable silence, listening to the night. He would talk to them of Margarita, while the pibroch in the summer evening stirred men's souls and set Cadogan's head nodding at the subtlety of the piping, and he, ever ready to listen and give sought advice, a reassuring presence to them all.

A hoopoe flew broad-winged across their path and Ingram followed its flight and felt the loss return. It would be difficult to write to D'Alby's father on his estate in England where hoopoes flew in the summer.

13

They could hear the cracking musketry quite clearly and already there were wounded trickling back into the village. Ramon nodded wisely; the battle was not far ahead. The road was cluttered with the solid bullock-carts and they passed a horse battery striving to force across the congested bridge. The gunners were grey with fatigue, worn out by the appalling task of bringing their ponderous weapons over the mountains.

Ingram leaned forward in his saddle to ask directions and the harassed battery commander pointed impatiently ahead. Hill's corps was in the defile there and Ingram saw the smoke of the skirmishers on the heights above the gorge. This was the end of his circuitous journey, of ever seeking the army and finding it had gone. The names were like D'Alby's list of places well remembered: Salamanca, Toro, Valladolid, Burgos with its ruined citadel, and now, beyond the pass, Vitoria. Here, the French had turned to fight.

There were Portuguese troops formed in column by the roadside and beyond them Ingram found the British division, sitting on their packs, waiting for the order to move. Hill was there with his staff and Stewart, the divisional commander. Above them on the hillside a furious infantry action was taking place. The dread grew in Ingram and he felt the prickling of his skin, the tautness of his genitals. He made himself turn to Ramon, who was sitting, white-faced and nervous.

'I don't expect I'll want my horse. You'd better stay here to take her. There's no point in coming further.'

The servant nodded in relief.

'Death to the French, señor.' But his voice quavered.

Ingram swallowed and kneed the mare forward to the generals' group. He saluted and Harringham, a major now, he noted, nodded in recognition.

'Back in the fold, Ingram? I dare say the Seventy-first'll be able to use you. Can't spare you a guide, of course, but you'll find them up there in the thick of things.' He pointed up the steep hillside. 'The enemy counterattacked on Morillo's Spaniards and we had to send your chaps up in support. The General can't move up the gorge until the crest is clear but Cadogan knows that. Hang on, I'll see if there's anything for you to take up.'

He moved over to General Hill, leaving Ingram to gaze up the gorse-covered hillside. He could see redcoats waiting in line about half-way up and further over a column was moving on one of the ragged trails. He thought he could hear the pipes, so that would be the Gordons, with the 50th in line. Higher, near the crest, there was light infantry in the drifting smoke. He swallowed. The 71st were heavily engaged.

Harringham was speaking to him. 'No, on you go, Ingram. Your colonel knows his duty well enough. The General is well satisfied.'

'Thank you, sir.' Ingram saluted and, signalling to Ramon to take his horse, he dismounted. He fumbled for his pistols and tucked them in his belt before starting to climb through the gorse to the fighting above.

It was hot work, scrambling up the rough terrain, and he was not cooled by the warm drizzle carried in on the breeze. The sharp needles of gorse tore at him and he had constantly to detour round thickets or where tumbled rocks blocked his way. He was sweating heavily by the time he came up to the line of the 50th. One of their officers nodded sympathetically.

'Are you going up to the top? You'll find a path further over on the left. I've been up and down it half a dozen times already this morning.'

The track was rutted and in places deep in slimy mud, and it wound interminably around the hillside, but it was an infinite improvement. Occasionally Ingram lost the way and had to retrace his steps, and as further irritation there were flies buzzing everywhere. Here and there were corpses and, worse, wounded men, already noisome with the insects. There were Spanish soldiers, and French, lying where he passed, and among them he saw, too, men from his own battalion. As the undergrowth diminished higher up the numbers of dead and wounded increased and the air grew thick with powder smoke.

Then he was over the crest and could see, in the hollow below, his own battalion and the other light companies waiting, in skirmish line, to storm the second summit. Tumbling and running down the slope, he emerged suddenly from a thicket and found himself among his comrades. Fox cried out to him and he turned to grin at his friend, but Colonel Cadogan was ahead with the forward companies and it was to him that Ingram had to report.

The Colonel looked down from the fine chestnut on which he was mounted.

'Ah, there you are, Mr Ingram. It's good to have you back. We've work enough for you. Colonel Cother will find you an appointment, I'm sure.' He turned away, his eyes keen on the fighting.

Cother grimaced at Ingram. 'Man, but ye're weel timed. Grant's wounded and Duff with him so I'll give ye Grant's company. Ye'll be the only officer.'

There was an increase in firing on the left and yells and cheering. The air was instantly buzzing with musket balls flicking around them. Cadogan wheeled his horse.

'Hall's flank is open on the left.' He faced the companies in the rear and bellowed, 'Captain Reed! Advance your company on the left, if you please. Captain Hall needs . . . '

He lurched forward in his saddle, then toppled over to the right and crashed heavily to the ground.

Ingram dived under the surprised horse, and there were others at his side. Someone was bawling for the surgeon. A musket ball had pierced Cadogan's back and their hands ripped at his coat in an effort to stem the bleeding. But they could see that he was weakening fast.

'Carry me where I may have a better view of the line.' His voice was firm but hoarse, and blood was in his mouth. 'There by the precipice.'

The willing hands lifted him gently and, staggering under his weight, bore him where he wished.

'A haversack for my pillow.'

Ingram was by him and arranged the haversack which a sergeant offered. There was blood on his hands, he saw, and pink froth.

'Where is Lord Wellington?' His voice was weaker now.

'There, sir, with his staff,' the quartermaster pointed and Ingram, following with his eyes, saw the valley of the Zadora and the massed troops waiting to embattle.

Huge French columns stood behind the river, blue stains on the green floor of the valley, with their eagles glistening in the watery light. Near a village in their centre was a knoll where a white flag stirred in the wind to mark King Joseph's headquarters. Already, smoke was drifting in banks as the cannonade began. From the hills in the west the British army poured in scarlet streams down to the bridges, and at their head could be seen, quite clearly, the escort and staff surrounding the grey-coated Commander-in-Chief. It was high time that this southern flank was cleared.

'Let the advance continue,' the Colonel whispered and he reached out his hand to Ingram. His clasp was weak and prematurely cold. 'Go on, George, your company is waiting. I will say goodbye.'

'Sir . . . '

The wind from the valley was chill now; Ingram felt it cut through his damp clothes. He saw George Clark, the pipe major, watching sadly and the others standing helplessly around.

'Colonel, permit me to take you from this cold,' the quartermaster spoke gently.

'Let me be. I will watch the advance. George Clark! Let the pipes play "Hey Johnnie Cope".'

Slowly Ingram rose and the mist was in his eyes as he saluted. They would advance to the same strains as when Cadogan had led them at the charge, to become the first troops into Fuentes de Oñoro. The drones began to pick up and Ingram felt his soul surge; this was the music that recalled the terrible Highland charge.

He ran over to his new company where the men were forming ranks. The pipes were wailing their message to everyone. It was in the sergeant's eyes as he saluted and handed over the command. Their blood was up, urging them to swift revenge. Ingram could hear the excited Gaelic cries behind him.

Cother cantered down the line.

'We'll gie them steel, boys. Fix bayonets. The Colonel's watching us yet. He'll no be shamed o' us. Let the Seventy-yin advance!'

They thrust forward, steady at first, while the officers and sergeants retained control, but as the pipes stirred their hereditary memories the Highlanders began to yell their battle-cries. The ancient slogans of Mackenzie and MacLeod, of Campbell and Stewart, called them on, and the Lowlanders too, roused by the music, and the Irish among them, and the English, all in their blood lust. The rigid line surged with their eagerness and changed to a shapeless wave of screaming, deadly men.

Ingram, borne along on this tide, had no more to do than keep himself at their head, aware of nothing but the need to go on, seeing only the terror spreading among the French ahead. He too was screaming in meaningless, forgotten Gaelic and everything was in a shadowy haze, with bodies falling before him and at his side. An enemy hesitated before turning to flee and Ingram cut him down and felt the numbness in his arm from the blow. There was an officer trying to rally his men. Ingram fired his pistol and the man fell over. Suddenly, the climbing was over and they were on the crest with the French flying from the summit.

The bugles were sounding the Halt and the pipes fell silent. Ingram controlled the hunger to give chase and strove to recover his scattered senses. He willed himself to sheathe his sword, to put away his pistol, and gradually his reason returned. It was cold now in the rain.

He had to find his sergeants; it was urgent to rally the company.

'Fifth Company! Stand to your ranks!'

The men jostled together, the sergeants pushing them into their places. They were chattering and laughing in shock and relief, while the more eager returned reluctantly from their blood-letting.

'Well done, lads, well done.'

'Are we not after showing the dago in them?' someone boasted from the milling crowd.

'Aye, but they'll be back. Form up there.'

The men were settling down and Ingram could look around. Ahead was a sharp dip and then a further summit and already the German rifle company was skirmishing forward in the green jackets which the French had learned to hate.

'The auld Sixtieth'll give us time to catch our wind, eh Mr Ingram?' Cother was grinning down from his horse. 'Is all weel with you? Ye didna lose too many men?'

'Well enough, sir, I . . . '

'Colonel Cother!' The voice was peremptory. The rider had emerged from a track through the scrub and was hurrying towards them. 'Why are you halted, sir? Why do you delay?'

It was Rooke, the senior colonel on Hill's staff. Cother eyed him coldly. 'And what delay would yon be, Colonel?'

'Why, that summit ahead must be taken. Look, the rifle company are on their way already. Colonel Cadogan would never have allowed that.'

'Colonel Cadogan is wounded, sir,' Cother spoke heatedly.

'Cadogan is dead.'

‘Aye,’ sighed Cother and those who heard moaned in anger and sorrow.

‘The men are gey weary, sir, and there’s been ower sair loss. Whaurabouts the rest o’ the brigade?’

‘They are engaged below, covering your left. That summit ahead is clear. Look, even Morillo’s Spaniards advance.’ The white-coated columns were moving obliquely across the lower slopes on the right. ‘I scarce thought to hear such nonsense.’

Cother was furious. ‘Nonsense is it? By God, Colonel Rooke, I cry ye a damned fool for we’ve lost one in five this forenoon and the men are no fit for a whilie yet. But I’ll no have them defamed, so forward we’ll gang. Aye – and proud o’t.’

They rode off together in loud acrimony but Cother was shouting the orders for an advance and Ingram turned to his company. They should be sharing out their cartridges before plunging off against an unknown hilltop like this, but clearly there would be no time. He could only dress their line and check that their weapons were loaded.

‘Pipes and bugle, fall in on me!’

Then they were off again, the tired soldiers scrambling and tumbling down the steep slope from the crest. The thick gorse forced the ranks to bunch and neither Ingram nor the cursing sergeants could do anything to maintain their formation. However, they were able to pause at the bottom and make some endeavour to restore order, to repair the ravages of the whin.

‘You men there! Form off on the corporal!’

Somehow Cother was still in the saddle, turning back to them, leading them on. The pipers stumbled breathless over the difficult terrain yet managed to keep wind enough to play. Over on the left Hall marched at the head of his company, calling his mother’s kinsmen forward in their native Gaelic. But there was no time to greet Hall in the race for the summit. Morillo’s column was just ahead, still marching obliquely across their front. It was strange conduct; they must have lost their direction. Ingram examined the advancing column; it was wheeling now to face them.

‘Sir . . . ’ The sergeant was pointing anxiously and Ingram saw the eagles for the first time. These were not Spanish soldiers.

‘Jesus . . . ’

‘They’re on the left also, sir,’ called the second sergeant.

Cother, too, had seen and was calling to halt and fire, but his words were crushed by the terrible blast of the French volley.

Men were falling everywhere. The sergeant at Ingram's side pitched backwards, shrieking. Someone's dropped musket went off. Ingram bellowed to his company to stand and fire, but another volley smashed into them and then those sinister white coats were looming out of the smoke.

'Fire!' Ingram yelled.

The column was undeterred and ripped another volley into them. The left flank was falling back and Ingram, watching Hall's company break, could see no sign of his friend. The French were driving hard and threatening the rear. The terror was growing within him.

'Front rank! Fire and retire!'

But his bugler was down and the withdrawing rank caused panic in the rear. The surviving sergeants were overwhelmed and then another volley came rolling down the hill. Ingram tried desperately to keep control of himself and ran with his men calling them to order, but the French were in pursuit, and the panic became universal.

He was struggling through the gorse, oblivious as it tore his skin, unaware of the rocks barking his shins. Musket balls were all around him, vile spittings in the air, and behind were the baying cries of the enemy, and movement was so slow and the slope so terribly steep. He jostled with the others towards the top, but even there, there would be no safety. There were no troops in support, only the continuing pitiless chase. He sobbed in exhaustion and dread.

Yet as he fought his way over the crest he saw ahead the steady line of formed troops. Such was his fear that he almost flinched, but these were British soldiers in their faded scarlet.

'The Fiftieth!' he gasped. 'Oh glorious, the bloody Dirty Shirts.'

It was splendid to see them there, in stolid line, ready to meet the French. Their colours, though hanging limp in the rain, were tattered and proud. D'Alby and Penderleigh should have been with them now.

He passed gratefully between two companies on to the flat of the hilltop. Shaking he was and his lungs hurt as he gasped for air. It was difficult to remember his duty, that his men relied on him. He had an increasing sense of shame at his panic and he wondered if they had noticed, if the other officers would cut him now, as a coward.

The 50th were in action now and their steady volleys acted as a balm to him. He stood erect, his head clearing. The remnants – they were no more than that – had gathered on the hillside in complete disorder. There was no sign of Cother and most of the other officers were missing. Major MacKenzie was still alive, with a bugler at his side. Sergeants moved out as markers and the bugle sounded to form company. Gradually, almost painfully, the disorganised huddles of shocked men began to take shape until at last they were recognisable again as an infantry battalion.

They were dreadfully reduced. In those few minutes in the hollow they had been cut down to half their strength. No more than sixty remained of Ingram's company, which had been a hundred strong. He inspected his exhausted men and wished he knew them better. There were few enough to whom he could put names; even the two sergeants who had survived were relatively unknown to him. They deserved better than his craven leadership.

He was about to summon the sergeants when he saw the major approach.

'How is it with your company, Mr Ingram?'

Ingram spread his arms.

'Fifty-four men and two sergeants, sir, and the piper. No officers bar myself.'

'Aye, just so,' said MacKenzie. 'You did well enough there, though you should never have held on so long.' Ingram was astounded. 'It was a damned bad business. Colonel Cother is missing, and God knows how many others. Poor Harry Hall is gone. There's your vacant captaincy if you have the stomach for it.'

Ingram nodded. Somehow it seemed inevitable. Grief would come later. MacKenzie eyed him curiously. 'Aye,' the major said, 'a bad business. Well, we won't be in action for a while yet, I doubt. There's an ammunition mule come up, so distribute twenty rounds a musket and then have your men lie down. I'll send a junior subaltern over to you but there are no sergeants to spare. You'll have to promote one of the corporals – I'll confirm it if need be.'

'Thank you, sir,' said Ingram.

'You'd do well to take Hall's captaincy, Ingram. It would be in the general good.'

In front, the French attack was reaching its crisis as the strong columns climbed that awful incline. The Gordons had taken their place in the line and away on the right, unmistakable this time, were Morillo's Spaniards. The allied volleys repaid their debt on the very slopes that had known Ingram's blackest moment. As the columns wavered the allies charged to sow panic and death among the French, over ground where Ingram's battalion had been so nearly destroyed.

The wind from the valley had died to the merest puff, killed by the concussion of the guns, and now, despite the drizzle, the afternoon was warm. Ingram removed his cap and rubbed the perspiration from his head. There was no water to be had; a brained corpse befouled the only spring.

'Where's that mule?' he asked impatiently.

It arrived in course and the armourer sergeant watched hawk-eyed as each man came forward with his cap held out to take his cartridges. Only when they were done could the men lie in rest, while the stoop-shouldered armourer moved on to the next company. A tired subaltern reported to Ingram and they settled down together by a rock to watch the battle on the plain below. In the smoke down there the French were retiring before the red tide sweeping across the river. British troops had reached the nearest village and the white flag had disappeared from its knoll as the French commander withdrew his headquarters. Far to the north they could detect cavalry charging into action. The din was terrible – the dreadful pounding of the guns, the chatter of musketry, and the other noises, the drums and trumpets, the cheers and the screams, the incidental sounds of war floating up to them in the damp air.

Fox found him sitting there and Ingram rose to clasp his friend's hand.

'You picked the day to return to us,' the voice teased.

'Thank God you're unhurt.'

'You've heard about Hall?' asked Fox.

'Yes. Poor Harry . . . '

'Well, you've got your blessed captaincy now.'

Was there jealousy in his tone? He sounded bitter and Ingram felt distant and could find no reply.

'There's Kate . . . ' he said.

'Aye. You'd better tell her yourself.' Fox pulled out his watch. 'That's been six hours already. It's a long day.'

He saw Ingram eyeing the timepiece and grinned at his expression. 'You've an embarrassing memory. I'll be all right, don't you worry. Listen! They're calling "Stand to"; I'd better get back. I'll see you later.'

The French were mounting a new assault and the urgent bugles were summoning them back into the line. Fox turned round and waved cheerily to him and pointed to the front. A spray of blood burst from his waist and he fell to his knees in surprise, then slowly toppled on his side. Ingram cried in dismay and leapt forward, shouting for aid. Fox looked up at him in astonishment and growled, 'The bastards. I thought . . . '

Ingram tore at the buttons of his friend's trousers and ripped the flap open. Blood was spurting from the wound and he rammed his fingers in to stop it.

'Leave it, George. It's gone into my belly. I can feel it.'

There was terror in his voice as he strove to keep control of himself. The battalion line was advancing now. Ingram's duties called him away. Fox saw it in his face.

'Leave me. It won't be long. . . . The watch. Take the watch. Keep it. I'll not need. . . . ' His painful sobs were urgent and Ingram did as he was bid, before reluctantly leaving him to his own dread shadows.

Ingram had no time left to think of Fox for the enemy columns were pressing hard. Distressed, he had to force aside his gloom and appear cheery and confident to his men.

'Forward, boys, we'll pay Johnny Frog in kind!'

A few more paces brought them to the edge of the hollow.

'Steady, lads. Check your locks.'

The white-coated French were struggling up the corpse-strewn slope.

'Present! Wait for the bugle, boys.'

There were officers at the head of the column, and skirmishers whose wicked fire was disturbing the lesser spirits.

'Steady in the ranks, there. We'll have them in a moment.'

The bugle rang in three sharp notes and before they could be repeated the muskets crashed all along the line. Smoke belched thickly around them. The men were reloading already, without orders. Ingram moved to the right flank of his company.

'First Division! Present and fire!'

The fire from the nearest muskets scorched his face. As the men grounded arms to reload he moved along the front.

'Second Division . . . '

The rippling fire poured down into the column below. All three British battalions were firing steadily in the most devastating musketry the world had known. The Spaniards, too, were blasting at the troops confined in the hollow. The columns would be in ruin, hidden in the smoke down there. Ingram ran back along the front of his company.

'First Division!'

Up came the muskets again, but even as they fired the Cease Fire was blown.

'Fix bayonets!' MacKenzie's hail was clarion clear.

There was a murmur of excitement as the steel flashed. This was the business the regiment understood best. The pipe major gave his signal and the great pibroch gave way to more strident music. It was 'Hey Johnnie Cope' again.

Ingram drew his sword. 'Hip! Hip! Hip!'

The men cheered loudly all along the line. Three times they cheered and then the bugle was blowing the charge. The line swept forward into the banking smoke, down the rugged, trampled slope. The noise of the cheering men was terrible as they charged through the half-light and, as they emerged from the hanging smoke-screen, the wavering French columns began to break. The enemy's front ranks pressed back into their comrades, and their officers could no longer urge them forward. The panic began there, in the front, and as the frightened men sought to save themselves it spread like wildfire through them all.

The solid phalanx dissolved as individuals broke away and suddenly the formation was a mass of scuttling men. Some turned to defend themselves but there was no pity from the British bayonets. Nor was there concealment or protection for those who sought to hide or were too laggard in their flight. They scattered away to the left and were pursued, and they scrambled up the facing hill and the chase was unrelenting. And all the time the bugles called 'Pursue' and the pipes sang and the drums beat as the British and Spaniards drove all before them and slew those who stayed behind. Up through the gorse they advanced, past where the 71st had been broken, and on, until at length they reached the crest of the hill, and there they halted.

Ingram could pause now and give attention to his men; another company was being sent forward as a skirmish line. There was no semblance of order in the excited crowd he led, shouting and jeering at the fleeing French.

'Weel, yon Jonnies'll ken us anither time, sir,' someone called to him.

'Aye, and they'll be back if you don't form up there. Sergeant! Dress off the ranks!'

They moved cheerily enough, pointing enthusiastically to the plain below, and Ingram saw that the entire French army was in retreat, streaming back towards Vitoria.

'Auld Nosey's ta'en anither victory frae the King o' Spain,' a voice cried.

Ingram's subaltern grinned sardonically. 'If Joseph Buonoparte was indeed in command it's scarce surprising that the Peer can claim the day.'

'Hm.' Ingram was noncommittal. The 50th were moving forward again. There was more skirmishing and killing and dying to be done.

14

The shadows were long in the evening sun before the exhausted soldiers marched down from the blood-soaked ridge. As the cavalry drove the French east in rout and the victorious disorder and drunkenness resounded from Vitoria itself, the battered 71st trailed along the dusty road. Heedless they were of the plunder which other troops were taking; reckless they were of the greatness of the victory. Those who saw them pass were moved by their blank, shocked faces, by the silence in their ranks, by the stillness of their pipes. Of a thousand men there marched but three hundred.

They halted in a wood to bivouac and at last Ingram could turn to his sergeant – the sardonic subaltern lay behind with a ball in his groin – and order his company to dismiss. The men slowly began to cut wood and build their fires and Ingram, like many among them, felt the loneliness cut him for the first time. As the officers drew together he knew that there was no one among them whose company he sought. There were strange faces and too many of the old ones were absent. All his friends were gone. And over the whole battalion hung the same gloom, for the Colonel who had so often encouraged them in lesser moments was no longer with them.

Yet they ate well that night for the commissary came up with rations for a thousand men and they had tobacco enough, for in the morning the Colonel had contrived to acquire half a pound for every man.

Ingram had no stomach for food, no craving for tobacco and he sat, surly, by himself, scowling into the night. It was not easy to forget the folly by which Hall had died, the jealousy which Fox had shown. He wondered irritably why Ramon had not yet appeared; the other servants seemed to have arrived and the women too, to judge by all the weeping he could hear.

'Ingram,' an officer was pulling at his sleeve.

'What is it?' he snapped.

The man lowered his voice and pointed with his chin. 'Mrs Hall has just come up. She's looking for her husband. I think . . . '

'Yes. Of course.' He stood up quickly. But what the devil could he say?

He saw her at once, moving uncertainly among the fires. Surely she could see the way that men were avoiding her glance, and then, with sickening dismay, he saw that she was pregnant. It had been six months since their last meeting.

'George!' She was worried to address him thus, and surprised to see him. 'Where's Harry?'

'Kate, I . . . ' He hesitated and she knew at once.

'Is he alive?'

'No.' There was nothing else he could say.

'I see. Thank you.' Her voice was flat. She did not move.

'The ensign's party is on the hillside now. They'll bring his effects in.' It was invariable practice to send an officer and twenty men back over the field to collect the arms and accoutrements and to drive off looters.

'Yes.'

He was going to tell her about Fox, but that would be meaningless.

'If there's anything I . . . '

'I think I want to be alone.' There was still no emotion in her voice, and she moved away without faltering. Ingram decided to follow discreetly, to watch over her. He wondered how soon the child would be; a couple of months perhaps, not much more. He wished he had not rejected the cigars when he had the chance. He stepped quietly after her.

'Jorge! Thank God you are safe!'

He leapt with shock at the burst of Spanish. Margarita was there, Ramon grinning at her side.

'What the devil . . . ' He spoke at first in English and then remembered himself. 'How in God's name . . . ?'

'I came by Segovia. Avila has fallen, Marcelliano is . . . '

But Ingram's mind was on the heartbroken woman stumbling through the trees.

'Ramon, look to Mrs Hall; she is widowed.'

'Your friend Hall is dead?' Margarita asked, concerned.

'Yes, and Fox too.' He realised she had been talking about Biarroco and the dreadful thought struck him.

'Is Marcelliano . . . ?'

'No. At least I think not. I came north to find him. Fernando is ahead of me.'

He nodded. These matters were unimportant now.

'And you found me instead.'

'I was on the road to Vitoria, just behind you it seems.' She eyed him gravely. 'I heard about the fighting on the hilltop. I was afraid that . . . '

Ramon was calling urgently. Ingram was instantly anxious. 'Look, I must . . . '

They ran through the woods together and had not gone far when they heard the racking sobs. Kate Hall had fallen in a ditch and was sprawled against the bank, lost in her grief. Ingram leapt in beside her and tried to lift her.

'Kate . . . '

'Oh Christ, oh dear God . . . ' She had broken down completely and fell into his arms. He could feel the tears wet against his neck. Her body shook against him and he felt her child cold against his belly.

It was dreadful to stand there, knee deep in the stinking mud and gaze past her weeping at the pattern of the trees in the night. To look helplessly up at Margarita and Ramon and know that there was nothing any of them could do to ease her. She was mumbling meaningless things now and Ingram caught the odd phrase.

'He will never know his son . . . '

'There,' said Ingram, 'there, there.'

Minutes dragged through the misery of the night before at last her weeping eased and they could lift her from the trench. Margarita helped him to support her back to the fires and there they laid her down and wrapped his blanket round her. She lay still but unsleeping and her eyes stared blindly into the unspeakable future. They sat nearby, Ingram and Margarita, watching over her, and Ramon slipped quietly into the shadows to seek out her servants and gather together their possessions and their little comforts.

Ingram and Margarita stayed in silent vigil throughout the night and as the stars moved imperceptibly across the sky their unvoiced thoughts in some strange fashion drew them closer than ever before. His arm was round her and her head on his shoulder and the comfort of it soothed his sorrow. Sometimes she slept and her steady breathing was gentle against him. Once when the cramp became too harsh he moved his position and she, stirred by his restlessness, wakened and looked up at him.

'My darling,' she said and then went back to sleep.

He wanted her then, with the rousing desire of all the celibate months and the closeness of her body. It would be easy now, perhaps, with her loving of him and in their present mood. Yet she was proud and the wood was a sterile place where death was companion to all. He fought with his pride and his fear of rebuff and he lost; there would be a time later, elsewhere. And the brooding night dragged on until, at last, sleep came to him.

It was rain that woke them, splashing on their faces, soaking through their clothes. Ingram stirred in discomfort, the fires were spluttering and hissing as the water spattered through the thick leaves of the wood. He drew his cloak around them and sighed despondently. As far as he was aware tents had been gathered in for the summer.

The woman in his arms was asleep yet, but there were soldiers stirring in the wood, and dawn could not be far away. Gently he eased her back and when she woke he whispered, 'I must attend to my men,' and, rising, left her.

A picket from the quarter guard challenged him softly as he moved through the dripping trees.

'Friend. Mr Ingram,' he responded. 'What time is it?'

'It must be just gone four, sir. The corporal is not long after posting me.'

'Very good.' It would soon be dawn. 'Do you know where the Colonel is?'

'The Colonel is dead, sir.'

'Yes.' The habits of his mind had caused his error.

'But if it is the Major you are looking for he is over yonder by the burn.'

The little group of the battalion staff were huddled together on the bank of the stream, their blankets drawn round against the rain. It was Gavin, the quartermaster, who saw him first.

'Here's Ingram now.'

'Morning, Ingram. You've saved us the trouble of looking for you.'

It was strange to hear MacKenzie's Highland accent in place of the Lowland speech of Cadogan and Cother. Yet his uncle, the paymaster, was broad in Scots.

'Aye, it's a dreich morning, George; a sair return for ye.'

'I was on the very point of convening the company commanders.' MacKenzie turned to the new adjutant. 'You may attend to it now, Mr Law. Well, George Ingram, have you decided to take poor Harry Hall's captaincy?'

He was completely surprised. 'I'd forgotten all about it, Major.'

'Aye, just so. Well, I'm taking no chances with you this time. The Colonel and the Lieutenant-Colonel were quite determined that the first vacancy should be yours so as I'm left in command I'll do what I wanted done in October and appoint you. It'll be an acting captaincy in the meantime but you'll get your confirmation.'

'Thank you, sir.' Dead men's shoes, he had said when Cadogan had promised him his chance.

'It's a good company, the Second Company. Keep it so. You've good sergeants, Ross, and your old friend, MacLeod.'

So MacLeod had won his third stripe; it was pleasant to think of working with him again. But the other company commanders were assembling now and there were all the details of reorganisation to be gone through. Men who had dropped out during the battle had rejoined in the night but even so a third had fallen. Others were missing. The men had to be redistributed among the ten companies and there were promotions to be made to fill the gaping vacancies. There was a shortage of officers and Ingram had only one subaltern instead of the establishment of three. Equipment would require replacement and there would be clothing to mend, and ammunition to be issued.

'Some of my rascals fired nigh fifty rounds yesterday,' one captain said.

'Aye, just so. Well, there you are gentlemen; if Lord Wellington intends a pursuit of the enemy we'll be having a busy morning.'

It was a weary battalion that undertook the work; men with stiff, bruised shoulders, ringing ears and aching heads, that shook sadly to see in the daylight the pitiful size of the reconstituted companies. Yet they worked away, repairing broken straps, stitching tattered trousers, requesting new footwear for old, sundered on the rugged hillside. Above all, they cared for their weapons, washing out and cleaning their blackened muskets, replacing spent flints, oiling wearied locks, and honing blunted bayonets.

MacLeod had welcomed him with a smart salute and a grin.

'Och dear me, sir, you're just back and there's all this organisation for you.'

'Well, you've got your third stripe, Sergeant, so you can take your share.'

'Aye, and you've got your epaulette, sir. Congratulations.'

He paused and tilted his head.

'I was right sorry about the Captain and Mr Fox, sir.'

'Aye.'

'I've sent a couple of the men over to look after Mrs Hall – and your friend of course, sir.'

'Thank you.' He could rest easy on that score in the meantime. 'Now where's Sergeant Ross? He's the senior isn't he? We'll have the company fallen in.'

But there were barely sixty men in his command where yesterday there would have been a hundred. There were faces he could put a name to and others well remembered, but some were unknown to him, recent drafts presumably. He began to walk along the line, pausing to talk to every man.

'Campbell, isn't it? All well with you? Good. How many cartridges have you left?'

MacLeod was beside him noting the answers. Here was an unknown face, but familiar somehow.

'You joined the battalion in March didn't you? I remember you passing through Plasencia. What's your name?'

The man looked puzzled for a moment and then said:

'Yes, sir.'

MacLeod said, 'MacMillan, sir. He's a crofter from Gigha and he does not have the good English.'

'I am sure you know your duty, MacMillan,' Ingram said distinctly.

'We'll do fine at the duty, sir,' the crofter grinned proudly.

Ingram passed on, wondering how an island tacksman had been lured away by the recruiting sergeant. Presumably at Inverary, or Arrochar, perhaps, or some other tryst along the drove roads. But the man beside him had come from the pends and vennels of Glasgow.

'Are we gaun efter the johnnies, sir? Then we maun rin gey hard to catch the chiels.'

Ingram began to realise that for all their exhaustion and sorrow the men were filled with pride. Already they knew that their battalion had taken by far the heaviest casualties on the previous day. There was a rueful satisfaction to be had in that and, he supposed, in the simple fact of survival. All in all he felt satisfied.

These men could fight again, today, if some black chance should deem it necessary. Later, if time allowed, there would be the burials.

It was not until the men had fallen out each to attend to his little tasks of repair that Ross approached him privately.

'Stand easy, Sergeant. What is the problem?'

The sergeant tried to maintain the wooden face that he felt discipline required but the concern was deep in his eyes. He had clearly devoted thought to his words and spoke as if he was in recitation.

'It is the men from Appin, sir, that followed Captain Hall. These are good Highland men, sir, and loyal soldiers.' Ingram felt dismay growing within him; were they protesting that he was a Lowlander? But it was something else. 'They have wives and children and ageing parents, that they have not seen since listing, that are left behind to tend the lands. They followed Captain Hall, sir, they were his father's tacksmen; it was their duty.'

'You are one of them, are you not?'

'I am so privileged, sir.'

'And now he is dead you all want to go home?' Ingram rasped.

'Devil damn it, no, sir. We have taken the oath.' Ross's eyes were angry at his ignorance. 'It is the land, sir, that belonged to the Captain's mother who is a good Highland lady like himself. But it is his father's now and he is a Sassenach and does not understand.'

'Sheep,' said Ingram, remembering something Hall had once said and beginning to understand.

'Aye, sheep. Och, you understand fine, sir. There's not a man that kens you that does not respect you, for all that you have only the English. Aye, it is the sheep that the Captain's father would be putting on the land and him dead that would put stop to it.'

'I am sure that Mr Hall would not resume the lands of the soldiers that followed his son.'

'Aye? His son was not. He spoke to us of it. But you, sir, you have been at the pleading with the Lords of Session. You can indict him.'

'Interdict,' corrected Ingram automatically. 'You should be a lawyer yourself, Sergeant. Your plea persuades me. I will do what I can.'

'I ken you will. It would have been the Captain's wish. But you're the Captain now, sir.'

As Ingram walked away he felt that there must be easier companies to command than this, with its high proportion of clansmen. Even the Glasgow men were easier to deal with, but now he knew he had the company's loyalty and they would follow him to the death. Remembering yesterday, he felt his stomach writhe at the thought. There was treason there too, for, barring good will, there seemed no legal bar to Hall's father putting sheep on the land. He would write shortly when he had had a chance to talk to Kate on the matter.

There was little time to ponder the subject for Woolcombe, his subaltern, brought news that the pursuit had commenced. The battalion would march at noon. He had just enough time to visit the women before beginning the company's arrangements.

Margarita's smile was warm.

'Ramon has been taking very good care of us. There is tea here for you.'

It was stale of course, but so hot that it scalded him and he was grateful for it.

'We are ordered in pursuit,' he said. 'We march at noon.'

'Señora Hall cannot travel. She will wish to . . .'

'Yes.' Hall's corpse still lay where it had fallen.

The widow was sitting by the fire and he knelt before her.

'Kate . . .'

The laughter had gone for ever from her eyes and left an empty shell as though she too had been slain.

'I am going home, George. I will stay with him for a while, but I am going home.'

'Aye . . . but the child . . .'

'I will bury him and then I shall go home. His child will not be born in Spain.'

'Aye . . . If there is any comfort I can . . .'

'Look after the men of Appin. They are in your care now. Harry would be so glad . . . His father cares nothing for them.'

'Sergeant Ross told me about the sheep.'

'Yes, the sheep. Harry would never permit it, but now . . . They've been so kind to me today, Livingstone, young MacGregor and the others.'

'I'll write, see if it can be stopped.'

'Dear George. And now you are marching away; I know the signs so well. And Humphrey Fox gone too. How our little company is broken.' She clasped his hands. 'I know you have your duties. I know so well. Goodbye, George. May the Good Lord keep you.'

Margarita took his arm and led him from the fire before speaking.

'I will stay with her. It is better that she is not alone.'

'Yes.' He had not considered what Margarita would do. 'I'll leave you Ramon. He can stay until Catherine has gone.'

'And then we will both return to you.' It was said softly and her smile was sad. 'There have been too many partings.'

He nodded in acceptance, ignoring the practical difficulties. It seemed quite natural that they should remain together now. He wondered vaguely about her search for Biarroco but strangely she answered before he could ask.

'Fernando will find Marcelliano and lead us to him.'

He could take his leave and know that the loneliness would be buried here, with his friends. His company awaited him.

The sky was dismal as the battalion marched from Vitoria. The pursuit of the French began in the rain and it was rain that enswamped it and allowed the enemy to slip into France. For five miserable days Hill's corps laboured over the mountains through ribboned mires that denied description as roads. At night the slimy things that were the soldiers huddled exhausted under their blankets to lie in the morass and dread the next gruelling day. On the fifth night they lay outside Pamplona and knew that the march was over for the French garrison had been strengthened for a siege.

The allied force settled down to the preparation of lines of contravallation. While the work progressed the besiegers learned that San Sebastian was also to be invested and everyone understood that if these two cities fell Spain would at last be rid of the French. However, as the days passed there was rumour that Soult had assumed command in southern France and was organising relief expeditions. Clearly the watch on the frontier would require reinforcement and accordingly fresh deployments were made. Stewart's division was ordered east to hold the Pyrennean passes and the 71st gleefully prepared to forsake the siege. At this stage Ingram still had no word from Margarita and he was in mixed mood when he entered the earthworks for the last time.

The major of engineers scrambled out of the trench and stood beside Ingram on the parapet.

'Damned good, Captain, this position is almost complete. Your men have done damned well.'

'Thank you, sir. They say you cannot better a Highland crofter with a spade.'

'Do they so? Well your fellows have earned their respite. When do you march?'

'In the morning.'

'Hm.' The major had his glass out and was surveying the grim walls of the city. Pamplona was well defended. The major grunted again and refocused the telescope. 'Hm. There's a group of staff officers there on the bastion. They'll be feeling secure enough, I don't doubt. Here, have a look.'

He handed the glass to Ingram. Through the powerful lens the walls looked even more impressive and Ingram could almost feel the rough texture of the stone, see the weeds peeping through the earthwork of the outer parapet. He swung the glass up towards the bastion and was glad that he would not be leading a storming party into a breach against this mightiness. Then his eye was on the array of blue uniforms and gold lace. There were white plumes aplenty, and the glitter of medals and orders. He could distinctly see several officers with telescopes scanning the allied trench-works.

'I expect Cassan will be there himself,' said the major.

Ingram wondered which of the men on the wall was the French general. He handed back the telescope. 'I suppose they'll know we're about to open the approach.'

'Yes. They'll know all right. They're wondering where we're going to start. I dare say they'll be prepared to hold out. It'll be a long affair if we've to force a breach.' The major snapped his glass shut. 'Well, there's no point in speculation. Let's see if your fellows have those gabions ready yet.'

They walked along the parapet to where Ross and his party were working, stripped to the waist, to fill the rough wicker baskets with earth and stone. The sergeant saw their shadows fall across the trench and turned round, his eyes twisted against the sun.

'Will you be wanting the gabions set in place, sir?'

'No, Sergeant, just stack them along the rear of the trench.' The major turned to Ingram. 'No point in letting the frogs guess where we're opening the approach. The pioneers can move them up tonight.'

Ingram could visualise the soldiers working in the torchlight hoisting the heavy baskets up as a protective parapet as they dug the zigzagging trench of communication forward to the position where the battery was to be sited. The French artillery would find them out soon enough and this whole area would soon be under fire. Bringing the guns along this system of earthworks would be an unpleasant and perilous occupation, confined by the trench with the scant additional shield of the wooden mantlets. But Ross was waiting for orders.

'Very well, Sergeant. Take your men back to the assembling point. I'll bring up the rest of the company.'

There was laughter in the ranks during the short march back to camp and Woolcombe commented on it as the company dismissed.

'They'll be in fine fettle in the morning. All the old songs, I warrant. God grant it keeps dry.'

They walked together back to their quarters. Ramon was waiting for him. He must have come from Margarita.

'Ah, señor, here we are in this fine camp, and now you are moving on again.'

'Where is Doña Margarita?'

'Those mule-head green-coats on picket would not allow her to enter the camp.' The Portuguese scowled. 'We managed to find a place two miles back on the road. It is better than the inn at Jerte.'

'Saddle my horse. We'll go at once.'

Woolcombe grinned when Ingram explained to him. 'Off you go, sir. I dare say I'll manage to look after everything here.'

However, when he applied to the adjutant, that officer shook his head. 'I'm sorry, Captain, my orders are that no officer is to be permitted to leave the camp.'

'I quite understand, Mr Law. I'll have a word with Major MacKenzie.'

'He's at Division; there's a conference.' Law smiled sympathetically. 'You could always try Major Walker.'

'Aye. I suppose one can try.'

As he expected, Walker was obdurate.

'We are marching tomorrow, Ingram. As it is we're in the presence of the enemy. Can't have company commanders skylarking around the countryside.'

'I only wish to bring her into our lines to join the other ladies.'

'Out of the question! You can't do a thing like that without the consent of . . . It's not as if she's your wife. She's . . . She's a foreign national.'

'Then at least permit me to visit her.'

'Impossible.'

Ingram fixed the other man's eye.

'I consider it to be a matter of honour.'

They held their gaze in anger, then Walker scowled.

'Two hours then,' he snapped, 'and not a minute more.'

She welcomed him as her lover and led him from the squalor of the inn out to the open hillside and it was a balm to him. Together they sat watching the green of the land deepen in the evening sun, and in silence, with so much to say and no time for the saying. When he told her their time must end she held him close.

'My darling, it does not matter. Tomorrow I will march with you as I have done before.'

Sadly, Ingram shook his head.

'No. It is impossible. I must leave you here.'

'I want to be with you. To share your camp, your tent.' There was challenge in her eyes.

He caressed her hair. 'We will be on outpost duty. The French . . . I daren't take you. Later, when things have settled, we'll find a place in one of the villages.'

'So I must remain in that miserable hovel.'

'I'll send for you as soon as it's safe.'

She was silent and in silence they walked back to the inn.

At the door he stopped and turned her to him.

'You understand why you must stay?'

'Yes. I understand.'

'I must leave now.' There was no point in prolonging his farewell.

Fox's watch was in his hand and he gave it to her for he had nothing else in token. Then she was in his arms and soft against him and her lips were warm upon him. Yet he forced himself away and the sadness was in her eyes.

'Keep safe for me, my love,' she murmured.

'I will.' But his voice broke in his throat and he turned from the door to the yard outside where Ramon waited doe-eyed with the horses to escort him back to the lines.

15

Ingram watched MacKenzie move his knight to cover the threatened square and then grinned ruefully at the paymaster.

'I was afraid you would foresee my attack, Hugh.'

'Aye? I hae been at the sodgering ower lang tae be ootflankit. Man, is this no the grand pursuit on a day like this?'

Ingram nodded. Even here, near the top of the pass, at a height of some two thousand feet, the July sun was warm and the mountain air clear enough to diminish the malodours of their encampment.

'I'll wager the old Moors guarding the pass on a day like this played chess like us now.'

'Aye, like enough. There'll be mony a sodger laddie stood his watch ower this pass in his time.'

They lapsed into quiet contemplation, half aware of the other lounging officers around them, of the orderlies and cooks beginning to prepare lunch, the men lazily cleaning their equipment among the tents. From the higher slopes could be seen the valleys falling away on the south to Maya and the road to Pamplona, on the north to France. But on the shoulder here they could see only the nearby rises and folds of a landscape that could have been their own highlands.

'It's your move,' said MacKenzie.

An officer, coming off duty, paused to watch Ingram's move. His fingers teased to loosen his stock as he gave his grudging approval. 'Aye. Maybe.'

Ingram eyed him balefully.

'Were these French or advancing cattle that your picket saw this morning?'

'Oh, cattle.' The stock was free now, and he sighed with relief. 'General Pringle knows better, though. Just out from England, in command for twenty-four hours and showing us how to do our work. He's moved up all his four light companies to Gorospil Knoll. That'll frighten Johnny Soult and his thirty thousand men.'

'Ye are certain it was cattle that ye saw?' asked MacKenzie searchingly.

'Saw them with my own eyes.'

'Weel, it's tae be hoped ye hae the better een nor your sergeant wha thocht he saw the French. Gin ye're wrang we'll be hard pressed wi' the present dispositions.'

MacKenzie was right. If the French chose to make a determined attempt to force the Maya pass the British would be in considerable trouble. Many officers had expressed their concern about the positions General Stewart had allocated to his two brigades. At least their own brigade was consolidated on the western side of the saddle and Cameron, the brigade commander, had the three battalions ready at his disposal. However, on the east, where the main road crossed over to Maya, Pringle's inexperience had scattered his brigade piecemeal on the basis that the troops could quickly come up in an emergency. Any strong enemy force could push them aside and pour down into the hard-won valleys of Navarre.

One of the subalterns looked over at them and spoke with slow effect.

'If it was cattle you saw, then their cow-bells have a damned funny ring. Listen.'

In the stirring bird-call of the wind they could hear a new sound growing, an alien crackling.

'Musketry, by God!'

They were all on their feet now, straining to hear, staring vainly beyond the nearby crag where the Portuguese battery was in position. They could hear it quite distinctly now, and the men too had stopped to listen.

'That's a major attack,' someone said.

'Rubbish! The battery hasn't fired the alarm.'

'You can hear the volleys. Listen to that.'

Ingram turned to the man beside him. '"Cattle", I believe you said.'

'I swear . . .'

On the crag above four guns fired in quick succession.

'Christ.'

'There's your alarm now.'

'Weel, gentlemen, nae doubt ye'll be busy enough.'

'To your posts, gentlemen, if you please.'

A drum was beating harshly somewhere.

'I'll just get my sword.'

MacKenzie caught Ingram by the arm. 'First time wi' your ain company, George. Mind on Vitoria and ye'll dae weel enough. Dinna be ower lang; it's my move ye'll recollect.'

Already Ingram's company was falling in and Woolcombe saluted formally as he arrived.

'This sounds damnably like the real thing.'

'Yes. Get the roll-call started. I want to get up to the alarm-post immediately.'

He fretted dreadfully over the few minutes taken by the roll-call and inspection, but Woolcombe was quick to report that all was correct and they could join the other columns hurrying to their posts on the west end of the col. It was only when they had done so and the company was formed properly in the battalion line that he could spare time to look around for sign of the enemy.

About a mile and a half away at the other end of the col the light companies of Pringle's brigade were fighting for survival on the Gorospil Knoll. Their scarlet coats were clear against the bracken but all around them in the battle-smoke the green hillside was befouled by a seething blue. Another blue mass, with white grub-like legs, was pushing past the fighting, crawling relentlessly along the road. Ingram was appalled. The French were in overwhelming numbers, a division perhaps, if not more.

Nervously he looked to his own front, where the road wound up from Urdaux. That was where the supposed cattle had been seen. There was no sign of movement yet, but another division would surely be toiling up the road, still concealed by the dead ground.

The 50th were marching past on the high road, presumably being detached to the east to aid Pringle's surprised brigade. The noise had intensified, so clearly the battalions from Maya had arrived to counterattack up the slope on the other side. But they would be too late to save the beleaguered companies on the knoll for the blue wave had swept over them and Ingram could see little knots of scarlet moving down to the north, prisoners carried back against the tide. So five hundred men were dead or captive.

He was aware that the men had fallen silent and saw Woolcombe watching stony-faced. He must stop them from reflecting on the disaster.

'Sergeant Ross!'

'Sir!'

'MacMillan does his duty well, does he not?'

'Yes sir.' The sergeant's reply was no more imaginative than Ingram could have expected, but the men were listening in curiosity.

'And as his English is not the best in the company could he take a message in Gaelic?'

'Yes, sir, if I make him repeat it.' Ross was looking puzzled but some of the men were grinning.

'And does not Major MacKenzie have the Gaelic?'

'Indeed he does, sir.' Enlightenment flourished on the sergeant's face.

'Then send MacMillan with my compliments to the Major and ask consent for the pipes to play.'

'The pipes to play, sir?' MacMillan's voice called from the ranks. 'It will be my pleasure to request the Major, sir.'

He fell out and marched away like a veteran and Ingram, hearing the laughter of his company, felt his mind easier. Woolcombe walked over, smiling.

'I'll make note yonder fellow speaks better English than he's acknowledged.'

'It'll be easier to bear with the pipes,' Ingram grinned.

'Yes indeed. Colonel Cadogan wouldn't have needed to be told.' Woolcombe gaped over Ingram's shoulder and then pointed with his chin. 'Christ, there's a general!'

Ingram looked round and saw the riders on the road, but he did not recognise the man in the major-general's coat. A face among his staff was familiar.

'There's Thorne – that must be Pringle. What the hell's he doing here?' It was quite extraordinary that Pringle should abandon direct control of his own brigade in a crisis like this.

'He's senior to Cameron; if General Stewart . . .' Woolcombe stopped. In the absence of Stewart command of the division would fall to the inexperienced Pringle.

'That can be the only explanation,' Ingram stated. He hoped Stewart would appear before it was too late.

'His second day of war,' Woolcombe said slowly. 'It should prove interesting.'

It was as they had feared. No one seemed to know where Stewart had gone and Pringle assumed command. Rumour came to them that his own brigade had met bloody repulse, and now the 50th were under severe pressure. The right wing of the Gordons was dispatched along the ridge to their support, as if a half-battalion could stop a whole division.

Ingram watched Major MacKenzie in conversation with the staff officer who had just arrived. Walker, as junior major, had joined them and Law, the adjutant, was there. He was reminded, strangely, of similar conferences with Cadogan and Cother which he had attended. Now they were breaking up and Law was riding over with orders.

'The right half-battalion to support the Ninety-second,' he cried, hastening past. 'Your company in column of march, please, Captain Ingram.'

'Pringle's got no idea, sending us forward in dribs and drabs like this,' Woolcombe observed. 'There's only the two half-battalions left on this flank if the frogs come up from Urdaux.'

Ingram grunted. Woolcombe's persistent criticism of their seniors was beginning to irritate him. Certainly there was validity in his comment, but the studied pessimism did not help. The men seemed happy enough at the prospect of action.

'To your post, Mr Woolcombe,' he commanded. 'Sergeant Ross! Move the company to the right. Piper! Fall in on me.'

It was a small column of only five companies that swung out on the road behind Maxwell MacKenzie and his adjutant, and as they climbed the road along the saddle Ingram felt the old dreads growing within him. At any moment the French hordes might swarm around them. When they came to the crest of the rise he was almost physically shocked by the sight before him.

Just ahead the 50th, in ruin, were striving to reform and away to the south the wrecked battalions of Pringle's brigade were being driven off by the enemy. But the most terrible thing of all was the tiny line of the Gordons drawn two deep across the crest of the ridge. Outnumbered twenty to one the four hundred men stood, steadily pouring fire into the French masses at a range that was under a hundred yards.

MacKenzie galloped back along the road shouting for the column to wheel into line behind the precarious Gordons. It was desperate to form quickly as it could only be a minute before the Highlanders had to fall back. Now Ingram's company were approaching their post and Sergeant MacLeod ran forward with his halberd to mark the line. At a signal from Ingram, Ross ordered the halt and then turned the company to face the front. It was a moment's work to dress the ranks.

'Check your locks!'

They could expect to be firing those muskets at any instant. Presumably it had been decided that a formed line would be a more effective barrier than a skirmish line but surely the Gordons in front would disprove that theory.

Yet as Ingram looked to the front he saw that the Gordons were still holding. It was a terrible thing to witness. There was a rampart now to defend the line; a rampart of the heaped bodies of their fallen, deep and bloody, seething with the wounded, and the stench of blood carried to his nostrils on the wind. And before them was another mound of corpses, their slain enemies piled high where they had fallen. Still they fought on, closing on the centre to fill the yawning gaps in the line. There were only two officers left now and few, pitifully few, men. The enemy were beginning to curl round the flanks. They could last no longer.

At last the survivors began to withdraw, closing their broken lines, halting to maintain their fire and then withdrawing again. Sometimes they disappeared completely in the swirling smoke and only the thin music of the pipes signalled their presence, but then their bonnets loomed from the smoke, fewer than before, but still fighting. Then they were safe and could march through the line of the 71st.

'Give them a cheer boys!' someone called. 'Well done the Ninety-second!'

There was a swagger to their kilt, but pride would wait. At present their faces were blank in shock; the larger part of them lay behind. Ingram swallowed; it was the turn of the 71st.

It was the barrier of bodies that delayed the French; such was its depth that it hampered their advance. The 71st fired its first volleys into the enemy as they climbed the obstruction, and the carnage was fearful. The French were in complete disarray, yet still they came on. A mounted officer was trying to reorder their formation, but he fell to some marksman's bullet.

'Fire by divisions,' Ingram cried.

The French sharpshooters were picking away at their ranks and there were spaces to be closed up. Ross and MacLeod were pushing the soldiers into their new positions.

'Close up, you buggers, watch your dressing there.'

A man toppled forward, clattering into Ingram, and then

slipping to the ground. The line was moving back by inches behind its own growing rampart of dead and wounded. And the mass of blue was moving forward again.

Woolcombe was shouting in his ear. 'We'll never hold them – we'd be better skirmishing.'

'Get back to your post,' Ingram snarled. The 71st had to hold on until the 50th was ready to bear the strain. He looked along the line. There could not be more than two hundred men left standing; his own company had only about forty men left out of sixty.

'Close up!' The sergeant's call was monotonous.

A bugle called stridently from the centre.

'Skirmish order. Fire and retire,' Ingram noted. 'Thank God.' As skirmishers they would be less easy a target to the enemy. 'Mr Woolcombe! Take the second section. Fire and retire. First section. Steady!'

Woolcombe's men fell back from the line to take up new firing positions in the rear. Ingram watched carefully, judging the moment when he too could retire, waiting to fire a last volley. The other companies were behaving likewise, holding off the French until the last instant.

Now was the time.

'Fire!'

The men were ready for his next order; the enemy was very close.

'Skirmish order! Retire!'

Breaking with relief from the close-ordered ranks the men scurried back towards the straggling line in the rear.

'Don't run there!' Ross bellowed. If they were allowed their head at this juncture it might be impossible to stop them.

Woolcombe's party were scattered tactically in ones and twos ready to meet the onslaught. MacLeod nodded grimly as Ingram passed through the position with his men. The heather was thick here, dragging at their ankles. There was firing on the left flank already. Ingram judged that they had come far enough.

'Halt! About face!'

The men quickly spread themselves along an extended front and made ready to open fire. Here and there were tussocks and dips which afforded a little cover. This was very different fighting from the ordered ranks of the deadly volleys, this was the individual action for which they had been trained. Woolcombe's half-company passed through into safety.

'Fire as you will!'

The better marksmen could take advantage of the freedom from controlled firing and soon were picking off individuals among the enemy. A captain with his head bandaged was pushing his men forward against them, but Thomson shot him and he rolled over in the heather and lay still, while his men hesitated. But the French were too many to be delayed and they came on again, firing with determination. And Thomson was down and his comrade kneeling helplessly over him. Woolcombe was in position again and, behind, the 50th drawn up in line.

'Fire and retire!'

The men were darting back from their puny cover, hurrying towards the safety of the line. But Thomson's friend was trying to lift him.

'Leave that, and get back,' Ingram shouted.

'I'll no leave him, sir, he's bleeding sair.' There was the challenge of terror in the man's face.

'Get back, you bloody fool. You can't save him.'

The man scowled and, turning his back to Ingram, slipped his arms round the wounded man and began to drag him across the hillside. This was defiance and folly, but MacMillan had come back, and a couple of the others and the big Highlander had Thomson over his shoulders, staggering under his weight while the others fell back in a protective screen. There were cheers as they brought him to safety.

Somehow it no longer mattered to Ingram that he had been defied, that the standing orders requiring the wounded to be left unattended by the fighting men had been disobeyed. He was grinning with the others. It was important now to provide Thomson with assistance to the rear. But there was barely time to arrange it before a new crisis developed. Another French column was advancing up the road from Urdaux and the half-battalions in reserve would soon be under pressure. Here was Cameron, hatless, urging them to fall back in order.

Back along the ridge they moved, the ruined Gordons, the 50th and the five dwindling companies of the 71st. And the weary men fought all the way until at last the enemy, disordered by their long battle, eased in their pursuit and the British could pause to reorganise behind the two fresh half-battalions. Ingram realised with a shock that they had retreated behind their own encampments. On the crag the Portuguese gunners were hurrying to bring their guns down the rocky slope. The rearguard was being driven in and there were enemy skirmishers near at hand. General Stewart had appeared at last and was trotting past with his staff, endeavouring to bring matters under control.

'He's left it too late, sir, I am thinking,' MacLeod was speaking softly to Ingram. 'They'll never save the guns now. Look yonder!'

The Portuguese had pushed the cannon into a ravine and were running for their lives.

'Should've pulled them out earlier,' Woolcombe agreed. 'The Peer won't be happy.'

No allied gun had been lost since Wellington had taken command after Corunna.

'Aye, there's been affairs better run that I can call to mind.' MacLeod sounded tired. 'Now if Colonel Cadogan . . .'

'That's enough!' Ingram snapped. 'Look to your men.'

The fact was that he knew they were right and was badly worried. The pass was no longer tenable and there would be all the horror of a retreat for those fortunate enough to survive. Yet it was quite conceivable that Stewart would be blind enough to try to hold on till the last man.

Woolcombe had stumped off, offended, but MacLeod was still there, with mild reproach in his eyes.

'The men are weary, sir, and hungry, and yet they have to stand watching Johnny Frog eat their dinners.'

He pointed towards the camp and Ingram saw that the French were among the tents, looting and plundering the small personal belongings. The meal which they had been about to eat was now feeding the enemy, but worse was this thieving of the little things that eased their campaigns. All their baggage had been lost.

'It's a long day, Sergeant.'

'Aye, and a long campaign for those that live to see it, sir.'

The hours that followed were a giddy nightmare of smoke and shot, defence and retreat, of confusion and death, of hunger and exhaustion.

At one point, running breathless up a hillside the men could go no further and Ingram could recollect later that they had turned to fight while their bursting lungs retched for air, and MacLeod moved along the line calling the drill-time. Later, when there was no ammunition, they huddled on an outcrop and threw stones down upon the enemy, until rescue came.

It was not till the early evening that help came and fresh troops arrived to counterattack the equally exhausted French. And the remnant of the Gordons charged with their only surviving piper playing 'The Haughs o' Cromdale' and disappeared into the bloody dusk to take vengeance from the dying day. MacLeod reappeared and asked if they would stand, to hold the pass on the morning. Ingram saw the greyness in the man's gaunt face and shook his head, not knowing.

In the event they could not hold and the orders came through just after dark. The gravely wounded would have to be left.

'That'll mean Thomson, sir,' said MacLeod. 'Ah, dear me. And MacMillan's dead, that could have carried him.'

'Yes,' said Ingram blankly. There were so many to be left behind. He would speak to those he could.

Woolcombe was very weak, though the surgeon said he should live.

'I'm sorry,' said Ingram, 'the frogs'll look after you.'

But Woolcombe caught his sleeve and his voice was a plaintive bleat. 'Don't leave me – for Christ's sake, Ingram.'

'I'm sorry. Boney's nearly beaten. We'll have you back soon enough.'

'Christ – don't leave me . . .'

There were others too, all crying to be saved, some strong enough, fighting to come with them. Ross was one such.

'I thought you were killed,' said Ingram.

'I've been spared for other work. I will not be left behind, sir.'

'You're in no condition . . .'

'I'll come just the same, sir.'

He had a musket for a crutch, and MacLeod had a friendly shoulder for him.

The paymaster, MacKenzie, loomed up in the dusk. 'Aye, George, a sair business. Ye'll no hae seen my nephew Maxwell?'

Ingram could not remember when he had last seen Major MacKenzie.

'I'm sorry, Hugh. Perhaps he's been taken.'

'Aye. A sair day. And Cameron's doon and Stewart hit in the shank. And the French awa wi' my chess-board that I hae carried syne Hindoostan. Aye. But I doubt Maxwell's made a widow o' his bonny Peggy.'

A corporal approached and saluted Ingram.

'Major Walker's compliments, sir, and wad ye see your company aff on the road.'

It was in the order of things that the battalion had a new commanding officer. The retreat was beginning.

It was a wretched business, the long disordered columns of dazed, exhausted men straggling down the road, impervious to the cries of their abandoned wounded. At first there was starlight to show the way under the merciful blanket of darkness that hid their suffering, but then it clouded over so that even the road could not be seen, and it began to rain. Their misery was immeasurable. A horrible night in wet, irreplaceable clothes, knee-deep in flowing water, legs aching and the chill growing in their bodies, and in the pitch blackness of it the units intermingled in confusion and spent men fell to be left to the enemy.

Ingram tried to keep his men together, walking extra miles as he and MacLeod hustled round them like dogs with cattle. There were encouraging words to be wrought from his spinning brain, and assistance here to a failing man. And MacLeod was beside him muttering gentleness to the weak, order to the tired. The muddle of it all overwhelmed them in the end and there was only careful footing to be found on the wet paving of the road, and the pain of legs and feet that had gone too far. At the halts they slumped where they were and slept, and it was terrible to waken and begin again and feel the gnawing hunger and the throat parched, despite the water running on the hillside.

Just before dawn they crossed the Bidassoa and entered Elizondo and here at last they halted to reorganise and rest. There were torches spluttering from the walls and a rider peered faintly at them.

'Is that you, Captain Ingram? Good. Move through the town, if you please – there's a guide here to the battalion lines. The commissary train has come up.'

There was an issue of bread and biscuit and the fires were lit already. Ramon magically appeared from nowhere and Ross, haggard and grey-faced, turned up as Ingram was calling the roll. And as they waited to fall out and eat the unhappy ritual went on.

'MacKendrick.'

'Sir.'

'MacMillan.'

Dead. Ingram had seen him fall.

'Sinclair.'

Silence. No one knew.

Stewart, Angus.'

'He fell out, sir, in the night.' His brother's voice.

'Stewart, Donald.'

There were few left from Appin.

'Thomson.'

'Ye left him behind! Mind?'

Ignore it, remembering.

'Urquhart.'

'Ah'm here, sir.'

There were only twenty-seven of them.

'Stragglers to report to me. Sergeant! Carry on.'

Ramon had found him shelter in a house by the main road and the warmth was glorious. He wondered if he could find dry clothes anywhere; even his cloak had been in his valise and lost to the French. God knew where his horse had gone. Back to her original French owners presumably. It was damned annoying that no one had looked to the horse lines. He grinned to himself in realisation that he had time to feel sorry for himself, and nodded pleasantly towards the fire. Sleep would be good.

'Hey! Señor! Señor!' Ramon was calling urgently.

Ingram sat up sharply; there was real anxiety in the Portuguese's voice, and he could hear MacLeod shouting too.

'Christ. Is there to be no peace?'

He forced himself from the chair and limped stiffly to the door. The group of soldiers in the road were arguing furiously.

'What's going on?' he demanded.

They opened up before him and he noticed the peasant in their midst for the first time. The man turned to face him and he saw that it was Fernando.

16

The little Spaniard recognised him at once and tensed instantly.

'Hold that man!' Ingram cried. 'He has murdered two of our officers.'

There were hands on his arms immediately, Fernando snarling angrily at his captors. He spat in challenge at Ingram and murder was glittering in his eyes.

'He was passing in the road, señor. I was sitting by the door,' Ramon chattered in excitement.

Ingram nodded.

'What are you doing here? Where is Major Biarroco?'

Fernando swore unspeakably.

'He was coming into the town, señor.' Ramon was actually pulling at his sleeve.

Ingram tried to clear his tangled brain.

'Shall I search the prisoner, sir?' MacLeod suggested.

'Yes, for God's sake. Watch him, Sergeant, he's probably got a knife.'

MacLeod's face was grim. 'Is this the wee bastard that Ramon was telling me of? Then we will have to be most careful. I mind of Captain D'Alby from after Fuentes de Oñoro.'

There was devilment in the sergeant's expression.

'Hold him gentle now, lads. I would not want him getting hurt.'

Ramon was dancing in anxiety, muttering about Fernando having been on the road. Ingram tried to think, to fit the thing together.

'He was walking towards the bridge, señor.'

'The bridge?' Instantly his mind was clear. Fernando had been heading towards the frontier, towards the enemy. The Spaniard yelped in sudden pain.

'Stop that, MacLeod!'

'Ach, I'm sorry, Captain. My knee slipped with the road being wet!'

Ingram pushed through his men to Fernando who was hanging limp and grey-faced between two hefty privates. The man looked small and helpless, but even yet he had an aura of dread. Ingram remembered his terror of this man and reaching out caught him by the hair and pulled his head back.

'Why were you going along this road?'

The eyes came alive again with all their old hatred, but the man said nothing.

'Is Major Biarroco in the mountains?'

There was no reply and Ingram pulled the head back further.

'What are you doing here?'

Fernando scowled and for a moment it appeared that he was going to answer, then his lips puckered and he spat, full into Ingram's face.

Ingram reeled back in disgust and MacLeod, enraged, pushed forward and swung the full weight of his body behind a punch which smashed into the Spaniard's jaw. The little man's head snapped back and his body swung round with such force that the soldier holding his left arm, taken by surprise, had his grip broken. Fernando spun round knocking the other soldier off balance and, released from his hold, fell sideways into the mud.

'You daft tykes,' snapped MacLeod. 'Pick him up.'

'Have you got his knife?' Ingram asked.

The men were clustering forward towards the sprawling figure. Already Fernando was scrambling away on his hands and knees.

'Catch him!' MacLeod yelled.

But the Spaniard rolled over, confusing the leading men, and then sprang to his feet. Someone swung a musket at him but he leapt back, snarling, and spitting blood and broken teeth. He swayed unsteadily and for a moment Ingram thought that they would catch him, and then the knife was in his hand.

In awful clarity Ingram saw his men move forward with their muskets raised like clubs and realised that they did not know their danger. He pounced forward and caught the leaders by the shoulders.

'Get back. He can throw it.'

And then as they passed behind him he looked up and saw the triumph in Fernando's eyes and knew that he was alone.

'Watch yourself, sir!' MacLeod's voice was in his ear.

He actually saw the man's wrist flicker and then the blow knocked him hard, and he noted in surprise that he felt no pain. Yet he had been thrust sideways and was still standing and already Fernando was darting across the opposite terrace towards the trees. And still there was no pain. Puzzled, he turned round.

MacLeod was kneeling on the ground, swaying from side to side, and his face was deep in concentration. Then his hands were clawing at the dagger in his belly and he pitched forward into the reddening mud.

Not twenty-five yards away his killer still ran free. There was a musket in Ingram's hands somehow and he cocked it quickly and raised it to his shoulder. The darting figure danced on the top of the muzzle. He squeezed the trigger and felt the life in the weapon spring against his shoulder. The smoke was a veil and then whisked away and the target was gone, thrown untidily down in the field.

He handed the musket to its owner. The shocked men were gathered around him.

'Get that bastard and bring me everything you find on his body.'

They were off instantly, vengeful hounds, hoping to find life.

Ramon and two of the others were kneeling by the sergeant.

'Henderson's run for the surgeon, sir.'

'Yes,' said Ingram. They all knew it was useless.

'He saved your life, señor, pushing you.'

'Yes.'

'Maybe the surgeon'll gie him some laudanum.'

'Nae guid, Wullie. He'll hae nae belly for it.'

The stench was terrible. Ingram knelt in the gore and bent down to MacLeod's face. It was covered in filth.

'He near smoored in the glaur, sir. We'd tae turn his heid.'

'Yes.' It would have been better if they had let him suffocate. His tongue and lips were bitten and bleeding as he clenched his jaw to silence his screams. Ingram could see the muscles' tension. The eyes rolled up at him and Ingram gazed back in sorrow and reached his hand out and stroked the forehead. There was nothing to be said that would be understood. 'The doctor will bring laudanum,' he began, but the eyes had lost their lustre and the jaw sagged open as if in one last merciful scream.

Ingram stood up, slowly. The others sighed and shook their heads. The filth was in a spreading pool around them. Ross was standing there, gazing in disbelief. Death was the prerogative of battle and disease.

The major was there too, mounted, with the battalion staff.

'What in God's name . . . '

'A Spanish renegade, sir. He didn't have a chance.'

'My God. You'll have to get him off the road. The French are in presence again; the whole division is moving. I want the battalion on the road in twenty minutes. There won't be time to bury him, I'm afraid.'

'I understand, sir.' He realised that he had been hearing the alarm bugles for some time. He felt more tired than ever.

The men came running back from the field and the corporal reported to Ingram with grim satisfaction.

'The bastard's deid, sir. Nae heid. He'd a' the usual junk, tinner-box, a popish cross. The usual. But we found anither fancy knife, sir, and this letter. Cannae read it mahself – it's no in English.'

Ingram took the letter with interest. 'Keep the knife, Corporal, and give everything else to my servant.'

'Captain Ingram!' A staff officer was calling urgently. 'Get that body moved. Clear the road. The artillery is coming, sir.'

Ingram crammed the letter into his pocket. 'You men, move the sergeant. The rest of you get to your posts. Don't you hear the alarm? Sergeant Ross! Come with me.'

As the French torrent poured from the mountains Hill's corps reeled back in a day of forced marches and keen pursuit. The rear-guard actions were bitter affairs in the unremitting rain. Persistent misfiring by dampened muskets made it perilous to hold on for the few precious minutes required to allow the tail of the column to clear. Time and again Ingram's battalion halted to play their part and suffer further loss, and then it was on again and the hurried scramble to escape through the woodland and rejoin the line of march.

The pace was too great for many of the weaker men, hobbling along on legs that were agony to move, feeling the whole breathless weight of the hours without rest, so that they flagged and fell out of the march and were left behind. In Stewart's division those who remained were scarcely in better case.

The baggage echelons were painfully slow and the Portuguese and Spanish drivers had to be forced to their work, lest they fled. Yet a terrified man could still find some impossible way to break a solid wheel or shear an axle and so abandon his cart to the mud. These deserters mingled in rabble with others in flight, the people of the villages, fleeing from a terrible enemy that was returning after so short an absence. In places the road was almost impassable, clogged with broken carts and scattered chattels, and the troops had physically to force their way through.

'There is consolation, sir, that the johnnies will be having the like difficulty,' growled Ross.

Ingram grimaced in agreement. The sergeant's face was almost green with pain and exhaustion, and he seemed to have shrunk in stature, such was his misery. Yet he kept going, hopping along with a musket as a crutch and the butt chafing at his armpit where his jacket had worn away and the flesh was torn and bloody. Twice already they had stopped to change his bandages and now his thigh was bleeding again. Ingram marvelled at his tenacity. The bugles were sounding the alarm again.

When they halted that night Major Walker summoned his officers to him. There were not more than fifteen men assembled in the clearing. Ingram sighed in despair. The battalion had been reduced to quarter strength since the morning of Vitoria. He wondered how long they could carry on; whether they could face another major engagement.

'Gentlemen,' said Walker, drawing their attention, 'the situation is grave. We know that the divisions which engaged us were badly mauled, but Soult forced the pass at Roncesvalles without serious loss. His main body is marching on Pamplona, and Pamplona must not be relieved.'

They nodded grimly and wondered how the enemy was to be stopped.

'All available troops are now being assembled in front of the city and I understand that the Duke of Wellington will himself be in command.' The major looked round them confidently as he gave this news, but in the firelight his face seemed older, aged in two days. There was an edge to his voice, telling of the strain of his unexpected command. 'His Grace will require our presence in the field so we march on. There is little time. However, this battalion is spared rearguard duty; that falls to the Portuguese Brigade so we'll let Hamilton's caçadores take care of things.'

'Thank Christ for that,' someone muttered.

Walker glanced sharply. 'It will be hard enough for us. I don't want any criticism of our discipline or rate of march. Keep the men moving, that's all that matters. Don't allow sullenness or complaint. There are problems enough. The commissaries are staving the liquor barrels so we must try to keep the men from getting at the spirits.'

'Some hope,' a voice commented, drawing laughter.

'Just keep your men in hand. Things are difficult enough,' the major complained. 'We march in an hour.'

Ingram sighed again. It was a proven impossibility to keep the troops away from drink. There would be drunkenness as a further hazard on the march. It might be better to leave the barrels unbroached and let the French face the problem when the baggage fell into their hands. He wondered if he could contrive to rescue a little brandy before it was all poured away.

There were, of course, flushed faces when they marched and several of the soldiers were unsteady on their feet, staggering against their comrades, causing confusion in the ranks. Ingram lost two of his men that way, and another, a steady young soldier, fell out, broken by the rigours, and they had to leave him sitting by the roadside.

In darkness the rains made nonsense of their forced march and in time they were compelled to halt. Anxiety for the morning refused them sleep and when dawn broke they were on their way once more, making their best speed to join Wellington in the line. They could hear the pounding of guns and knew that battle was joined, and desperately they urged themselves to be in time. But the miles were too long and when they came down into the valley of the Ulzama they knew that they were too late. At the bridge near Beunza they learned that Soult had failed to break through. He was waiting now for the divisions which had pursued them. The morrow would renew the battle.

They bivouacked near the village of Lizaso and Ingram and his fellow officers found shelter in one of the larger houses. It was dreadfully cramped, of course, sleeping three or four to a room, and the servants crowded in the stable, but they were able to assemble together in the main living-room and ignore the busy cooks round the fire and the steam rising from their sodden clothing. Someone had produced a jug of rum.

'It's splendid to have quarters again,' said one of the young ensigns.

'Aye.' MacKenzie was dour, his mind on his nephew's missing face.

'They'll be arranging to exchange him in no time, Hugh,' Ingram encouraged. With luck there would be more French prisoners after tomorrow.

'Aye? Then ye maun tell his Peggy gin ye daur sweir he's alive. It's God's grace she bided at Pamplona.'

Ingram nodded. He had spent many of the past hours pondering Margarita's fate if she had been permitted to accompany him.

'Then God grant that she may remain safe.' Walker stood and raised his glass. 'May the morning bring victory.'

They growled in approbation. Outside were the fifes and drums of the gathering line, the clatter and rumble of the artillery moving up. Somewhere a kettledrum boomed and a squadron of dragoons wheeled into position, and, nearer, the sharp call of a bugle band as the Rifle Brigade quick-marched in their faded green uniform. The army was disposing itself for a great battle.

The fate of Spain might be determined on the morrow. Defeat would open Pamplona to the French, undo the summer's work. The besiegers of San Sebastian would be imperilled, forced to withdraw; retreat from the Pyrenees would return north-west Spain to enemy control. No new campaign would be possible before the onset of winter and the spring might bring new conscript armies swarming across the frontier. Yet victory at this place would throw the French back across the frontier and ensure the taking of the two great city forts and the liberation of all Spain. The road to France would be clear.

Ingram shivered in his wet clothes and sniffed. He was chilled and the cold was stuffy in his head. He wiped his nose with his sleeve, but the serge was wet and unsatisfactory. He picked at his plate of boiled pork without enthusiasm and sniffed again. He must have a handkerchief somewhere and, putting down his fork, he began to search in his pockets. His searching fingers found the letter.

Oblivious of the conversation around him he took out the damp piece of paper and looked at it stupidly. He had forgotten all about it. He pushed aside his meal and spread the crumpled sheet on the table. The wafer was unbroken and turning it over he saw that the address was smudged and bloodstained. Reaching over he picked up a knife and quickly slid it through to break the sealing wafer. He unfolded the letter, spread it out again and picked it up to read it.

Expecting to see Spanish his mind was already thinking in that language and thus he was completely taken by surprise. It took him several moments before he realised that the letter was in French. It took him even longer to understand its meaning; his French had never been good and he had not used it for a long time. Moreover, in places blood and damp had obscured the handwriting causing near illegibility.

The superscription meant nothing to him but though the identity of both addressee and signatory were unknown to him he noted that the former bore military rank and that the names appeared to be French. What the devil had Fernando been doing carrying a letter for the enemy? A nervous prickling flushed over his skin for as he read it became apparent that this was a military dispatch. Apart from his concern at its bearer he realised that the document might contain urgent intelligence and anxiety grew at his negligence in leaving it forgotten in his pocket.

The writer paraphrased reports from the French commander at Pamplona, outlining the deteriorating condition of the garrison and the progress of the breach. A statement of British dispositions followed and Ingram whistled at its accuracy. It seemed probable that had this information been in Soult's hands before his assault the situation would have been even worse than at present. The unknown writer pleaded for a relief expedition and then went on to state that the French would find the roads clear of guerrilla activity and that the British were being troubled by banditry perpetrated by the guerrilla bands. It appeared that the rising at Avila had encouraged disaffection.

Ingram sat back on reading this. The Frenchman was making extravagant claims. Certainly it was true, as the letter stated, that a Spanish division had been committed to extinguishing Biarroco's rebellion and that there was considerable disorder in certain of the irregular troops, but Mina and Pinto and all the others were loyal enough. Surely the writer was hoping for commendation by submitting over-optimistic reports. The following sentences were obliterated and then Ingram read:

'. . . work is done. He has established connexion with Pamplona, has occasioned the disorders among the guerrilleros, has encouraged their banditry. He it was who raised Avila, whose efforts continue to harry the English communications, spreading false rumour, succouring and encouraging enemy deserters. He bears this letter and I entrust it to safe hands. Your Honour will not have forgotten him for it was he who did so much to obtain the Ballesteros affair. I commend him to you in the strongest terms. Major Biarroco is my finest agent and has done great service to France.

'For God's sake bring relief to Pamplona. Spain may yet be saved.'

Slowly Ingram spread the missive on the table and read again the critical paragraph. He examined and re-examined the French construction but there could be no mistake.

'Ill news from home, Ingram?' His neighbour's face swam. 'Didn't know we'd had any mail.'

'No – I . . . ' He wanted time to think but already too much time had been wasted. Why Fernando had been carrying the letter and not Biarroco, the latter's whereabouts, the extent of Margarita's involvement were all questions which would have to wait. His ambivalence had allowed this treason to continue and clearly the enemy was being well advised of allied movements.

Ignoring his companion he rose and walked round the table to Walker.

'Major, a word with you, please. This matter is urgent and important.'

His voice was steady, but unusually loud and conversation paused in a surge of curiosity. Walker did not move from his place, but grunted assent and Ingram, aware of his hushed audience, found difficulty in expressing himself, stumbling over his short explanation.

'You say you took this letter from MacLeod's assassin. I recall the occasion.' Walker eyed him coldly. 'That was two days ago. You didn't think to open it till this moment?'

'No, sir.' It was shameful that the entire company was listening.

'And this Major Beo— what's his name – is he related to your lady friend? Same name, isn't it?'

'Yes, sir,' Ingram admitted miserably; 'she is his brother's widow.'

'I see.'

The silence in the chamber was almost painful; even the orderlies watching in awe.

'And why do you tell me this at this late stage?'

'Obviously Headquarters must be advised.' This cross-examination was beginning to annoy him.

'You think so, do you? Bit late isn't it, on the eve of battle? For one dago traitor.'

'It's more important than that, Major.' There was an edge to his response.

Walker examined him balefully and then changed tactics.

'And who's to carry it, eh?'

'Well, sir . . . ' That at least should be obvious.

'How the devil am I to manage, Ingram? You can't be spared – you know that. And you've lost your horse.'

'There's that, too,' Ingram agreed, knowing that there was no alternative. It was infuriating publicly to be addressed like a newly joined ensign.

'Well, you'd better take Gavin's horse – and no sleep for you. I want you back here by four o'clock. I suppose you'll see Harringham.'

'I think that would be best, Major.' Certainly Harringham was the officer on Hill's staff who knew most about the background and intelligence was his responsibility. He would be busy enough at the moment preparing for tomorrow's engagement. There could be no question of troubling Hill with the matter at such a time.

Harringham smiled knowledgeably and prodded the superscription. 'Fourchant, Colonel Louis-Marie. Soult's Chief of Intelligence. That's to be expected. The writer's well known to us. Le Marquand – it's his hand all right. He's a wily bird – didn't know he was still in Spain. This was careless of him, though. If I'd had it a couple of days ago we might have picked him up. Pity, that.'

'Yes.' Ingram wriggled uncomfortably.

'One of those things. You weren't to know. It's a golden rule, though. Always read the other man's mail immediately. Still, we'll be able to use this. We can stop those reports from Pamplona now we know about them and then we'll have to trace the intelligence on our movements. Bit alarming that. His nibs will be delighted and I dare say the Peer will have a word to say. It's as well you brought this in. No laurels in it for you though.'

'No.' Ingram smiled.

'It'll finish Biarroco. We'd guessed he was an enemy agent. He's safe under lock and key. This will be enough to hang him. Otherwise it'd have been the devil's own job to collect evidence.'

The words rang in Ingram's head. Harringham's face seemed miles away, shining bright in the lamplight.

'Surely there is ample evidence against him.' There was uncertainty, self-doubt in his voice.

'You'd think so, wouldn't you? But who can trace the witnesses? Most of them won't talk anyway. The dagos can't even establish that he actually deserted. It's a delicate political matter, and he's got too many powerful friends. But treason, aiding the enemy, that's different. No, this letter's the thing that'll hang him.'

'Oh.' The chill in his body deepened.

Harringham's expression was keen. 'You met him on several occasions. He'd be an easy fellow to like.'

'Yes.'

'Hm. That's bad luck. There's the woman too. Yes, we know all about that, Ingram. I dare say we'll be able to keep her out of it.'

'Thank you,' he mumbled, his head spinning.

'Bad business altogether. Hm. Only met him that once, in Aranjuez. Good horseman. There's that grey. I don't suppose . . . '

'La Paloma. She was killed.'

'Pity. She'd have bred well.'

Ingram was thinking rapidly, suddenly conscious of the contradiction.

'Sir, on that occasion he was engaged with a French column. Outside Avila. They fought a pitched battle. And earlier, when I was at Avila, he had a French squadron massacred. He ordered the prisoners to be butchered.'

'Yes, I'd wondered about that. He had to convince his men. Perhaps he does actually dislike the frogs. Anyway, he wouldn't have been so dangerous if his men hadn't thought he was on our side. Nothing like the odd atrocity to please people like José Perez. Pretty cool, though, when you think about it. One of the reasons we lacked evidence. He's a ruthless bastard.'

Ingram felt physically sick. He recalled the captured hussar, nailed to the door, and Fernando standing with the saw. He wanted to hear no more, to be away. He made to rise.

'That's all right, Ingram. Bit of a shock, eh? Not really a nice man. Well, I won't detain you. I dare say Walker's anxious to have you back, though I don't expect there'll be much call on the Seventy-first tomorrow. You fellows have been through too much just recently to expect much in a major engagement.'

Harringham rose and escorted him to the door, extending his hand to say goodbye. 'Wicked affair, but you've done your duty honourably. Don't suppose you want to see him, but Morillo's provost marshal has him securely under lock and key.'

The Spanish sentry moved aside and watched without interest as his officer fumbled with the keys. The lock ground harshly.

'You will excuse me, señor, but I must be present at the interview.'

Ingram nodded. The heavy door creaked open.

Biarroco was sitting on his bed at the far end of the cell, gazing arrogantly at the door from his wretchedness. Gone were his fine regimentals and in their place was ragged peasant dress. He was unwashed, his cell filthy, his waste in a stinking pile in one corner. He was manacled. And yet his unshaven face had dignity.

Seeing Ingram, he grinned toothily and spread his arms in welcome, but his chains clinked and confined the movement. He could not rise.

'Jorge, my friend. Have you come to take me from this hole? Shall we drink together in Avila?'

Ingram swallowed. 'Major Biarroco, I have to advise you that I took Le Marquand's letter from Fernando. Its contents are known to myself and to the Adjutant-General's department.'

Biarroco's smile froze and his hands dropped with a rattle and he lowered his eyes. 'I see.' He raised his head again. 'It is strange, is it not, that it should be you who betrays me. Perhaps I should have left you to the French hussars.'

'To your friends. Whom you butchered.'

'My friends?' The smile was back, ironic. 'I detest the French. They served my purpose, that is all.'

'What purpose? Treason?'

Biarroco sucked his teeth. 'You didn't listen to a word I said in Plasencia. You didn't understand a single word, did you?'

'Fine dreams, Biarroco. A Spain for the warrior hero. You said nothing of helping her enemies.'

'I could have made Spain great again. A nation of conquistadores!'

'You're mad! Insane, dammit! Look at the suffering you've caused. All the useless death. My friends, your friends, the men who trusted you.'

The prisoner sighed in exasperation. 'Go away, Ingram, with your little mind and its duty. Leave me in peace. Lieutenant Peña! Relieve me of this meaningless conscience.'

But when the door was open he called to stop them.

'Hey! Jorge! Take care of Margarita for me. And when you see Avila again, take wine in my house.'

'I will do these things, Marcelliano.'

Biarroco remained motionless in his squalor, watching them with his ironic smile until the door clashed shut and removed him from their sight. As the key grated the lock and the sentry moved back to his post Ingram felt that Biarroco was watching still, seeing their boots crash on the flags as they walked along the corridor.

'Must he be kept in that filth?' he protested angrily. 'Look, I don't know whether he is a madman or a ruthless traitor but . . .'

The Spanish lieutenant had no emotion in his voice. 'He is a leprous dog, señor, to be put down.'

17

The guns of Sorauren had spoken and with Wellington's voice, and had broken Soult's hopes of victory. And in the west, seven miles away at Beunza, where Hill was being mauled again, the guns of Sorauren had wrought victory from defeat, pursuit from retreat. The French, cast back, fought hard to regain the passes, defending every ridge and hill and village, until at last they slipped back whence they had come and the advancing allied army could breathe once more. In that fighting the 71st lost another hundred men, but wreck though they were they had to stand with the other regiments and defend again the passes that were the gate to France.

Thus it was that one day in late August Ingram stood watching the snow flurry across the high pass of Roncesvalles. He drew his greatcoat closer around him and scowled. Winter had come early to the mountains.

Satisfied that there was no activity on the French side of the pass he turned round to watch his men work at the blockhouse. They had been working since light and, despite the bitter cold, sweat ran from their pores. Yet it was too chill to leave off their greatcoats and so they toiled encumbered, digging at the frozen, unyielding soil, dragging out reluctant boulders, building up the walls with numb fingers. Even the mortar was stiff in the cold and sluggish like the weary men who plastered it over the half-built defences.

Sergeant Ross looked up from his task and peered back down the new road where other men laboured with spades and picks, levelling and paving. He spoke to the man beside him and then turned and walked down over the heather to Ingram.

'The column is on the road, sir.' He grimaced at the weather. 'The squaddies will not be sorry. I doubt it is more August-like on Rannoch Moor today.'

Ingram nodded. The new tents should be with the column, and a few comforts to ease existence in this place. He could expect liquor for issue and perhaps some fresh vegetables. There might even be firewood instead of the coarse heather roots which would only smoulder. In a few more days it would be the turn of another brigade and luxurious warmth in the villages below.

But the column would also bring new tools, more materials for construction, an engineer to find fresh tasks, to criticise and alter what was already done. He nodded again in resignation.

Ross permitted himself a smile. 'The paymaster's with them, sir. And your servant.'

'Ramon?' Ramon would have news of Margarita; it was four weeks now since he had been sent to her and there had been no word in all that time. His hand fluttered for a moment at his neck where her crucifix had hung. Ramon had carried it to her that night, before Sorauren, when the thunderstorm roared in the skies and Biarroco lay awaiting his end. And in all that time there had been no news.

He strode up to the blockhouse and Ross, beside him, pointed out the column winding into view, showed him Hugh MacKenzie, heavy on his horse. Ramon, a little ahead, saw him and, waving, kicked his mule to a canter.

The men had stopped working and were leaning on their picks and spades, watching and chattering in interest. Ross was about to protest but Ingram, in charity, intervened.

'All right, Sergeant. They've worked well enough this forenoon. Let us hope there may be tents to erect. Take your rest now, lads, but keep from taking cold.'

He moved forward alone to meet Ramon. The boy was positively hurtling down the road and, as he approached, drew the unhappy mule to a terrifying stop with a gleeful shout, and waved cheekily at the laughing soldiers. He leapt from the saddle and bounded to Ingram. 'Mother of Sows, it's good to be back, señor.'

'Good,' said Ingram drily. 'I trust you enjoy living up here.'

Ramon grinned and scratched himself and then fell silent.

Ingram could wait no longer. 'Well, Son of Sloth, did you do what I bid? Did you see Doña Margarita?'

The boy's face saddened and he spoke slowly.

'Yes, señor. She gave me this, to give to you.'

From his pocket he took the thing and gently clasped Ingram's fingers around it. When Ingram opened his hand he saw what he already knew, that it was Fox's watch. He saw the gold dull in the grey light and felt the empty mist across his vision. Ramon's eyes were deep, understanding pools of hazel.

'There is also this letter, señor.'

Ingram took the paper and it felt thick and swollen in his fingers, though he knew there was one, single sheet. Absently he slipped the watch into the pocket of his greatcoat and, turning from them all, from Ramon, from the curious soldiers, from the approaching column, he walked silently away. In the shelter of a half-constructed wall he sat down and broke the seal. The sheet fluttered in the wind and threatened to blow away, but he held it firm, and as the snow flurried around and whisked away, he read:

'Sir,

'Your letter tells me what you have done and now the news comes to me that Marcelliano has been hanged.

'In all my life I have loved but three men. One as a husband, one as a brother and the third, yourself. The first was crucified by the French and betrayed no one; the second was hanged for his treason yet betrayed no loyalties of his own; the third was bound by his duty and his was the betrayal of the second.

'You did your duty to effect. At the court-martial it was the letter alone that secured Marcelliano's execution. It is my hope that your concept of duty satisfies the loss occasioned to your honour.

'Ramon has been kind enough to assist me on my road and will tell you that I am now destitute and have lost all. Luciano's loyalty is well repaid. The family estates are confiscated. I shall seek consolation in Mother Church and will pray to Santa Teresa for your soul.

'I am, sir,
Your former friend,
Margarita de Cabezon-Menorez de Biarroco.'

He sat gazing at the neatly written sentences until the words danced on the white page. The wind sucked and pulled at the paper and blew cruel on his fingers. Snow whipped over the wall and gathered on his shoulders and sought out the gap at his collar. He sat there motionless until the letter dissolved into a spinning wheel of sorrow and its coldness brought him to slow awareness of his physical chill. Ingram folded the sheet and slipped it into his breast and then he rose, suddenly to feel the cramp in his limbs and the cut of the wind from the south.

Slowly he walked back to the road. The snow was beginning to lie in the sheltered hollows and where the column had halted the mules stood miserably with the white flakes clinging to their coats. All work on the defences had stopped as his soldiers unpacked the heavy panniers, breaking out tents, piling supplies. Everyone seemed engrossed in the tasks and no one had time to pay attention to him. Even Ramon had disappeared on some labour of his own. Ingram thought that he should be supervising matters, but there appeared to be no need, and he felt useless, rejected.

He found Ross directing the efforts of his men to arrange all the clutter of supplies, while a lieutenant of sappers fussed over his precious equipment. The sergeant gestured angrily. 'Take care of that, MacGregor, it is not a peat that you are carrying, you young gommeril.' He grinned at Ingram. 'It is all this fine contraption for the lieutenant here, sir. And themselves handling it like it was sacks of meal.' He cocked an eye at the engineer. 'Yon is a man who has his own way with things. Grand news about the Major, sir.'

'The Major?'

'Major MacKenzie, sir, that . . .'

'Sergeant! Your attention here . . . Oh! I beg your pardon, sir.' The sapper's tone was urgent. 'I didn't see you. Brown, sir. Royal Artificiers.'

'Ingram.'

'I have taken liberty with your men, sir. My equipment. Perhaps you would wish . . .'

'That's all right, Mr Brown. You know your own affairs best.'

'Your servant, sir.'

'Yours, sir. Carry on, Sergeant.'

His presence was an irritation to the agitated Brown so he drifted away. There was this feeling of futility, of lack of purpose, of isolation. His own men did not need him; he was in their way. He wondered what Ross had been saying about Maxwell MacKenzie and determined to seek out his uncle.

The paymaster was warily superintending his own clerks, but on Ingram's approach he smiled in welcome. He at least could spare time for a friendly word.

'Ye'll hae heard the news concerning oor Maxwell?'

'Only that it is good, Hugh.'

'Aye, ye maun cry it guid. They hae wrought his exchange and he is fit tae serve. He'll be wi' us the morrow's morn.'

'I'm glad, Hugh. I'll not be sorry to see him back.'

'Aye. He's a wee thing different frae yon Campbell, Walker. I never kenned a guid man yet frae Inveraray toun.'

MacKenzie paused to shout at one of his men. 'God spare ye, Duncan. Hinna ye learned yet tae lift a pack-saddle? Yon's a mule, no a march-dyke. Get the driver tae help ye.'

Ingram made to move, not wanting to cause further distraction, but MacKenzie caught his arm.

'There's guid news for yourself, George. Ye're in the Gazette.'

Later the words would bring satisfaction. His captaincy was official at last and his seniority ran from the date of the notice in the Gazette. The date was important, it must have been at least a month ago; already there would be captains junior to him. His rank, too, was a valuable asset, available for sale. But at the moment he merely nodded and said, 'Oh.'

'Man, but ye're droll. I hae seen mony a body languish for sic news. I'll be adjusting your warrant, ye ken. There's a month's arrears o' pay for ye. It's ten shillings and sixpence a day noo, Captain Ingram.'

'I'm sorry, Hugh. Oh, I'm mighty pleased, you know. It's just . . .'

'Ach, I ken fine. It's yon letter that Ramon brought ye. There's nae siccan pain in a' the warld, but it aye heals wi' forgetting.'

Ingram grinned sheepishly. He supposed the whole battalion had guessed what was troubling him. But there were elements that they did not understand.

'Aye.' MacKenzie patted his arm. 'Here, I maun cheer ye. There's mair nor yin letter for ye. The mail is in – no that I've just the moment to distribute mail – but here.' He opened a portfolio and flicked through a sheaf of correspondence. 'A letter frae home for ye.'

Ingram took it and smiled his thanks. He wandered away, absently opening the envelope, hoping that it might contain some tidings different from the usual plaintive complaint. It did not, of course. His parents had not been slow to note his gazetted captaincy and see its significance to their own hardships. It was pathetic to read the pleading words, to know that the whole question of his financial arrangements would be the subject of further protracted correspondence. For the thousandth time he cursed his brother who, unmoved by his family's circumstances, remained secure on the family estate and ranked with his father's creditors. He folded the letter and put it away. It contained not a single word of congratulation.

He paced thoughtfully away from the hubbub around him, past the half-built blockhouse and down through the heather to the crag where he had stood earlier. The wind keened over the ridge, whipping the skirts of his coat, biting at his exposed neck. He remained still, in silence, and let his mind have its course.

In time MacKenzie came to him, stumping down the rough slope to stand gazing down the valley for a moment's quiet before speaking.

'James Ross is biding ye. There is your company's camping ground tae be sited. And the adjutant wad hae a list o' men for picket.'

'Yes. I'll come now.'

MacKenzie was thoughtful, his eyes resting on the vastness around them.

'Ye ken, we lost twa mules in a ravine, coming up the road. I was minded on yon mule that went missing the day we got orders in Don Benito. Man, ye were in a frenzy ower that. It'll be a year syne, tae the day near enough.'

'A long year, Hugh.'

'Aye, lang enough. I doubt the sun shines there yet.'

'Do you wish you were back there, Hugh?'

MacKenzie eyed the snow dusting the mountains above, watched the cloud rolling down the gullies.

'Back yonder in the sun? No. Ye get tae thinking o' them wha lie ahint ye. It's memories ye hae tae owercome. A man maun bide tae his duty; that's that that's brought us here. No. There's nae wish tae be yonder in the sun. Here's the place. Look ye at yon road. That's the road tae France and we maun march there gin I'm no mistaken, aye and afore the harvest is weel gleaned.'

Ingram's eye followed the road down the valley, winding round the great buttresses, twisting into the gorges. The war would be carried that way, into the enemy's homeland.

He took Margarita's letter from his breast and as the older man watched he tore it into little shreds and cast them to the wind. Then he turned away and slowly walked back up the hill to his waiting company. And the tiny pieces of paper danced with the snow flakes in the wind as it carried them down into the valley towards France.